T0196745

Natural Drift

by Ron Boggs

iUniverse, Inc.
New York Bloomington

Natural Drift

Copyright © 2009 by Ron Boggs

All rights reserved. No part of this book may be used or reproduced by any means, graphic, electronic, or mechanical, including photocopying, recording, taping or by any information storage retrieval system without the written permission of the publisher except in the case of brief quotations embodied in critical articles and reviews.

This is a work of fiction. All of the characters, names, incidents, organizations, and dialogue in this novel are either the products of the author's imagination or are used fictitiously.

iUniverse books may be ordered through booksellers or by contacting:

iUniverse
1663 Liberty Drive
Bloomington, IN 47403
www.iuniverse.com
1-800-Authors (1-800-288-4677)

Because of the dynamic nature of the Internet, any Web addresses or links contained in this book may have changed since publication and may no longer be valid. The views expressed in this work are solely those of the author and do not necessarily reflect the views of the publisher, and the publisher hereby disclaims any responsibility for them.

ISBN: 978-1-4401-3338-1 (pbk)
ISBN: 978-1-4401-3340-4 (cloth)
ISBN: 978-1-4401-3339-8 (ebk)

Printed in the United States of America

iUniverse rev. date: 4/3/2009

For my brother, Dennis, an enthusiast—

"I tell you there're few things in life more exciting

than watching your bobber go down."

D.M.B. (1943-1999)

RANKIN COUNTY
MONTANA
YELLOWSTONE COUNTY
GILLETTE COUNTY
TOWER COUNTY
T.8 N.
R.23 E.
T.8 N.
R.22 E.
TO BILLINGS
EVERHART
176
CITY OF
GRANT
34
GREENWALL
McNally
Creek
Vermillion
River
Bridal
CUSTER
THORDAHL
RANCH
Long
Bow
Stanley's
Veil
NATIONAL
MINE
COOPER
RANCH
County
Forest
Preserve
FOREST
IRISH KINGDOM
PALISADES
RYAN
RANCH
TO SHERIDAN, WYO.
NORTH
To Yellowstone
National Park
HARLAN
RANGE
SCALE
IN MILES
0
5
10
15

CHAPTER 1

(Tuesday, October 18)

From a block away, Sheriff Axel Cooper saw her on the deck of the Grant Café, a main street restaurant. She had made it down from Billings. He couldn't help but smile.

As he approached her, Dr. Anne Lynwood jumped up from her chair.

"So," she said, "what did the governor line up for you?"

They met with a loose hug and he gently pushed her auburn hair back behind her ear and kissed the nape of her neck. As they moved to the table and sat down, he touched his index finger to his lips. He took off his broad-brimmed hat and raked his fingers through his grizzled hair.

"The raid is on," he said softly. "To hit the ranch before sunup Thursday, we've got to leave town tomorrow, late afternoon. The whole crew is already here. The 'Light Brigade' is still working on their signals. Stayin' at the Matterhorn."

"Wow, the 'Light Brigade.' I thought they got wiped out in the Crimean War. 'Into the Valley of Death rode the six hundred.'"

Axel smiled. "Strobe lights and 50,000 watt spotlights. Part of the intimidation plan."

"So, what are *you* going to do? What's this all about?" she asked. "A big secret?"

"Course. We want them there when we get there." He breathed deeply and leaned across the table. "We're gonna raid a meth lab at a ranch out east. The Feds are running it and, man, *are* they. I've just spent six hours in a time-warp. Fifty years in the future. The POB, Pre-Operations Briefing, don't ya know. It was as though I was in a foreign country where they spoke their own language and had a whole different way of doing things. A lot of strange dudes." Then, as if confiding a secret code, he whispered, "They don't need me. Really, I don't think they even want me. I'm just another burdensome prerequisite. I'm the *local liaison*. It's like the federal forty-two-page book on Montana ranch raids calls for a local liaison. So I am their guy!"

He smiled broadly and flipped his palms up to frame his face like a circus clown. Just as quickly he dropped his hands to the table and returned to a serious look. "And then there's Ham Frazier, my old boss. He's pretty gung-ho."

Axel took a deep draw of the beer that Anne had brought out to the deck table from the bar. "Good Stuff!"

He sat up straight. At just under six feet, Axel was not tall, but his erect posture, trim waist and broad chest gave him the appearance of greater height. He shook his shoulders to work out a muscle twitch. "Ham behaved himself. He was quite civil, showed extreme patience with the Feds—on the verge of sucking up to them. The Feds loved him. Maybe it's just me who can't get along with him. I was ready to ask if he had qualified as a local liaison, so he could take my place. No need for both of us." He laughed aloud. He took another swallow of his beer and then peered into the liquid through the clear glass stein.

Anne waited quietly, watching Axel's every move.

"Actually, one of his guys, a young trooper, asked one too many questions and Hilton, the U.S. Marshal from Denver, called him out. Never to return." Axel paused and took another sip of beer. "I think Hilton isn't interested in explaining himself to anybody, let alone to a twenty-six-year-old trooper. Kid asked a reasonable question about backup support. Hilton said the answer is 'above your pay grade, and if I were you, I'd focus on showing up on time!' Definitely an edgy guy."

Axel let that sink in and then said, "Ham told me that the governor wanted him to line me up, but Ham told the governor to call me himself. Got a laugh outta that. Ham hasn't forgotten either. Thing is, he's more local than I am. I only qualify as a local with folks who aren't from Montana."

Axel Cooper held the distinction of being the first elected Montana County Sheriff in the last sixty years who wasn't born in the state. Anne twisted her mouth to an awkward smile. Anne was a native Montanan, and Axel knew that it takes a long time to become a Montanan to Montanans.

"What happened at the meeting?" she asked. She picked up her wine glass and took a sip of the hearty cabernet.

"Those Feds from Denver got a different view of the way the world works and a vocabulary to match." He slowly turned his head back and forth to scan the empty tables on the deck of the Grant Cafe. "It's a plan only a bunch of techno-geeks could come up with. I swear they went to school in Cal Tech's military logistics department. They've got probability distributions on the most salient variables—the MSVs. Satellite photos, coverage matrices, cognitive disorientation, perceptual exhaustion, terms of engagement, objective lethality. Sounds like an Internet world-dominance game."

He paused to take another sip of his beer. "Ya know, Jefferson, our dear, professorial governor, heard this plan and labeled it 'elegantly simple.' Could he really come up with that line himself? 'Bout as elegant as a sledge hammer. And 'simple' no, that doesn't apply either. Simple like the electrical wiring of a new car. 'Elegantly simple,' no way!"

Axel slid his chair closer to hers. "One thing for sure, we've got to keep this under wraps until the raid's over. Nine of us. Hit the ranch just before sun up, Thursday morning."

He paused for a moment. Then he asked her, "Have you heard anything about the Irish Kingdom lately?"

"You guys going to the Kingdom?"

"Yep! One of their seasonal operations. Pretty far up the hill. On the other side of the Custer National Forest past Arlyn's place." Axel's brother Arlyn had a small ranch on McNally Creek about twenty miles east of Grant.

"The Irish Kingdom. Mmmmm. Seems everybody's got their own view. Some talk about it like it's a private club, others a secret society, a wing of the IRA. I think that's a stretch. I think it's a pretty loose family group that cooperates when it can. Not so much illegal as sort of outside the system. They certainly aren't really public. Keep to themselves. There was one kid in high school, Patrick O'Neill, who always claimed his granddad was the big mover and shaker with them, the king of the

Kingdom. Dad, he did business with them in the seventies. But, I think he got stiffed. Never got paid after he delivered the goods—windows, I think. When he told them that he'd have to take the windows back, they said, "go ahead and try." Can't say he holds them in high esteem. Long memory."

"Windows?"

"Yeah, they wholesaled everything, he and my Uncle Don. Doors, windows, farm equipment, plastic pond liners. They loved the role of the middle man. I swear Dad could fill an empty warehouse with ten telephone calls and sell it all with another hundred calls. Dad'd be a good resource if you needed a Who's Who in the Kingdom. Christ, he'd give you the scorecard for the last fifty years."

"Well, I'm not ready for that. The Feds think there's a meth plant working in the Kingdom, and they're going in to bust it. One of the out-ranches at 7,000 feet east of Mt. Elliott, off the backside of Dead Horse Plateau. Crestfallen, that's the name of the ranch. Nobody lives there full-time. Close it up for the winter."

"Yeah, *Crestfallen*?" she laughed. "Doesn't sound too positive."

Axel stared straight ahead, twirling the remaining liquid in his glass.

"Well, somebody named it that. I gotta believe this is a renegade operation. From what I've seen, the Kingdom's almost mainstream nowadays, legit. As Rankin County Sheriff, I get zero business out of the Kingdom. It's got to be a couple of young guys can't hack ranch work. This isn't a sanctioned profit center."

She pursed her lips in concentration.

"Are you serious? A commando raid? That's what your session today was about? They still do stuff like that? Sounds like the Mexicans attacking the Alamo. Remember Grenada? D-Day. Any paratroopers? What do *you* have to do with it? Out east there's a lot of federal land, Forest Service, BLM, Park Service. Is it even your jurisdiction?"

"Yeah, it's my jurisdiction. Well, we start in the County Forest Preserve. Go across some Forest Service land, but the ranch is private property. In the county, but, that's not the point. The whole shebang is a federal thing on an old warrant. A fugitive from a federal indictment. That's why it is the U.S. Marshal rather than the FBI. They say they need me as an insider—lay-of-the-land sort of thing. No, I'm not looking to arrest anybody. Halfway through the first presentation today, topography, I figured brother Arlyn's better equipped for this than me, and with all their maps and satellite photos they know as much about Dead Horse Plateau as I do. Hell, I'm just a guide."

"So … you're what … some kind of Sacajawea?" she asked, referring to the female Shoshone guide of the Lewis and Clark expedition. "But a raid? In the middle of the night? Do they have a drama deficiency or something?"

"Basically, they want to drop down on the ranch from the backside, down from Dead Horse—surround 'em before dawn. Call 'em out. Reinforcements on wheels appear only after we've secured the ranch." As he started to describe the plan, Axel realized how wild-west it sounded.

"Over Dead Horse Plateau in October?" she said.

"At night."

"At night?" She pushed out her chin and tilted her head. "So, at 10,000 feet, it's been snowing off and on since Labor Day. Is there any accumulation? This *is* on the north side. You could make good time across Dead Horse, if you don't get blown off, but once you drop down off the far side, even with a full moon, which you won't have, you'll be lucky to make two miles an hour. You might miss the snow, but it sure as hell will be cold. Good wind across that plateau could make it feel ten or fifteen degrees colder. Hope you've got a helicopter?"

"No, too noisy. We're driving to the end of the gravel to the Ajax trailhead, then hiking up, across, and down." He modeled a flat-topped plateau with his hands.

"You're hiking the whole way? Have you done this before? Do you know what you're getting into?"

"Well, I drove an ATV up there yesterday afternoon. Took a coupla hours. Trails up and across are pretty good. No real snow. Couple of patches. Going down at the right place could be hairy. There's a bit of a trail through the woods. I left a bunch of traffic cones to mark the way. Measured out the miles and marked the cones on the Plateau. Nine-mile hike. Tough part's gonna be the last stretch, coming down to the ranch. About a mile through the woods."

Anne smiled at Axel. They both knew that regardless of her concerns, the hike was going to proceed according to Axel's plan. "So, what do you think of the U.S. Marshal? Hilton. Did he wear a star with a big 'U.S.' stamped in the middle?"

"No star. Not yet, at least. Yesterday I talked to a friend of mine, Jim Faraday. We worked together at the Montana State Patrol. He's with FBI—Denver now. He called Jack Hilton a George Patton on steroids. From today's meeting, I think Faraday's got it 'bout right. Hilton was in the Marine Corps. A major, a step above captain. Story is he got passed over for lieutenant colonel—too rough on the civilians in Iraq. Now he's a one-star general in the Colorado National Guard. Don't know how that works. He's about fifty. Shaves his head. Seems mad at the world. Gut 'bout as round as his head; three times as big. Got to be 6'3", 280. Big guy, more thick than fat, solid, pushy. Uses his body for physical intimidation. I saw a lot of guys like him when I was in the Coast Guard. Only get so far."

Anne nodded, but said nothing.

Axel continued, "He's got a real attitude. This is his gig and he'll take no flak from anybody. Apparently he's got some connections. Strong enough to keep him on the job, in spite of some reprimands and shooting two guys in federal custody—one guy a handcuffed mobster."

Anne's eyebrows jumped up on her forehead. She said, "How'd he handle the meeting? Today."

"Very much into control. He ran the meeting as though our raid was an elaborate military campaign. As though he was the supreme commander coordinating naval bombardment, air power and the marines on the beach. Very directive, 'better mind your manners,' stuff like that. Hilton's got a plan. Can't say he's told us everything. Like, why's there no one else from the U.S. Marshal's office in on this raid. This is formally a U.S. Marshal operation, out of Denver. But the team's made up of Hilton, two guys from the DEA, two South Dakota troopers, Ham and his two remaining MSP guys and me. The DEA guys don't even report to Hilton. He had a couple of his staffers here. But they're not hiking. Very strange. He's in a rush, like this ranch could disappear next week. He's a real smart-ass. He makes jabs like, 'Has Rankin County got mobile phones yet?' and tries to play us off against one another. Like I should care what some South Dakota trooper thinks of me. Spent ten minutes talking about the Langley Rules of Engagement—Level 5 plus. Special rules. Langley, like CIA Headquarters in Langley, Virginia. We can't shoot first. If they start firing at us, we can't even shoot back unless they're really good and have a good chance of killing us. So, we let them shoot at us and wait for them to get really close so we can shoot back at 'em."

Anne shook her head and said, "Sounds like a supreme court case to me. You'd better bring an objective observer or three to authorize return fire!"

Axel started up again, "Then in the afternoon, he's in the back of the room while a guy from the DEA tells us about how dangerous meth production is: exploding gases. So we don't blow up the place. Hilton lights up a cigar. We're in the basement of the county building—no smoking. So I told him he'd have to smoke outside. He stands up, stops the presentation, gets right in my face and says, 'Whatcha gonna do, Sheriff? Arrest me?' His stomach was about six inches from my fist. I swear he did it to create a confrontation. Smoke alarm went off before we came to blows."

Anne was back to working on logistics. She said, "And you'll have to have night-vision goggles. You guys sporting flashlights coming down off the Plateau, you're gonna look like the seven dwarfs with their lanterns. 'Hi ho, Hi ho, it's off to work we go.' Or the night grooming crew at the ski hill. 'Here we are!!' Who thought this up? Hilton himself or some committee of brainiacs? Tell me they're not from L.A. Are those terms of engagement normal?"

Axel had learned that Anne had a particular disdain for Los Angeles. She had little interest in most big cities. She would occasionally pronounce that God didn't put her on this earth to support mass transit in Manhattan. Today it was Los Angeles.

To many Montanans, Axel was an Eastern flatlander, a relative urbanite. So he was on high alert whenever Anne landed on an urban-rural issue. Axel wasn't an advocate for one over another, they were just different. He didn't disparage his hometown of Evanston, Illinois, the first suburb north of Chicago. It was just the place where he grew up.

While he had good family memories, he was happy where he was and wasn't looking to go back or even get into extensive comparisons.

His personal coming-of-age was in the Coast Guard in Florida, dealing with drug runners, drunken boaters and illegal aliens. After that, the sedate family insurance business had little appeal, so Axel chased down his older brother in south-central Montana. At first, it was going to be just a month break. But then he met a girl and started looking for work. The MSP needed troopers and his Coast Guard service gave him a ten-point bonus on the entrance exam, so he stayed. Now, Montana was home.

Brother Arlyn, an electrician and a part-time fishing guide, had once called Axel's life adventure a *natural drift*, comparing it to the desired movement of a fisherman's trout fly floating downstream at the same rate as the stream's current: going with the flow. Axel couldn't deny the lack of an overarching plan for his life, but wasn't ready to embrace Arlyn's analogy.

Anne was proud of her family's Montana heritage and her firsthand experience with avalanches, below-zero temperatures, six-foot snowdrifts, bears, moose, snow on the Fourth of July and a forty-eight-day growing season. "Simple," "independent," "basic," "pure," "strong," even "rough" were high-order attributes. Axel considered her disdain for Los Angeles another element of her Montana-ness, and let it ride.

"Well, Denver's not L.A., exactly, but might as well be. I don't believe most of these Federales have left the safety of their cubicles since training." Axel enjoyed his pronunciation of "Federales," with a phony Spanish accent, tacitly comparing them to the much-maligned Mexican federal police.

"But Jack Hilton's something else. He's never seen a cubicle. He's a wild man."

The waitress interrupted to bring out the dinners Anne had ordered, and as Axel called for another beer, they lapsed into silence. He picked up his fork and pushed the fried potatoes off to the edge of the plate.

After three bites of his steak he looked up at Anne and smiled. He leaned back. Her voluminous hair, which she usually tied back in a bun or ponytail, was loose and catching every deck breeze. The so-faint freckles across her nose and her gymnast's stature made her look much younger than she actually was. High cheekbones and a ready smile. A midlife Little Orphan Annie.

As the sun dropped below the horizon, a quick chill sent Anne and Axel off the deck into the restaurant. Nursing the last of his beer, Axel said, "I've got some pretty decent coffee at my place, and we might be able to catch the end of the White Sox play-off game from the neighbor's satellite."

She smiled at his indirect invitation to spend the night. It was not a surprise—she had her own key. He obviously was not up to saying, "Hey honey, let's go to my place and go to bed."

"I'm not really that into the White Sox," Anne said with a smile that made his pulse rush.

"Glad to hear it."

They settled the bill and walked the three blocks back to his house.

He'd started the rehab project two years ago. It was an authentic coal miner's shack, built cheap and fast a hundred years ago, long before a methane explosion closed the mine. It had two rooms up, two rooms down with a tiny cement-block cellar. The remainder of the foundation was comprised of un-mortared river rock supporting creosote-soaked railroad ties. Brother Arlyn, the electrician, had ruled the electrical system "fragile" before Axel ever bought the place. The farther he got into the rehab, the more complicated it became.

For the last year, Axel had spent most nights at Arlyn's ranch, a dilapidated house and barn on eight hundred acres without any cattle. The appeal for Arlyn was that it bordered the Custer National Forest and had frontage on McNally Creek, a red-ribbon trout stream.

Axel was developing a strange affinity for his "city house." It was his and his alone. It had character and what the Realtor called *provenance*. It had been through a lot. It deserved some attention. And besides, as an unmarried, small-county sheriff, Axel felt he needed a project to keep from getting into trouble.

Just before they rounded the corner in front of the house, Axel swung his arm around the small of Anne's back, so that as she turned the corner his hand slowly slid to her hips. Anne looked back at Axel in mild reproach. He fought to keep a straight face.

As he got out his house key and stepped up onto the porch to unlock the door, she moved up behind him and with her small but strong hands seized his hips and said, "Hey, Sheriff, did you bring your gun?"

Axel smiled as he swung the door open. He scanned the living room. Axel said, "Well, Pilgrim, I think we'll have to look upstairs. It's certainly not down here."

As Axel turned and swung the door closed, Anne again stepped up behind him so that when he turned back to the room, they were face-to-face, inches apart.

He beamed, embraced her, and closed his eyes. His fingertips brushed her hair as they inched their way up her back. She sighed and opened her eyes.

"Where did you say those stairs were?" she breathed, her voice heavy.

"I don't know …," he mumbled, nuzzling into the side of her neck, slowly kissing the pale, freckled skin revealed as her shirt collar fell open.

He drew her over to the single piece of furniture in the room, an old, dusty Lazy Boy.

"Axe, honey, can't we find something more comfortable? Like a rock pile maybe?" She was teasing. Sort of.

"Okay, you win. I don't mind," he said illogically. As she moved, he kept his roaming hands on her.

He side-stepped over the chair's massive armrest and slid into the wide chair and awkwardly pulled her down, face-to-face. She laughed as she turned and fell sideways into his lap, releasing an explosion of sawdust that neither of them noticed.

CHAPTER 2

(Tuesday, October 18)

A tall, raw-boned man with a long, weathered face, Sven Thordahl slowly crested the sharp ridge of the nameless foothill in his all-terrain vehicle.

He stopped and planted both feet on the ground. As he set the emergency hand brake and slowly swung his stiff right leg over the four-wheeler, Sven saw movement two hundred yards out across the canyon on the near-vertical rock wall. He froze and then settled his airborne knee on the ATV's padded seat. Then he slowly slid his knee off the seat and crouched behind the ATV. He was riveted on a large animal. It was almost solid black, and was slowly and cautiously picking its way down the sheer face. The rancher's breathing slowed.

Yes, it was a wolf, not a coyote. He whispered to himself, "Who in the hell thought up the idea of bringing wolves back to Yellowstone, a goddamned zoo without bars? Wilderness, my ass. Probably some desk jockey never worked a day in his life. Bad enough, they let stupid-ass buffalo in there; walking bacteria colonies. Wolves. Who needs wolves? Damnation, might as well hobble the rancher with on-site inspections from the animal rights brigade. Next, they will probably protest branding calves, tagging their ears. Inhumane. Today there's going to be one less wolf on this Montanan's ranch.

He slowly drew his rifle from the plastic scabbard bolted to the ATV, careful not to bang the sides. He cradled the rifle while he closely examined a bullet. It was one he had reloaded himself years ago. Can't take a second shot. Shots in this canyon could broadcast for miles. Two shots would be an unmistakable message that someone was hunting before the start of deer season. No, it has to be one good, clean shot.

Embracing the rifle, Sven slowly moved from a crouch to a kneel—first his good left knee and then the bad one, the one that would only bend half way, a souvenir of his days breaking in young colts—and then he lay down on the rocky ground. While humming a groan of arthritic pain, he rolled down the back slope, away from the ATV. After three full rotations, he stopped on his stomach, raised his head, and crawled forward to peer over the ridge. He was closer to the wolf but still above it. Sven drew up the rifle and, resting his elbows on the rocky ground, pushed forward the safety lever and sighted in on the slow-moving target. One shot, needs to be the head. He held his breath, cradled the rifle's circular front sight in the bed of the rear one and slowly squeezed the trigger. He closed his eyes.

The jolt to his shoulder and roar of the rifle hit Sven at the same time. He lay still and kept his eyes closed. The echo was more immediate and short-lived than he expected.

The wolf tumbled head first off the wall to flop chest first on the valley floor in a tangled jumble.

Sven peered over the ridge for thirty seconds before he spotted the black fur ball amid a triangle of large boulders a good ten feet from the base of the sheer wall.

He stood upright, re-holstered the rifle, strapped it down and mounted the ATV. He started it up and carefully eased off the hand brake and slowly, cautiously, backed down the lesser slope to the gravel trail. It was a short trip to the canyon floor. He stopped fifteen feet from the animal.

He slowly dismounted the ATV, retrieved the rifle, untied a short rope, and, with one eye on the wolf, chambered a second cartridge for possible use. He cradled the rifle in his left arm and with his right picked up a six-inch rock. He threw it underhand. It hit the blood-matted fur of the wolf's chest with a hollow thump. The body didn't twitch.

He moved forward and pulled the wolf's left rear leg out to look at the full profile.

He tied the hind feet together and with the other end of the rope cast a loop to fit over the ball of the ATV's trailer hitch. Then, dragging the carcass, he drove into the shadows of the converging walls, dodging the larger rocks. At the end of the canyon, Sven executed a sharp u-turn, stopped, dismounted, and dragged the carcass to the base of the wall. Then, in slow jerks, he pulled it twenty feet up the far wall, out of sight behind a large boulder. He positioned it behind the boulder and gathered up armful after armful of smaller rocks to cover it. Nature will have its way; the scavengers would arrive soon enough, but there was no need to make a spectacle out of it.

Breathing hard, he surveyed the final scene, noted his own sweaty brow and considered all he'd ever done in the name of protecting his cattle, his ranch, his livelihood and his way of life. This was just taking care of business. *Dad would've celebrated, skinned it and nailed the pelt to the bunk house wall.*

CHAPTER 3

(Wednesday, October 19)

The three black Chevy Suburbans had started out in Grant and dropped them at the Ajax trailhead at 6,500 feet. They hiked up through the Ajax pass to the plateau at 9,000 feet. Axel set the pace slow, knowing that too fast a pace early on could exhaust all but the most well-conditioned hikers. The trail was well marked and straightforward. But now, after five miles on the trail, his efforts were very deliberate. He breathed deeply. He had to conscientiously raise each knee as though he were ice climbing with three inch nails in the soles of his boots. It was work, but so far so good.

At the orange plastic traffic cone marking mile number five, Hilton came up to Axel, who'd been walking alone, leading the single-file line.

"You gonna make it, mister?" Hilton asked.

Axel kept walking and responded without looking at Hilton, "Damned right. Toughest part's behind us. It's working out. We're staying together. That's good."

"But can't we pick it up a little? Looks like we've got a cakewalk 'cross the plateau."

"We're doing fine. Our getting there early won't make the sun rise any sooner. We're together, nobody hurt themselves. Think we should leave well enough alone."

"Four miles to the ranch, right? Three to the woods? The sooner we get there, the longer the rest."

Axel stopped and turned to look at Hilton. Hilton also stopped, as did the whole group behind them. Looking up at Hilton, Axel said, "Marshal, my sense is that if we went any faster, we'd start losing people.

It's not a race, and hurry-up-and-wait just won't work." He flipped his head forward toward the other hikers, several of whom had taken off their backpacks and were drinking water.

Hilton took two steps forward to a small ledge on the side of the trail, which increased his height advantage over Axel.

"Ya know, Sheriff, I think we're looking at the reason that you belong in this miserable little town." Then Hilton spoke louder, loud enough to carry to all the hikers, "You're just a little man. If you were man enough, we could double-time it from here and have a three hour break."

Axel took a step back and said softly, "Why are you doing this? This hike's on plan. We both know you haven't told us the whole story. I'm the local liaison. I'm going to get this motley crew to the ranch in one piece and before sunup. If you've got some other plans, you'd better lay 'em on me right now."

Ham Frazier came up to the two. "What's the rub, boys?" He tilted his head up and swung it back and forth to eye each of the men. "Something happen? Change of plans?"

Neither Axel or Hilton responded.

"Well then, the rest stop's at mile eight. Gentlemen, we got some work to do. I say we get right on it."

Axel looked at Ham. "Yes, Commissioner, let's do it." He turned and stepped out to continue the hike.

Hamilton Frazier was a short, solid man with a white head of hair in a buzz cut. His neck was as wide as his head. His muscled face and deep-set eyes gave him the look of a wild animal. He was the longtime Assistant Commissioner of the Montana State Patrol and had been instrumental in Axel's abrupt departure from the MSP seven years ago. Axel had refused a reassignment to Kalispell, more than two hundred miles from his home, because Ivey, his wife, was dying of cancer. Ham Frazier gave Axel the choice: take the reassignment or resign. Axel resigned, his wife died, and a year later he was elected Rankin County Sheriff on the recommendation of the retiring sheriff.

Ham was one to speak his mind and could be a formidable opponent, whatever the venue.

As other hikers followed Axel, Ham looked up at Hilton. Neither man said a word. Ham waited for several hikers to pass before he joined the single file. Hilton brought up the rear.

While it had been a sunny sixty-two degrees when they left town, Axel could now feel portions of his face hardening in the cold, like so many moveable tectonic plates on the earth's crust.

During the slow, silent march across the plateau, Axel considered just how it was that he came to this place at the front of a law-enforcement squad trekking across a mountain plateau in the middle of a cold Montana night. Perhaps brother Arlyn's comparison of Axel's life to the natural drift of a trout fly floating down a stream was not that far off. He envisaged a fluffy, dry-fly responding in one way or another, to every rock, back-eddy, side-stream and change of gradient the stream had to offer. The movement was continuous, often without apparent cause or explanation.

When they reached the rest stop, Hilton called the group together for a review of their action plan. There were no changes. Hilton would choreograph the light show. The fire zones were to be established and respected.

The group dispersed on the tree-lined slope for each find their own sanctuary out of the wind, a chance to rest their legs and perhaps to sleep.

CHAPTER 4

(Wednesday, October 19)

The Harlan Range of the Rocky Mountains slowly exhausts itself over ten miles of progressively lower foothills just to the southeast of Grant. On this roller coaster to the high prairie, several Montana families had successfully raised multiple generations of Black Angus and tall, thin, intelligent children. The Thordahl family was one of these.

From the moment he got out of bed, Sven Thordahl had been thinking about the ranch. For him, this was a common theme. At eighty, he had long ago lost an active interest in the ranch's daily doings, but with his only child, Chester, lawyering in Billings, the ranch, his legacy, and the very purpose of his life were commonplace concerns.

Sven Thordahl was famous, perhaps the most famous octogenarian in the state. *The Billings Gazette* first drafted up Sven's obituary when he hit seventy. It read that Sven at twenty-six had won a Congressional Medal of Honor in the Korean War for single-handedly rescuing his platoon from an attacking company of Chinese Rangers at Yultong Bridge. In three minutes with six precision shots and two grenades, he had eliminated the Red Chinese company's leadership, killed twenty-two troopers and sent the remaining sixty into active retreat.

After the war, Sven came back to Montana, Rankin County, and the family ranch. He settled into cattle raising as his life's work. With his father as senior counsel, he aggressively expanded the family ranch, secured water rights and made the Thordahls rich.

As the sun rounded Mt. Elliott's craggy peak, Sven was in the barnyard double-checking the air pressure in the tires of his meticulously maintained ten-year-old yellow pickup. It was one of the first double-cab pickups, with a second row of seats. He popped up the hood, checked the water level in the battery and ran his hand over the electrical wiring leading from the battery to the coil, starter, generator, and lighting harness. He wiped his hand on the back of his pants and slammed the hood down with an affirming metallic thunk. He pulled himself into the driver's seat. The day had finally arrived. Time to head west.

After three hours of solid driving, Sven pulled off Interstate 90 on the east side of Bozeman. He nosed the high riding pickup through the dense suburban traffic into the heart of Old Town with its ageless bars, tourist restaurants and re-purposed hotels. He was after El Camino King Ferdinand cigars, six-inch long cheroots as big around as his muscular index finger. Clemente's News & Cigars was a treat and a large part of the reason that he routinely volunteered to pick up Megan, his son Chester's oldest child, at Montana State.

Today he was all business. Two boxes of twelve paid for in cash to the wordless high-school girl at the counter. None of the usual banter with Usebio, the aging Cuban owner. No exchange of stories of cold days on the Montana range for hot nights in Havana as Usebio and Sven, two unlikely confidants, shared memories of their youth.

Within five minutes of parking the pickup, he was back in it, working his way to the land of fast food and SUVs that had never tasted gravel trails. After eight minutes traversing city streets he parked in the far corner of a mall parking lot, five hundred feet away from the front door of the specialty store he had researched on the Internet. He left his hat in the truck, thinking he'd be less memorable without one. Montana Hobby was promoted as the biggest store of its kind between Seattle and Denver. Sven knew the brand and model he wanted but toured the open aisles looking for it rather than talk to a sales clerk.

The Cotton Hill Racer, a remote-controlled 1/12 scale dune buggy was his target. Not a child's toy, but the most popular base model among the novice class at last year's competition of the Western Remote-Control Off-Road Association. The kit had the best, most reliable long-distance remote-control operation available in a kit. Better remote systems could be purchased as components, but Sven calculated that to purchase components would present a higher customer profile than he wanted.

He walked slowly through the aisles and kept his eyes on the floor, six feet in front of him. He found the kit and talked to no one in the store. Paid cash. In and out of the store in eleven minutes.

He opened the box while still in the parking lot. Sitting behind the wheel he took out the major components. He stored the wheels and the short, orange body under the back seat of the pickup's double cab, but took the chassis, receiving unit, and transmitter and locked them in the stainless steel toolbox bolted to the bed of his truck.

Three blocks further, he pulled over to the curb near a construction-site dumpster and threw away the body and wheels. He was pleased that he and his old pickup raised no interest among the construction crew. As he moved back into traffic, he pulled out his cell phone. "Megan, it's Grandpa. You 'bout ready?"

"You betcha. I've got my stuff on the front porch. I'm ready when you are. Where are ya?"

"I'll be there in five minutes. I am turning off Chamberlain now. Bye." He looked at the LED timer on the phone. Fourteen seconds, start to finish. He was pleased.

As Sven rolled to a stop, Megan was on the curb with her back-pack.

"I can't believe you're still driving the Yellow Dog, Grandpa," Megan teased as she climbed into the truck. "One of these days it's gonna break down on the road and you'll be sunk."

He laughed, put the truck in gear and pulled off from the curb. "She's taken care of me for years. I figure she's got a few good ones left in her. I don't know a truck that got better care than this one." He then slowly turned toward her and said in a cold, flat tone, "And I like its electronics. Straightforward. Easy to debug. No computer chips, satellite uploads, or government tracking. Keeps me off their databases. I like that fine."

She looked back at him and said sadly, "Oh, Gramps, are you back on that? I thought you worked that out. You want me to drive?"

Sven looked straight ahead and didn't acknowledge her question.

Megan pelted him with questions as he worked his way out of town, and he said nothing.

Settling into the right lane on the interstate and shifting into third gear, Sven asked Megan about her fall courses.

"It's cool. I've got a couple of sweet classes—Anat/Phys lab is gonna rule. The best! We've named our corpse 'Annette.'"

Sven was often confused by the way Megan talked. It seemed every semester, there was a whole new vocabulary to learn. Sven admitted he didn't understand half of it. "Anat? Your corpse? You're cutting up dead folks already?"

"Well, not really. Annette's the only body in the lab. She's dead, ya know. I won't get my own until med school. So the T.A. dissects Annette, and we take notes. It's pretty cool. Way better than the frogs in high school."

"You started looking at med schools?"

"Actually, yeah! There's a really sweet program through the U.S. Health Service I'm applying for. That's one of the reasons I have to come home this weekend—I've got to have Dad fill out some forms. Because of my good grades, I can apply for early admission. It's a full ride plus a salary for the whole five years, and all I have to do is give them a six-year commitment once I get my M.D. So I get paid to go to school and have a guaranteed job when I'm out. My advisor says I've got a real shot at it. Payback is usually a posting in a small town. 'Bout the most specialized I could be is general surgery, internal medicine. Maybe gynecology or dermatology. Not much call for cardiac surgery in Grant. Anyway, it's only six years."

Trying to keep his composure, Sven took a deep breath and asked, "Are you gonna work for the government? Are you sure this is what you want to do, Meg? They could stick you anywhere—most likely on the reservation. Six years on the reservation in Lodge Grass could feel a whole lot like a life sentence."

"Grandpa, it's a super deal. It's totally outside the norm. They've got a short list of the best schools. The schools have to take you if you're in the program. Early admission. That means I'm not applying to fifteen different schools—and getting rejected from fourteen of them. No second and third round of MCATs, no game playing for a good internship, no interviewing and, best of all, no hitting Dad up for tuition every six months for the next five years. Do you know how expensive Stanford Medical is these days? Even with his help, I'd be a hundred thousand dollars in debt by the time I graduated."

Sven stared straight ahead at the winding road. He began speaking in a soft monotone, "First of all, if there's one thing your dad's got, it's money. Med school wouldn't put a dent in his estate planning. But, honey, I don't think you realize what you're getting yourself into."

And then before she could respond, he continued, "I hate to see you selling yourself short. The U.S. government is the employer of last resort. You'd be nothing but an indentured servant, almost a slave. Your youth will be stolen from you. Can't you see it at the university? Government crushes people. I'm sorry, Megan. It's just that you're so gifted. Special, really, I can't stand to see you throw it all away."

She answered without turning her head, "I'm not throwing anything away, Grandpa! I *want* to come back to somewhere like Grant, be a small-town doc. Without this deal I'll be paying off student loans 'til I am eighty!"

They drove in silence. After a long thirty minutes, they left the expressway and turned south following the Ballard River valley.

Sven broke the prickly silence, "All I'm saying, Megan, is that I want to make sure you've thought it through. Haven't you heard that the Thordahls got more money than the rest of the state? We'll find the money. I'm so proud of you, and I know your parents are, too. But it seems like this damned government of ours messes things up more than it ever helps out."

He slowly turned toward her and said, "It's like that damn mad cow mess. Feds let the Japanese slam the door on us. South Korea won't buy any of *our* beef because of some Canadian cows. I tell you, it just burns me up. The incompetence and waste the U.S. government puts out—and none of the resources going where they're needed most."

She said nothing as she stared out the front window.

Three minutes later, Sven looked over at her. He said, "Honey, have you seen what they're doing up there on the Bridal Veil Creek, above the ranch? The EPA gave those Canadian miners the green light a month ago. Untested. An experimental mine, after palladium. Up-country of some of the best pasture land in south-central Montana. It's in the Custer National Forest. Not ten miles from our ranch house. They never spent one red cent on testing for what it'll do to water quality, ground seepage and surface erosion. National security, my foot. We've got more palladium than we'll ever need. Recycle catalytic converters. Used mufflers. Bridal Veil may look like just another boney, snow-melt creek, but it's the lifeline of the Thordahl Ranch. They screw up that creek and we're done ranching."

"Careful, Grandpa, you sound like those ecoterrorists from Seattle," Megan said.

"It's all about the ranch, our ranch. The Thordahl Ranch. What's the water going to be like when it gets to us? You think they're not using our water for their drilling machines? We've got a deal that guarantees us exclusive water rights. What happens when the creek runs dry, huh? Or turns alkaline and we can't water the cattle? I'll tell you what. The Thordahl Ranch shrivels up and blows away, that's what happens."

"Is it really that bad, Grandpa?"

"Well, there's nobody making sure it isn't, I can tell you that." He turned to look at her. "Your folks think I'm over the edge—out in the twilight zone. But like paint on the barn—everyday we lose a little."

Three minutes later, he started again, "Ya know they asked me to give the Veterans Day Speech in town. Hell, I figured after that debacle at your high school graduation, I was off the list of approved public speakers. Anyway, I said yes, but I really need help putting it together. To me, everything's connected by the hand of our screwed-up federal government. But to anybody else, I sound like I'm bouncing off the walls, going from one topic to another and back again. I'm not a speechmaker. I'm rambling, disorganized, and probably drooling, but goddammit I got something to say. Doesn't that count anymore? Or has it all melted down to big smiles, political correctness and playing to today's gallery? You gonna help me put this brainstorm together? Write it down?"

Megan turned to look at her grandfather with his deeply lined face from his decades in the sun and wind. He was hunched over the wheel of his pickup peering into the twilight.

"Grandpa, sure I'll help. But I'm going back to Bozeman Sunday.

Let's make it a short, simple, focused speech. No need to talk about electronic surveillance or the fluoridation of the water," she said. "There's got to be something that can be done about the mine. They can't just be allowed to do that."

"Damn right. One way or the other, something's gonna be done. No way in hell are they gonna be mining on the Bridal Veil."

As they drove east around the northern edge of the Harlan Range, Sven wondered what time the sun would rise tomorrow.

CHAPTER 5

(Thursday, October 20)

Hilton roused the group and they quickly came down through the sparse pine forest and into a wide, u-shaped valley with a high ridge off to the left—the head of the Ryan Meadow. Off the plateau it was dark with no hint of sunrise, and the troop, without any lights, slowed its pace. Axel was pleased that the hike down from the plateau through the trees had worked out so well. He had delivered the team to the work site, Crestfallen, and he now considered his assignment over.

At the first sight of the ranch, Axel slowed and stepped to the side of the trail, allowing the DEA pair to take the lead. Slowly, others passed by him while he drifted to the back of the pack. When the leaders were fifty yards ahead, Axel was ready to catch up. In front, Hilton made a move.

Hilton pushed forward from the center of the pack. He dropped his head and pumped his arms, as if he were a marathon runner struggling to break away from the pack. He plunged past the state police contingents and the DEA pair to lead the slow-moving procession. Once he got in front, he stopped and turned to face them. The group stopped. Axel stayed on the higher ground as though to record the event playing out in front of him. Hilton puffed out his chest and pulled the cuffs of his dress shirt out of the sleeves of his insulated wool blazer, a move that reminded Axel of a fastidious Coast Guard band director preparing for the Star Spangled Banner. Hilton looked ready to address the group, but he said nothing. He folded his arms across his chest and took a wide stance.

Eyeing Hilton imitating a bald Colossus of Rhodes with the ranch over his shoulder, Axel had flash thoughts of the Ruby Ridge federal law-enforcement fiasco. Just last month, in Billings, Axel heard a presentation by the Idaho county sheriff who had served as escort for the federal task force at Ruby Ridge. They had assaulted a ramshackle private home in remote Idaho to serve an arrest warrant: a warrant for selling a sawed-off shotgun to an undercover federal agent. The agent had set up the target by repeatedly asking for the gun. It was certainly a minor offense, if it wasn't a case of entrapment. The Feds wanted to turn Randy Weaver into a federal informant to secure information on the skinheads at Hayden Lake. Instead they shot and killed his wife and fourteen-year-old son. The final score there was two dead civilians and one dead law enforcement officer. The Idaho sheriff's point of view was simple, "The Feds want immediate results and will bring ten times the necessary fire power, including helicopter gun ships. All suspects are assumed to be guilty and deserve to die." Axel was impressed by the sheriff's candor. Since Axel met Jack Hilton, the Idaho sheriff's credibility was on the rise.

Axel had walked the Custer battlefield and considered the role and psyche of the Crow Indian scouts who led the U.S. Army into the valley of the Little Big Horn River on that fateful day in 1876. Axel wondered if he was playing the role of the Crow scouts to Hilton's Custer. Axel snapped out of his daze as Jack Hilton started waving his hands over his head.

Hilton got everyone's attention. Without a word he turned and led the assembly out of the pines and down the sloping meadow. Axel stepped out briskly to catch up with the troop, but then was struck by the serenity of the scene before him. He stopped to get an overview of the small ranch with its few, twinkling yard lights and the yellow light bulb over the front door. From one thousand yards out and on the rise three hundred feet above it, the scene reminded him of the Christmas holidays back in Illinois when Dad, with intermittent help from Arlyn and Axel, would build elaborate Lionel train sets with miniature towns, papier-mâché mountain ranges, plastic forests, and match box ranch houses.

Come November, Crestfallen would be mothballed for the long winter. Axel had never seen the ranch and had never been within five miles.

Throughout the Kingdom, the only paved road was the Montana State Route 34, the direct route between Grant and Sheridan, Wyoming. The road was not a busy one. It threaded itself like a ribbon turning and twisting over the rolling hills and plunging down into the wide creek valleys marked by towering cottonwoods. In the thirty miles from Grant, the longest straightaway was less than half a mile. It was a two-lane paved blacktop with lane lines, well maintained, but with no shoulders. Two feet off the pavement on either side, the ground was often much lower than the road and sloped away fast. The road was notorious for its frequent, deadly, one-car accidents, often rollovers down to the irrigation ditch. The interstate route, while longer, actually saved a motorist a half hour of drive time.

Axel had told Hilton that he would not be surprised if there was a twenty-four-hour lookout scrutinizing each vehicle traveling on Route 34 as it passed through the Kingdom. Approaching Crestfallen through the high mountain, backdoor route was the only one of Axel's recommendations which Hilton accepted.

The Kingdom dated back one hundred years, a very long time in Montana. Local lore was that two blackballed Irish copper miners from Butte had started using the dry, sparsely-populated corner of the county as a hideout between criminal ventures. The Wyoming border, only five miles away, provided ready refuge from aggressive Montana lawmen. The outlaws married each other's sisters and started buying land and bringing in more of their family from Boston, Kansas City and Butte to run cattle, grow alfalfa and winter wheat, and hunt the local game to fill the larder for the long Montana winter. Over the century, they had been called cattle thieves, booze runners, poachers, unlicensed butchers, and pimps. But arrests were few and convictions by juries, composed of cautious ranchers who sought to mind their own business, rare. Axel knew of only one conviction and it was ten years ago. It involved a barroom fight that got out of hand; involuntary manslaughter. It drew only a thirty-day jail sentence from a usually harsh judge, effectively overturning the brave jury's verdict.

As sheriff, Axel had only one case involving a family member. Two years ago, a drunk eighteen-year-old drove his pickup with two cousins onboard through a sugar beet field before crashing into a farmer's barn. The boy's dad paid for the barn damage. The Rankin County Attorney, in a move Axel likened to a no-harm-no-foul approach of a pickup basketball game, accepted a guilty plea to reckless driving with a retroactive two-month license suspension and a $250 fine. Axel felt that the resolution was an undeserved gift and said so in *The Rankin County Courier*, the county's only newspaper. At the time, Axel hadn't viewed the incident as involving the Kingdom as much as an example of the unwillingness of the county attorney to support a crackdown on underage drinking.

To the Montana newcomer, the Kingdom could present itself as a remnant of a prairie utopian society of the late 1800s. Axel had even heard new arrivals speak of the Kingdom comparing it to the collective farms of the Hutterites, a German-speaking pacifist group, which had several farm colonies in Montana. Axel knew better, but still, manufacturing drugs was not anything Axel considered a bona fide Kingdom activity. This had to be a renegade operation.

This perspective had been the foundation for Axel's suggestion to Hilton in their first telephone call Monday that the best approach to serving the warrant was to talk to the leader of the Kingdom and secure his cooperation. In response, Hilton accused him of "wanting to sleep with the enemy." Axel calmly reiterated that he thought his approach had a substantially lower risk of injury, but conceded that the movie rights wouldn't have as much value. Hilton's response was to hang up the telephone.

As Axel had learned yesterday, one law enforcement organization or another had been stalking the suspected group of meth makers for four days since the South Dakota theft of 1500 pounds of anhydrous ammonia in a wheeled tanker. South Dakota law enforcement had done a good job. Apparently the theft occurred late one night. An old pickup with a trailer in tow was spotted by a patrol car heading west at 6:15 in the morning. Montana plates. Back roads. Very suspicious, but no theft had been reported. One of the South Dakota troopers who lived near the Montana border used his personal car to track the rig into Montana and off Route 34 into the Kingdom. By ten o'clock the theft of a tanker had been reported. The South Dakota troopers called the FBI, who referred the case to the U.S. Marshal's office.

The ammonia was intended as a fertilizer to enhance South Dakota sunflower production, but was also an essential ingredient in the production of methamphetamine, America's new illegal drug of choice. Farmers didn't steal fertilizer. The thieves were in the drug business.

When Hilton reached the ranch's first barbed-wire fence, he again spun around with hands raised to face the group. He removed his gloves, took off his backpack and again pulled the cuffs of his starched cotton shirt out from inside the sleeves of his jacket. From the back of the group, Axel noted how out of place, yet comfortable, Hilton looked, as though an early morning raid on an isolated ranch house was a weekly event for him. Hilton spoke in whispers as he assigned positions around the ranch house to the DEA agents and state troopers.

After several assignments, Hilton looked up at Axel, standing ten feet behind the group. Hilton nodded at him. Axel took this as recognition that he had fulfilled his trailblazer role and was now all but dismissed from duty. Ultimately, Hilton posted him only ten yards from where they crossed the fence, near the juncture of the back fence and the fast-running swallow creek, which carved off a third of the fenced enclosure. At eighty yards out, Axel's post was the farthest from the house.

The plan was to encircle the ranch house and then use synchronized halogen strobe lights to flash through windows and to call out to the dopers with a bullhorn to surrender *en masse*. Alleged to be modeled after the capture of Noriega in Panama, this approach was definitely not a Rankin County design. A female Assistant U.S. Marshal, who flew in by helicopter for yesterday's meeting, had presented fourteen PowerPoint slides with aerial photographs overlaid with a nine-pointed, star-shaped grid, which she called a coverage matrix, showing the engulfment in the house by overlapping seventy-five degree rifle-firing zones. Axel wondered if the presenter's vocabulary and perspectives were intentionally delivered to distance the Feds from the local common folk, who didn't work with "hyper-perceptual environments inducing cognitive disequilibrium" on a regular basis.

At yesterday's pre-operation briefing, the Senior DEA man, newly assigned to head the Denver office after closing down a Mexico City-St. Louis drug ring, concluded his orientation on "pre-apprehension" with the statement that: "Escaping felons are 78% less likely to run outdoors to evade apprehension at night. Night time is the right time." His crew cut and bravado sent a chilling shudder across Axel's shoulders. At a break, Axel was pleased to learn that the presenter was just that and was not to be one of the raiding party. But Axel had to agree with the guy that the last thing they wanted was fleeing suspects and a manhunt in the Harlan Range.

Jack Hilton wrapped up the POB with a remark that this effort was to set a new standard for a "high stealth, antiseptic interdiction."

While he noted that the POB presenters spoke with the confidence of evangelists, Axel's reaction was one of suspicion: these are inexperienced, isolated, self-important people with wildly unrealistic plans developed in a sterile laboratory. The immediate response of the Montana state troopers to the presentation was absolute silence with a variety of facial expressions, all of which asked, "Are these guys for real?" Axel wondered if he looked as bewildered, shell-shocked and disoriented as they did. The expression "shock and awe" from Rumsfeld's Iraq invasion plans came to Axel's mind: Shock and awe might be impressive at a video arcade or the invasion of Baghdad, but would it succeed in the Harlan Range of the Rockies? What did Ham think of this? After the DEA man spoke, Axel had looked across the room to Ham Frazier, who acknowledged his inquiry with a steady nod of his head. The effect was to cast further doubt on the whole operation.

Tonight all the hikers were well armed. Axel had a shotgun loaded with 00 buckshot and his holstered 9mm Glock. He had no thoughts of actually using either, but, as he had been taught over the years, he needed to make absolutely sure that, if necessary, his payload would be up to the job. The twelve-gauge held a three-inch shell with nine metal balls, each one-quarter inch in diameter. Axel had choked the gun's spray pattern down to where at thirty feet from the muzzle the pattern was two feet wide; at fifteen, it was less than six inches.

Axel was afraid to think about the totality of fire power. The Feds all carried hip-holstered 9 millimeter pistols, but Axel knew that was only the beginning. Several of them had bulky backpacks that could contain anything from bazookas to grenade launchers.

Ham appeared to have only a side-arm. Axel had been watching him throughout the hike tonight. Ham, the oldest hiker, had done well and had always been in the middle of the pack.

As the patrol silently settled into their spots around the house, Axel climbed down the creek bank, kneeled, and then eased himself down to the cold, rocky ground using the bank as cover. His feet were almost in the shallow water. Even in the cold night air, the moisture coming off the creek carried a surprising zest. Between the protection offered by the bank and the white noise of the gurgling creek and the rustling leaves, Axel felt insulated and secure. Furthermore, he found comfort in the fact that he was not on an escape route. Only a fool would run at the intersection of the fence and the creek. The meadow immediately beyond the fence offered little protection. It would take a runner a long time to run up the hill to reach the shelter of the tree line. Axel faced the corner of one wing of the one-story ranch house. A yard light illuminated several small-equipment sheds off to his far right.

Axel watched the young, crew-cut DEA agent, Derrick Samuelson, assigned to Axel's right toward the sheds. Samuelson opened his back pack and dumped its contents. He was equipped with a halogen light post on a collapsible tripod and a two-foot-long rifle with a telescoping stock. The post held two five-inch-diameter lights. To Axel's surprise, they were chrome-plated and looked like headlights on a 1920s luxury car.

Just as Samuelson set up the light post at his assigned position, Hilton came by and changed his position to be closer to the ranch house and further left, in front of Axel. Samuelson's new position was within Axel's prescribed zone of fire, effectively restricting his right side. On Axel's left, Hilton repositioned the female South Dakota trooper, closer to the ranch. Ham and one of his troopers with a light post were next. Hilton, himself, was further off to Axel's left and only thirty yards out from the front door. Axel calculated that the two placements in front of him narrowed his own field of fire down to only thirty degrees, less than half the theoretical area. So much for *that* theory. *Maybe Hilton's squeezing me out altogether.*

After five minutes, everyone was in place and lying on the ground. Axel could see no one. He could see Samuelson's light post and two others. All were dark. He had a good view of the doors and windows of the front and one side of the house. He consciously took slow, deep breaths, enjoying the sweet, moist night air.

Hilton's position in front of the house did not have a light post. The yellow glow of the porch light stopped short of his position. Hilton stood and swung his head ceremoniously right and left, like a ten-year-old about to cross the street. As Axel spied over the edge of the bank, Hilton took four elongated strides toward the house. MacArthur returns to the Philippines.

At the first electronic crack of Hilton's bullhorn, Axel checked his watch—5:22. Hilton's broadcast message to the ranch house was simple: "This is the federal government. Come out of the house with your hands over your heads. No weapons. Come out the front door. All together. Now." Thirty seconds later, he repeated his statement and took two further steps toward the semicircle of yellow light. Then, leaning forward, he shuttled off to his left behind a dilapidated, flatbed truck with sun-bleached fenders only twenty yards from the front door. He was joined by the male South Dakota trooper.

Once settled in behind the truck, Hilton waved his right arm up and down. The halogen lights came on instantaneously from the light poles and started a synchronized strobing. The flashing lasted for ten seconds. Then the lights stayed on for five seconds and started strobing again.

Axel saw no movement within the house.

The lighting program continued but after five minutes there was still no response from the ranch house. Hilton activated the bullhorn again. Its loud electronic pop ensured everyone's attention. This time, he stepped out from behind the truck and had the halogens turned off. Axel was surprised at Hilton's move toward the porch: such an easy target, so brazenly foolhardy. Through the bullhorn, Hilton issued orders as though he were directing a high school marching band. "We will take you into custody. We have fourteen agents and more on the road. We have warrants from the U.S. District Courts for Districts of Minnesota and Colorado. In ten minutes, we will use tear gas. Come out the front door with your hands over your head, fingers spread. No weapons." Hilton walked backwards to the protection of the truck and sat down, leaning against the creased rear bumper. The synchronized strobing started again.

There was no activity within the ranch house for several long minutes. Then, all at once, the lights inside the ranch house came on. In response, Hilton quickly stood, turned and drew his hand across his chest, from shoulder to shoulder, and the throbbing halogens stopped. Reflexively, Axel looked up to the truck to see if Hilton was moving. Hilton stayed standing behind the truck. He was focused on the front door. Axel could now see three or four distinct shadows inside the house quickly moving from one room to another and back again. Then, as though in coordination, all of the house lights went off. Then, as in a battle of light switches, the strobes came on again. In the flashing white light, the occupants running from place to place looked to Axel as if they were in an old-time silent movie.

Suddenly, in front of Axel, two men burst out of the house through the side door. To Axel, it looked as if they were on a stage at the theater. The flashes of strobes tracked their progress. They were hunched over, carrying rifles, and scurried along the side of the house. Then in unison, they turned and ran away from the house to Axel's right. Their goal appeared to be the closest equipment shed, the stolen trailer and a VW camper more than one hundred yards off. The steady crunch of the gravel filled the still night air. They did not go in a straight line. First, they ran parallel with the ranch house. Then they angled away from the house straight at Samuelson's strobe lights. Then back toward the shed.

After three quick strides, they turned again, away from the shed and toward the halogen lights, which illuminated their pale faces. Axel pulled down the brim on his hat and cradled his shotgun tightly under his chin. Then, as though the two runners simultaneously recognized the folly in assaulting the light tower, they turned further to their right and struck a path between Samuelson and Axel. They headed for the fence to Axel's right and now ran full speed with no pretense. Quickly they were behind Samuelson's lights and in the dark.

To Axel it looked like their path would hit the creek only thirty feet to his right. He whispered, "Turn left. Go to the sheds. Don't see me. Don't shoot." He could feel his eyes opening wider and hear the rapid thump of his heart.

Then the front runner stumbled and as he fell forward, he pushed the stock of the small rifle forward to break his fall. As the rifle stock hit the ground, his right hand slipped from the grip and tripped the trigger. The rifle shot flared in the darkness. In spite of closely tracking the runners, Axel was startled by the roar to the point that he craned his head further forward over the edge of the bank. As he did, a metallic thwack rang out from the shed. The second runner ran past the first and angled back toward the VW and, to Axel's relief, away from him.

Axel breathed deeply and silently scanned from one runner to the other, wanting the boys to reach their destination. The stumbler stayed on the ground, low, as though hugging it.

Suddenly Samuelson jumped up to his feet with his back to the ranch house. He shouldered his short, stocky rifle. He didn't shoot. Both boys were now between Samuelson and the sheds, but Samuelson's line of fire on the downed runner ran only twenty feet to Axel's right. Axel pushed himself over the edge of the bank and yelled to Samuelson, "Get down." Then he slid down below the edge of the bank. Samuelson was a bigger risk to his health than the runners.

Samuelson held his pose and squeezed off three quick shots aimed at the far runner, who was now closer to the shed than the stumbler. The shots were on fire, like bolts of lightning. The rifle's sound was unexpected—a muffled popping, like a toy gun shooting ping-pong balls—pop-pop-pop.

The three flashes splashed on the ground, off target: short, then long, then way too long. Axel prayed Samuelson would stop shooting. When the echo of the last pop returned off the shed, Samuelson flopped to the ground as though the puppeteer had cut his strings. *Great. Stay there.*

Axel slid down the creek bank to the point that he could barely see the ranch house and the sheds. He could hear the stumbler's deep breathing coming through the sparse grass. He had a fleeting thought of speaking up to warn the kid to stay down. But he said nothing. His yell to Samuelson had revealed his position. He wanted cover. After taking a long count on the ground, the young man shuffled up to a low crouch, and with the athleticism of youth, clutched his rifle and ran after his partner. Then at full speed, he suddenly spun and while still in a low, running crouch fired off two quick, errant shots from his hip at Samuelson's light tripod.

Samuelson didn't return fire. Axel breathed out. The boys would make the shed.

The flashing strobes continued with a steady beat.

Then, as though in youthful defiance of a scripted easy getaway, the shooter skidded to a halt on the loose gravel, yelled to his partner and reset his course—back to the fence and the creek behind it.

But after three quick strides toward the intersection of the creek and the fence, the runner drifted to his right, as though to avoid the fence. With every step, the shooter got closer to Axel. The far runner, who had almost reached the first shed, turned his head back over his shoulder, then slowed and, without stopping, turned obliquely to follow the shooter. The shooter slowed down as his partner stretched to catch up with him. Then, the boys were in lock step only three feet apart. Their new path led straight to Axel. They were in full flight straight toward Axel. Twenty yards out.

As his field of vision filled with oncoming runners, Axel voiced a quiet, "Oh, shit."

Axel could feel the pounding of their steps and hear their heavy breathing. His mind and body went to total automatic pilot. Animal instincts and years of training took control. In a single move, he pushed himself down to gain better footing in the rocky creek bed and then sprang halfway up the bank to a low crouch, shotgun at his hip aimed up at the lead runner. The runner fired at Axel without breaking stride. He was only fifteen feet away but he missed his mark as the bullet whizzed past Axel's left ear. Axel stood his ground. The two runners were almost side by side as they cleared the edge of the bank. Axel shot twice in succession. *Boom. Boom.*

He hit them both. The first in the chest. The blast stopped him in midair and threw him over backwards against the bank. The second runner was hit in the neck. His momentum carried him forward into the creek with his arms and legs at full extension, an athletic cartwheel. He collapsed in a jumble in the water among the rocks. His body writhed. He pulled one knee up to his waist and then shot the leg out straight, the toe pointed. His head flipped forward and then flopped back, exposing the pulpy, pulsating wound to his neck. He was still, his glassy eyes staring into the dark sky.

Clutching his shotgun, Axel lunged toward the bodies, swinging his head from one to another. His forearm suddenly ached from the tight grip he had on the shotgun, ready to use it as a club. The throbbing on his right temple forced him to close his eye. His breathing, through his nose, was deep and well paced, building a reservoir for battle. But the bodies lay still and quiet. He looked into their eyes again. The moisture was still there but both sets were fixed and beginning to glaze. There would be no more fight.

Axel saw a picture of the scene. It reminded him of Matthew Brady's grim civil war photos of dead soldiers looking like so many rag dolls thrown about. Despite the cold night air, beads of sweat formed on his face. He could feel the beads rise to the surface and the tingling sensation of them evaporating.

Axel felt the strength of his legs slide away and his knees slowly buckled. Suddenly half conscious, he let himself slowly collapse. He cradled the shotgun as he turned in a half faint and slid down the bank toward the water. A sharp rock cut his forehead and brought him back to full-consciousness. A steady stream of blood ran across his eyebrow back to his ear. The shotgun blasts had overwhelmed his hearing and fogged his total perception. Then he crawled up to the edge of the bank and peered over, as though he expected a second wave of attackers. He reloaded his gun. His head cleared and he once again heard the gurgling creek and the rustle of the drying leaves from the nearby cottonwood trees.

He surveyed the ranch. No movement in the silent feathery haze. The halogens had stayed off and Axel wondered where everyone had gone. He looked down at his right hand, which still clutched the shotgun, as though it had offended him. *Just what have I done?*

Then there was sound and movement from the ranch house. Axel saw more lights in the house and moving shadows through the windows.

Then the introductory pop of Hilton's loudspeaker. With crisp, clear, authoritative intonation he commanded, "Steady, full lights." Instantly the house was illuminated with amber-orange floodlights from the light poles. No halogens this time. Samuelson appeared and scrambled to his feet behind his pole. The screen door jumped open six inches and then slapped shut, emitting a puff of dust. Then it opened again, more slowly this time. Several jumbled sets of human hands emerged; hands held high in surrender. To Axel, they looked like starfish shimmering in orange Jell-O.

Slowly, three gaunt human forms squeezed silently through the half-opened door to the front porch; slowly as though the screen provided some protection and there was a chance that the humans would need to retreat to its sanctuary.

Axel pushed himself up to the top of the bank, as Hilton, still behind the truck, shouted "Get 'em ." A South Dakota trooper and a DEA agent sprang from behind the truck with rifles pointed in front of them as they ran at the porch. Their profiles struck Axel as the silhouettes of World War I doughboys executing a bayonet charge. In eight quick steps, they were on the porch, and using their rifle barrels as prods they herded the trio into the yard. The agents had the three lie face down and spread-eagled. Then Hilton stepped forward as the agents patted them down and took their wallets.

From a hundred yards away, Axel could see that Hilton was barking into a large, boxy, cordless satellite telephone with a short, stocky antenna. His words were inaudible but his body language conveyed a call for immediate action. Hilton was waving his free hand over his head. The one word Axel could discern was "now," which Hilton repeated every few seconds. Then over Hilton's shoulder Axel saw the bouncing headlights of a small convoy of vehicles led by a small ATV that had been hidden behind the last hill below Crestfallen. Hilton threw his head toward Axel.

Axel turned to look down at the would-be escapees. There had never been any doubt that they were dead: one of a center-chest wound and the other of a neck shot that had all but severed his head. The dry, rocky ground had soaked up the blood that hadn't drained into the creek. Axel stood slump-shouldered over the first body and swung his head slowly from side to side. He still held the shotgun, one-handed, pointed to the ground. He moved his lips in a silent prayer.

With shotgun in hand, he slowly clawed his way back up the creek bank and stood facing the porch.

Hilton moved forward to the three young men lying in front of the ranch home and now guarded by the DEA agents. Hilton had each of them slowly roll over onto their backs so he could see their faces. No one spoke, as Hilton examined each one in turn and shook his head as if to say, "You're not the one." After reviewing the third, he swung his head in a wide half circle, took off his hat with one hand and, with the other, slowly raked the loose skin of his forehead and bare scalp. As the approaching vehicles put him in their headlights, he quickly spun toward Axel and yelled, "God damn."

The new arrivals stopped their vehicles short of the ranch house but kept their headlights fixed on it with engines running. Hilton turned away from them, ran five steps toward Axel and stopped, throwing his hat on the ground. He yelled across the wide expanse, "Axel, goddamn it. I just knew you'd mess this up. Fuck me royal. Local support, my ass!"

Axel saw Hilton's outburst and knew it was directed at him, but could neither hear exactly what Hilton said, nor catch his meaning. Now he could see Hilton charging toward him like a football defensive back closing in on a would-be receiver. Hilton's head was angled to the ground. His eyes were focused three feet in front of him as he plunged forward with his arms pumping. He ran into the shadows and straight for Axel. He said nothing. Axel didn't move. Hilton cocked his head to the side and dropped his shoulder as he slammed full speed into Axel's side. Axel was jolted backwards, lost his balance, and fell to the ground on his back. He held on to his shotgun and the barrel clashed on the rocks.

"What the hell's wrong with you?" Axel shouted at Hilton. "You think I came here with this in mind. Get out of my face, asshole."

Hilton had bounced off Axel and stumbled forward. He quickly caught his balance and focused on the closest body in the creek bed for a moment. Then he ran back to Axel, who was sitting on the ground. With a quick two-handed thrust, Hilton slammed Axel flat on his back. Hilton jumped forward, straddled Axel and sat on him in an effort to keep him on his back. Pressing Axel's shoulders to the ground, Hilton lowered his face to inches above Axel's and screamed, "I'm in your face and I'm going to stay in your fucking, goddamn bloody face, now and forever. Fucking civilian. You ain't got a clue. Not a fucking clue. One of these guys is a federal undercover agent. FBI. You wasted him."

Axel grabbed Hilton's upper arms and yelled, "Undercover what?" Axel tightened his grip and tried to push Hilton off him.

The wrestlers rolled sideways and reached the edge of the bank. Axel freed his right arm and with a quick jab hit Hilton in the nose. Axel felt the nose cartilage collapse under his fist. Hilton's head jerked to the side and then snapped back with blood flowing freely. Then Ham and one of the South Dakota troopers ran up and seized Hilton from behind, pulled him up and off of Axel. Hilton fought the grip of the lawmen and attempted to jump at Axel, still on the ground. Both men were bloody.

To Axel, Hilton looked like a netted mountain lion, wounded, bloody, and bearing its full set of teeth. Hilton, still in the grip of the troopers, was bent over and drooling blood. He took slow deep breaths.

Axel scrambled to his feet and the four men stood apart from each other, ready to respond to the next false move. Hilton shook his head slowly, wiped his nose and mouth with the back of his hand and said across the square to Axel, "You … you screwed this up, big time. You did this to fuck me over." Then he paused as though to consider his next move. Then he drawled, "You're done. I'm on to you, dead man."

Ham swung his head to look at Hilton and then Axel. And then back at Hilton. Finally, as though rendering a verdict, he said, "Whatever happened here, there's nothing we can do about it now. This was self defense." He reached over and grabbed the front of Hilton's shirt and pulled him close. Ham cocked his head and said, "You got a problem with that?"

Hilton said nothing. Ham let go and Hilton, who towered over Ham by a foot, took two steps back. Hilton stared back at Ham and cleared his throat with a grunt. He spat a bloody wad toward Ham, just missing his boot. Neither man said anything. The stand-off ended when Hilton broke eye contact to look back to the ranch house and the line of vehicles assembled in front of it.

The new arrivals at Crestfallen were mainly more federal agents—DEA and Deputy Marshals. But there was a Montana State Patrol SUV. The federal personnel sought out and soon swarmed around Jack Hilton. After posting a guard on the bodies, Hilton led his contingent back to the ranch house. The guard, a uniformed DEA agent, turned his back to Ham and Axel.

"Let's get out of here," Ham said to Axel. "The Feds will secure the scene and do their investigation. They'll be here for days. Let's go. You don't need to be here. Need to patch your head up. You can sit in the warmth and comfort of your office and write up your account. Better'n being badgered by that asshole." He threw his head back over his shoulder toward Hilton and the ranch house.

Axel didn't react and stood like a stunned Neanderthal, slump-shouldered with his feet spread wide. He now held the barrel of the shotgun, still warm, while the stock rested on the ground. Silently, he rocked his head forward and back as though responding to an internal rhythm. Ham waited.

Finally, Axel pulled his head up, shook his shoulders, looked Ham in the eye and said, "You're right. Let's get out of here. Cold." Axel took two staggering steps and stopped. He regained his equilibrium. Then the two Montanans walked in silence up to the ranch house.

The shiny new Montana State Patrol SUV seemed strangely out of place. The driver retrieved a first aid kit and bandaged Axel's head. Then Ham and Axel settled into the back seat, and they left Crestfallen. Minutes later, as the SUV turned off the rutty, gravel county road onto State Highway 34 and headed west, a Blackhawk helicopter appeared, circling around Mt. Elliott, across Dead Horse Plateau, and headed for Crestfallen Ranch.

CHAPTER 6

(Thursday, October 20)

Sven hadn't gone to bed until after eleven, but he was up before sunup and made himself a pot of coffee. He checked the wiring on his pickup and the ATV. He left the sleeping ranch and rode his ATV up into the mountains to the test mine high up in the Bridal Veil Creek drainage, just below the falls that gave the creek its name. Today he would act on yesterday's pledge to Megan; he would stop the exploration.

Over the last three weeks, miners had drilled and blasted sixty feet into the sheer granite wall of Mt. Elliott. Sven had always considered the mountain and creek integral parts of the Thordahl Ranch, regardless of their federal ownership. This mine was an assault on his preserve. Today Sven took an indirect off-road route, avoiding both the hikers' trail and the old logging road.

The sun rose early this high on Mt. Elliott. At first light, Sven was surprised to see a helicopter slide around Mt. Elliott and head east.

At the mine nothing appeared changed from his last visit, three days ago. Today was a day for action, not just reconnaissance. He scanned the ten-foot-high cyclone fence. It was topped with a tight coil of razor wire. He closely examined the stainless steel eye bolts, cables, and turnbuckles holding the fence secure against the near-vertical wall of the mountain. What was so valuable or hazardous about the operation that it had to be so well protected?

All work had stopped four days ago. The workers had cleaned up the yard and locked the gate. *All the better. No witnesses.*

The massive gate was double-thickness chain link reinforced with diagonal metal bars welded to the frame of two-inch-diameter stainless steel piping. Each leaf of the gate was eight feet wide mounted on six-inch-diameter vertical posts that appeared to be set in concrete. Sven reflected that they'd had to drill down at least three feet into the granite to set the post deep enough to support the weight of the large gates. The fence was more than enough to discourage the passing hiker or even the opportunistic vandal. But Sven was more intent and prepared than either.

He turned back to the creek. The sunlight filtered through the aspens and reflected off the cascading water brought a smile to his face. He was doing the right thing.

Sven parked the ATV in front of the gate and dismounted. The gate's lock was his immediate objective. He walked up to it and shook his head. The lock was an antique, a big brass survivor from the days of key-entry padlocks to bonded warehouses. While the hasp was a half inch in diameter and the lock itself weighed more than a pound, he knew it wasn't as strong as it looked. He wondered about the choice of this lock. Was it selected by an old timer who hadn't kept up with new technology or a young buck who calculated that a proven limited-access key entry system was actually more secure than modern, digital combination systems? Either way, they were dead wrong. This lock's easier to breach than a dime-store bike lock.

He went back to the ATV and unstrapped the large plastic toolbox he'd carefully prepared last week. His immediate objectives were a set of C-clamps, a tungsten drill bit, and his portable drill. In short order, he clamped the lock to the solid frame of the gate and then drilled through the key entry. The lock fell open after a three-minute effort. He opened the gate slowly, examining it for contact sensors that might send electronic signals to security personnel. There weren't any.

The work yard in front of the mine itself was the size of a football field and filled with half-scale earth-moving equipment. Sven was amazed at the tidiness of the place. As clean as a sales lot for used equipment. There was no slag heap. Sven figured that the equipment was to excavate the mine and to carry the slag either off the mountain entirely or to a second, EPA-co-opted site, further away from tourists in a backcountry drainage. Other than a small front-end loader, the equipment was foreign to Sven, especially the vertical tank with a thin, almost miniature conveyor belt leading up to the top. Were they sorting loose rock, crushing it? He stared at it, leaning forward to examine the elaborate machine. He could see where material came out and where the raw material went up the conveyor to the top and into a tank. But where did the material go from there? He gave up and focused on his mission.

The mine ran straight into the mountain. He cautiously walked into the fifteen-foot-diameter opening. Even in the deep shadow, he could see the back wall ahead. Sven marveled at the accomplishment. The shaft was perfectly cylindrical except for the flat floor. The curved walls were smooth and as regular as a gravel-paved road. The footing was even more refined, a well packed, pebbly base as flat as a parking lot. He looked at his watch and turned to go back to the tool box. After allowing his eyes to adjust to the brightness of the unfiltered sun, Sven scanned the work yard and the opened gate.

He straddled the ATV, started it up and drove through the work yard. By the front-end loader he stopped, inspected and then picked up an empty heavy wooden box, left by the miners. The old oil-stained box looked out of place in the high-tech mine. As he drove into the mine, he could feel the walls closing in. He felt a tightness in his chest. He turned back to the bright entrance and expended a chest full of air. Only then did he realize that he'd been holding his breath since he'd entered the cave.

Over the next half hour, he taped four small dynamite packets to the roof of the cave. He was pleased that the tape stuck to the hard rock ceiling. He then wired in detonators and linked the four packets, wiring the final packet into the Cotton Hill Racer's receiving unit.

He thought about the fact that the unit's fresh nine-volt battery could be sending out a locator signal. He dismissed the idea with the consideration that even if it was, it wouldn't be for much longer. The sending unit remained in the tool box. Sven sat on the overturned box and admired his work.

A quarter mile down the trail from the mine, Sven stopped his ATV and took out the Cotton Hill remote-control transmitter. He turned it on and pulled the antenna up. He held the unit over his head. Then he pushed the accelerator lever switch to maximum.

The explosion reminded him of a mortar shot from Korea. It wasn't at all like exploding fireworks or a building explosion, but a low frequency thump as though a huge boulder had landed nearby. A thin cloud of dust floated downhill. Instantly, the air tasted like dirt. Sven fought the urge to drive back to see what damage he'd done. He got back on his ATV and drove away from the mine, took the first turn off from the hiking trail, drove through the creek, and cautiously worked his way down the hill to quietly arrive at the ranch house a half hour later for a peaceful morning breakfast.

He was looking forward to a horseback ride with Megan.

CHAPTER 7

(Thursday, October 20)

At 7:47 AM Ange Clauson of the County Sheriff's office received a telephone call from Huntington British Columbia Mining's security office in Salt Lake City. The caller was a male technician who reported that he was charged with monitoring video feed from twenty-two North American mine sites. In a flat, atonal Midwestern voice he said, "We have a possible break-in at our Bridal Veil Mine just outside of Grant. 7:03. We have video images of what appears to be a tall man on an ATV. The camera was activated by breaking a laser beam five feet in front of our gate. We've got only 10 seconds of film—straight time. The camera wasn't well adjusted. All I've got is a picture of a couple of wheels, a right pant leg and a scuffed up boot. The right flank of an ATV—red and well-used. It looks like a guy with a bum leg. Can't bend his knee. In our FMT System, if there's movement in the activated target zone after ten seconds, the shutter is supposed to go to three-second bursts every thirty seconds for the next four hours, subject, of course, to our intervention. But that didn't happen. All we've got is the first ten seconds. Could you guys check it out?"

His report was straightforward. No excitement, no alarm. Ange thought maybe it was his third such call of the young day.

Ange looked at the detailed County map she kept at her desk for just such occasions. She also looked to the door to the office corridor and Axel's office. "That's back in the Custer Forest, right? Beyond the Thordahl Ranch? Do you have directions?" She paused.

The Salt Lake City security man responded, "Yeah, I got directions."

She had spotted the trail on the map and jumped in with, "Wait,

I've got it. There's a patrol car out now in that part of the county, and I could probably convince him to swing by the mine. Can a four-wheel-drive get up that trail? If so, we could have somebody there this morning." She wasn't ready to call this a high priority. She didn't like the pushy attitude of the Salt Lake City caller.

"That would be good. I'm in Salt Lake. Never been to the site. My map has the trail intersecting State 34 about twenty-three and a half miles southeast of the intersection of 34 and 176. That make sense to you? Can you have the deputy report back to me when he gets there?"

This request was over the line. Ange certainly wasn't going to have anybody getting back to this caller. She replied, "Tell ya what. Give me your name and phone number. If we need to talk to you, we'll call. Otherwise you call us back. You've got our number. OK?"

He gave her his name and number and hung up. She wrote herself a note and pinned it to the cork board above the phone. Later.

CHAPTER 8

(Thursday, October 20)

Axel and Ham sat together in the back seat of the MSP's SUV. Its bright, clean interior struck Axel as an extreme contrast to the cold, dark creek bed. Axel, with his wet, bloody clothes and the bandage on his head, felt out of place. The driver, a young, uniformed state trooper, had nothing to say. He hardly moved his head as he continually scanned the road ahead. He wore mirrored sunglasses and acknowledged Ham's few softly spoken commands with a barely audible, "Yes, sir."

The trio rode toward Grant as the sun rose over their left shoulders. For the first ten miles, neither Ham nor Axel spoke.

Then Ham started a monologue in a low, soothing voice. Axel hardly paid any attention. His mind was still back at the creek.

Ham's story was that just last year he had worked on a Patriot Act task force. The group had been led by the FBI out of Seattle. Three Arabs and four Canadian nationals came across the border floating down the Flathead River. They had a rented cabin at the end of the road in Polebridge. The standoff ended in a twenty-minute, seventy-six-bullet shootout and the deaths of two suspects and a federal agent, a veritable phantom who only first appeared at the start of the shooting. Afterwards, no one acknowledged knowing him. His body vanished from the scene as inconspicuously as he had arrived. Ham's conjecture was that he was either CIA, military intelligence with FBI handlers, or just a contractor, a hired shooter. Ham described how the Feds sought a gag order from a federal court to clamp down on what they called "uncorroborated, independent accounts." The goal was for the lead FBI agent to be the only source of information and disinformation. The FBI's story was to be the only story.

Gazing out the window at the passing foothills and the long shadows of the early morning, Ham said, "Every shot was analyzed: timing, shooter, objective, and destination. The FBI got the event and its reports classified under the Patriot Act. Never saw one word in public. It's a federal go-to-jail felony to talk about it. Hey, maybe Hilton's got a warrant for me."

Axel was lost in thoughts of the early morning's events.

They arrived into the awakening town with the sun. When Axel saw a familiar truck, he had a moment of panic. So what does he do now? What does a fellow who just shot two people to death do an hour later? He squirmed in his seat. He shifted to his right and stared out the window, then left and right again, as though he was viewing the town for the first time.

The town had been originally laid out on a grid in the flat bottom of a broad u-shaped valley, with the Vermillion River off to the east side. Most of the town was to the west of the river. The main street, Broadway, lived up to its name. Fifty feet wide, it was the only street that ran the complete length of the town. It gained a hundred vertical feet over its fifteen blocks within Grant. It ran parallel to the Vermillion River four blocks to the west.

There were three bridges. The Route 34 bridge was the biggest and busiest, but that was a relative term because except for the few families on the east bank, the sparse Irish Kingdom traffic, and the occasional tourist seeking the back road route to Sheridan, the bridge saw little action. The two others saw less.

Thus, Axel was surprised when the driver turned off 34 east of the river onto a quiet street to take the old upper bridge, built over the steel frame of two recycled flatbed railroad cars.

Taking the old bridge avoided a long, conspicuous promenade down Broadway and allowed the MSP SUV to slide into the small parking lot behind the County Building without meeting another car. From the backseat Axel gave the silent driver a soft pat on the shoulder.

As soon as they stopped, Ham opened his side door. He ran behind the vehicle and opened Axel's door before Axel had moved or had even considered getting out. Axel smiled at his own stupefied condition and allowed Ham to hold his elbow as he got out of the high-clearance vehicle.

As they rounded the corner to enter through the building's main door on Broadway, Axel looked up and down the street—up, until it trailed off into the foothills and down, through the dusty, sleepy commercial district with its wood-frame store fronts and an occasional two-story portico shading the sidewalk, an authentic Western façade. Axel had once mused that all the town needed was a horse-livery service on Broadway and it could serve as the movie set for a remake of the movie *High Noon*.

The trio stopped at the front door. Axel gripped and then let go of the door handle. He flipped his head to the left and silently led the group around the building to the side entry that led straight to the sheriff's office, thus avoiding a number of the county offices. As early as it was, there were bound to be people already on the job. The troopers weren't the only ones managing Axel. Axel was managing Axel.

As they rounded the corner, Axel considered that the building well represented the county: strong, resilient, and hard working. The County Building was a formidable three-story stack of creamy-tan Madison limestone blocks. Each block weighed more than a thousand pounds. They were quarried at Henrietta, cut to specifications at Park City, then numbered and assembled into walls in Billings. Then the walls were taken down and the blocks were shipped by special train to Grant and there reassembled in two weeks' time—complete with sixty-foot-long Douglas fir floor joists, maple flooring from Michigan, and wide, deep-set sash windows from Seattle. One of Axel's predecessors claimed that the building may have been built in 1929, but it was really 350 million years old—dating from the original shallow sea that covered much of North America and its sea bed that formed the limestone deposits. Today, Axel marveled at the strength of the building, illuminated in the beamy, bronze, horizontal morning light.

Axel always connected the strong, earnest building with the county's resilience and pride of independence, and now feared that he had breached a public covenant and disappointed the proud citizens of Rankin County.

CHAPTER 9

(Thursday, October 20)

Hilton had long planned a mid-morning press conference in Billings to announce the unequivocal success of his early-morning raid. It was to be his finest hour, another defining moment in his stellar career. He had enlisted a Department of Justice public communication specialist from Washington to outline a press release. He recruited a chemist from DEA to calculate the anticipated annualized output of the Crestfallen production facility based on the size of the tank of anhydrous ammonia. Hilton coached the young chemist into a $100 million estimate.

A helicopter was to ferry Hilton to Billings to meet the press. Instead, Hilton cancelled the press conference and had the specialist send an edited e-mail to CNN, Fox, NBC, ABC, CBS, fourteen radio networks, the *NY Times*, the *Denver Post*, the *Seattle Times*, and the *Billings Gazette*.

> For Immediate Release
> 8:00am, October 20
> Billings, Montana
>
> Today the U.S. Marshal's office in a pre-dawn interdiction secured the capture of a federal fugitive and succeeded in derailing the start-up of a $100 million methamphetamine laboratory in rural Rankin County, MT.
>
> A multi-agency task force led by U.S. Marshal Jack Hilton of the Denver office apprehended Robert T. Johnson, a convicted federal felon who had been released on bail pending sentencing. Johnson failed to

> appear for his sentencing hearing in Minneapolis and was believed to be traveling west.
>
> The South Dakota State Police were instrumental in focusing the search for Johnson. On October 16, the South Dakota State Police reported to federal authorities that an anhydrous ammonia trailer was stolen from a farm outside Lowther, South Dakota and was towed west into Montana and ultimately to an abandoned ranch high in the Harlan Range.
>
> Federal authorities tied the two incidents together and, utilizing a new Rapid-Strike Planning Process, launched the assault on the ranch within 72 hours of confirming the location through satellite photography. The assault team included elements of the U.S. Marshal's office, the DEA, the South Dakota State Police, Montana State Police and the Rankin County Sheriff's Department.
>
> Upon assessment of the facility, the DEA officially estimated that it had a full-production weekly capacity of hundreds of pounds of crystal meth, with a street value of $20 million. Raw materials on hand could have supported five weeks of full production.
>
> At least two suspects ran from the ranch house as the task force closed in. Shots were fired and two suspects were wounded by a Montana law enforcement agent. Their identities and the extent of their injuries are being withheld pending further confirmation.

One reporter from the *Billings Gazette* showed up at the local federal building. No one from the U.S. Marshal's office appeared. A stack of the press releases were on the table in the basement press room.

Hilton flew to Billings on the first helicopter out of Crestfallen. As it banked to turn north away from Mt. Elliott, a small, single-engine plane flew over it on a take-off pattern. The plane was quick and climbing fast. Hilton swung his head to follow it. He asked the pilot, "Was that one of ours?" The plane continued to climb in a wide arc. Hilton craned his neck to follow the plane as it headed west into the face of the Harlan Range. The helicopter pilot tracked the plane as it flew away, but said nothing and accelerated as he reached altitude and headed north.

By noon, Hilton was back at Crestfallen with three Deputy U.S. Marshals from Billings and a senior DEA field officer. By 3:00 PM four FBI agents were on the scene and promised a comprehensive investigation.

CHAPTER 10

(Thursday, October 20)

As they entered the side door of the Rankin County Building, Ham reestablished his gentle grip on Axel's right elbow and ushered him into the sheriff's office. Ange Clausen stood as the two men entered. She stared at the bandage on Axel's forehead and the blood on his jacket. Through the exterior glass door, she saw the MSP trooper with mirrored sunglasses blocking the entry.

Axel said nothing as he passed Ange's desk, but he slowly bobbed his head to tell her that he was OK and it was fine "for this guy to help me back to my office." Ham and Axel continued across the lobby toward the hall and Axel's office. Ange stood and stared.

Ange Clausen was a Rankin County celebrity. She was a looker and she knew it. More than one middle-aged Rankin County cowboy regularly dropped into the sheriff's office just to spend some time with Ange. Axel had to shoo one guy away with threats of arrest. She had been the star on the Grant High School basketball team when they won the state championship in the mid-1980s. Her two teenage boys now led the Grant High School Cavalry in basketball. She still carried herself with the poise and balance of an athlete and retained her tall, lean figure. Last year, she had gained another boost in local status as the wife of Topper Clausen, the head lineman for the local electric co-op, who last winter had braved sub-zero temperatures and a thirty-mile-an-hour wind to repair a faulty circuit breaker at the top of a sixty-foot tower, only to have the telescopic hydraulic boom freeze solid. He was rescued four hours later with full press coverage and the boisterous cheers of a crowd of onlookers. They had brought pitchers of beer with them when they left the Broadway bars.

Ham and Axel went through the lobby door, took three steps down the hall and turned into Axel's office. Ham positioned Axel behind the desk and closed the door. Axel sat there, stock-still. He zipped his jacket up to his chin.

Ham looked down at Axel. He said, "You stay there. Don't answer the phone. Don't talk to anyone. Not even Ange. I'll talk to her." Then he playfully leaned his head forward, shook it quickly and said, "Nooobody," the sound reverberating in the small room. He popped his head up, smiled, and said, "I'm going for coffee, need cream?" Ham headed for the door.

"Noooobody," replied Axel in an artificially deep, slow baritone. "No cream either," he yelled as Ham closed the door behind him.

Returning with coffees, Ham walked up to Ange's counter. He stopped and collected his thoughts and then flatly reported, "I'm Ham Frazier, Deputy Commissioner of the MSP. The morning raid at Crestfallen. Well, it didn't go down like we planned. Two guys came out trying to escape. Took a shot at Axel. Missed. He shot back. Killed 'em both." He paused to consider whether to say anything more about the shooting. He decided not to and continued, "He's in shock, sorta. I'm gonna tell him to take some time off—ten days, two weeks, whatever. We'll bring in some troopers. I'm gonna to stick around, help coordinate. Can you put together a roster of the deputies, today's shifts and schedules?"

Ange stood up slowly and smoothly as though she was being raised by a helium balloon. She brought her hands up to her ears and said, "Oh, my God."

Ham continued, "Axel'll be OK. He's just got to work it through. Shit happens." His eyes were riveted on her to make the point.

Ange spoke again, "Oh, my God. Two guys. Axel shot two guys dead? This morning?"

Ham looked down at the floor. "Yes. Now we need to keep our cool. We need to help Axel." He raised his gaze to look her in the face. "He did the right thing. He needs our help. Do you understand? We've got to help him and not get folks riled up. He's absolutely without fault. But, there's goin' to be flak. Fed's aren't happy. We've got to help him fend it off. You with me?"

Ange, while slowly nodding her head, let herself descend into her chair and, when settled, looked at the interior office door leading back to Axel's office.

"Holy moley. How did it happen?"

Ham paused, looked out at the trooper guarding the side door, and said, "Short story's what I gave you. It was dark. We had the ranch house surrounded. Feds had strobe lights on short poles. The U.S. Marshal was on a bullhorn. Two guys came out running. Zigged and zagged a bit. One runner tripped and his rifle went off. Hit a metal shed. One of the DEA guys shot at the downed runner. Some kind of zap-gun. But he missed. The guy got up and shot back. Then both runners were up and running helter-skelter. Then they came right at Axel. Shooting. He didn't have a choice." He paused. "He didn't have a choice. I hope to talk Axel into staying here for today and tomorrow. Go home Saturday. Could you call his brother Arlyn? Have him bring in a couple changes of clothes. No sheriff outfits, just jeans, shirts, socks and underwear." Then he looked at her sternly with his eyebrows furled, "Don't be retelling this story just yet. I'll do what I can to get the story out. But let's keep it under wraps until I can talk to the deputies. Can you bring 'em all in, even the off-duty ones, say … " He looked at his watch. "Ten o'clock? We've got to manage this so folks don't go off half-cocked."

Left to himself, Axel's thoughts surged. He replayed the vision of the boys running at him in the dark with the strobe-lit ranch house behind them. It was like a film clip that ran in a continuous loop. When he did look around the office, he focused his attention on the oversized double-hung window behind the gritty Venetian blinds. Then he began talking aloud to himself: "Yes, I shot them. They were running at me, ready to shoot. One of them shot at me. I thought I was just about dead. Just about dead."

Ham was in the hall outside Axel's office when he heard Axel talking. With a paper cup of coffee in each fist, he burst the door open and shouted, "Who are you talking to?"

Axel jumped halfway out of his chair, then fell back down again and said nothing. Ham spotted the telephone a good four feet from Axel's hand and realized that Axel had been talking to himself. "Here, coffee," he grunted and pushed the paper cup in front of Axel. He sat down across the desk from Axel, scooted his chair close to it and placed his own cup on the desk. He caught Axel's gaze and held it, as though examining his face for acne scars.

"Axel. Axel, I can't stay with you all day. Wish I could. You hear me?" as though talking to a child who'd just awakened from a nap.

Axel responded slowly and picked up his coffee. "I'm here, Ham. You've got my attention. Christ, you rattled the pictures."

"Axel, number one, you were absolutely justified in this shooting. I saw everything. You did what 99% of trained officers would have done. The 1% who wouldn't shoot would be dead. You didn't start the shooting. We all saw it. The kid tripped. The DEA guy shot lightning bolts at one, and then the bad guys came for you to avoid the lights and the DEA guy. One of 'em shot at you. No culpability. Totally without blame. Hear me?" Ham coughed and increased his volume. "You are totally without blame. Understand?"

Axel had taken a sip of the coffee, breathed deeply, unzipped his coat and settled into his chair. He looked at Ham, through his moist eyes. While Ham's words had come at him too fast to completely register, he heard most of them, and felt the support Ham was sending. Blinking away the moisture, Axel replied softly, "Thanks Ham, but, but I shot 'em. Did you hear what Hilton said? I was on the ground. Hilton's on top of me and says, 'One of these guys is undercover FBI.' Just out of the blue, FBI undercover."

Ham jumped out of his chair. "Criminy, man. FBI. Undercover. He never told us that." Ham sat back. After a moment, he said, "Regardless, you did the right thing. For all we know, they were bad dudes, ready to blow you away as soon as they saw you. You got that? Listen to me. Hilton's got a lot of explaining to do. Undercover FBI. I can't believe he didn't tell us. He'll have a three-ring federal circus on his hands, and I don't know that he can handle it. He'll do everything he can short of torture to hog-tie that DEA agent. My sense is that Hilton's not a stand-up kind of guy. He's made a limp career out of dodging responsibility. You talked to Faraday about Hilton, didn't ya? Me too. Hilton'll look to pin this on anybody. Anybody. I'm sure he already started." Ham wanted to say, "His number one target will be you," but he knew that Axel had enough to deal with and would probably come to the same conclusion himself soon enough, if he hadn't already.

Ham started up again after a pause. "Trooper, you gotta take care of yourself. Put yourself on leave. If I could suspend you, I would. No work. Paid leave for the next ten days. Our State Patrol handbook calls for three week's paid leave for any shooting, irregardless. Rankin County probably doesn't have such a plan. You've got to get the jump on this. Don't try to do any county work, you'll just screw it up. Right now, take yourself off the duty list. Paid or unpaid. You can't be working with people. You can't be a leader. Minimum ten days. You hear me?" Axel continued to slouch in his armchair. He nodded his head.

Ham couldn't tell if Axel was half asleep or in a stupor. One way or the other, he wasn't sure that the message was registering.

Ham started again. "Get yourself a pad and paper. Write down everything said and done—by anybody. Start with the first you heard of this adventure. Detail phone calls. Every conversation you had with Hilton. Every detail of the Pre-Op. Every thought and opinion you had. You need pages and pages. It's a brain dump. But don't talk to anyone about it. This is your uninfluenced memory."

Ham paused to take a sip of coffee. Axel watched him closely, but said nothing. Axel leaned his head against the back of his chair. Ham started in again. "Write down your thoughts of the presentations, the presenters, Hilton, what you thought of him at every step. Why you did what you did. What you thought he thought. Doesn't have to be full sentences. Don't stop 'til you finish. Tomorrow, rewrite your notes. Tie things together, put it in chronological order. Then trash your first draft. Tear it up and never look at it again. Better yet, burn it. Your second draft will be your whole memory."

Axel tossed his head from side to side, which Ham understood as evidence of Axel's consideration of his advice.

Then Axel said, "Ham, thank you for getting me out of there. We both know the Feds are going to have a turkey roast. I'm OK. I got a job to do. I can't take ten days off. I got six deputies and sixteen daily patrols. The Rankin County Sheriff's Department doesn't run itself. I've got to prioritize what needs to be done." While still in his chair, Axel shrugged off his jacket and put both palms on the desk in preparation for standing. Then he started to get up.

Ham popped up and threw himself across the desk in an effort to push Axel back into his chair. Axel scooted his chair backwards. The chair banged against the back wall, jarring Axel and tossing him forward.

Lying across Axel's desk, Ham yelled, "The hell you are. I'll get the governor to declare martial law before I'll let you think it's business as usual. Hell, we'll get the Montana National Guard in here. That won't look too good on your résumé. Couple of voters might find that odd. Uniformed troops in Humvees. Hey, Axe, killing folks ain't in the job description. Nobody knows how to act. But I tell you this. It's one hell of a mind-bender. You need to relax."

Axel sat back in his chair, now three feet behind his desk, and sighed. His arms flopped over the arms of the large leather chair. His hands dangled six inches above the floor like dead weights.

Ham sat back into his own seat and stared at Axel.

After a long silence Axel said, "OK. But, I can't charge the county for not working. I'll take a week's vacation. Unpaid leave. You can run the place, set the schedules. Maybe the deputies will learn something from your troopers. How do we do it?"

"Easy. I've got a complete communications center in my car. Who's your First Deputy? Got any prisoners here? I'll set the schedule. We'll get two or three MSP units from Billings."

"Whoa, buddy. Slow down."

"Here's what we do. You take leave but stay here at the jail. Tonight and tomorrow night. Have food brought in. Any prisoners we take up to Yellowstone County. You stay inside all day. Sleep in a cell. We get a couple of two-man state squads to do county 24-7 road patrol. We do it all the time, one county or another. No biggie. I'll direct your deputies. You stay away from the phone. Wear casual clothes and act like a prisoner. Have food brought in. It was a long night. You need a rest." Ham was thinking fast. "You need to consolidate, get your story down cold. Write your report."

"What about my deputies?"

"I can handle that. I'll give 'em the straight scoop, otherwise they'll make up their own stories and complicate things further. Ange and I will keep'em busy. Don't worry. Rankin County's the number one priority of the State Patrol. This week, next week. After that it'll be somebody else. I'll write out a script for Ange. You're taking at least a week off, and the MSP is here for two weeks. All existing plans for staffing patrols and shifts stand until further notice."

As Ham was leaving the room, Axel, slouching in his chair, said, "Aye, aye, sir!!"

Ham stopped at the door and turned back toward Axel. He fixed his eyes on Axel and said, "I've shot a few guys trying to kill 'em. Afterwards, there's no *right* way to act. But you can't undo the fact that you shot 'em. You can't forget. It's a head game. Best outcomes I've seen are the guys who find a place for it, put it there, and learn to live with it. Tomorrow will be better than today."

Ham closed the door behind him.

Axel stayed in his office reworking the morning's events. About half an hour after Ham left, Ange came back to his office with a message from Ham with the names of the dead men: William J. Ryan and Douglas Burns, who, indeed, was an undercover FBI agent.

Axel was aware of his fragile emotions and wondered how his feelings would change as the days went by, and if there were names that would apply to them. An immediate thought was that, since the event happened only hours ago, wasn't there a mechanism to restructure the event to reach a better outcome? His mental approach was to find a turning point, a decision made or a step taken, to choose the other alternative, and then run the time machine forward to a conclusion that did not have him shooting anyone. As successful as he was at alternative endings, he soon came to realize the silliness of his game and the sadness of not being capable of escaping reality.

Axel followed Ham's advice, and Ham was as good as his word on taking over Rankin County. Ange called Arlyn to bring in two changes of clothes for Axel—no questions asked. No prisoners, so Axel unceremoniously moved into the secure three-cell suite. He took a shower and ate a scrambled-egg sandwich from the Grant Café.

After the sandwich, Ange briefed Axel on the call from Salt Lake City. She relayed the description of the ten seconds of videotape. Ange hadn't yet dispatched any of the current patrol to the mine but suggested that somebody go up there so she could call the guy back—at least. Axel sat quietly in the cell and told Ange to get a copy of the video and have Ollie look at it. "Ollie can handle this."

The thought of Ollie Macy made Axel smile. Ollie was the First Deputy Sheriff, a Grant native and ten-year veteran, Ollie wanted to solve mysteries and was as enthusiastic as a new recruit. He wanted the full back story, motives, independent evidence and all the new equipment. He looked younger than his age and his flat-top haircut, flattened nose, and protruding ears reminded some of a ventriloquist's dummy. But he was Axel's loyal, go-to assistant who knew how to take orders and get the job done.

Ham's idea of staying in jail to consolidate and avoid people, and the inevitable rehashing of the shootings, worked well for Axel, but he wasn't a purist. He needed to talk to Anne and Arlyn. He wanted them to hear from him that he was handling the impact of the shootings, and hear the full story from his lips so they would know how to deal with the inevitable half-truths and speculation. He wanted them to know that he was the same man he was yesterday, and he wanted them to tell him that he wasn't alone. But first some sleep, if possible.

Settling into the jail, Axel had the feeling that yesterday was years ago, when he'd been so young and innocent.

Another person he had to talk to was Hank Anderson, the owner-editor of the *Rankin County Courier*—a friend and confidante.

Axel wanted to tell Hank the whole story. Hank would listen patiently and then test him. He would ask the hard questions and force Axel to answer them. Hank would also help him sort out what really went on and organize Axel's thoughts.

Over the years, Axel had had many off-record, candid, private discussions with Hank on issues of county government, the sheriff's department, and individual cases. They hadn't been background interviews: not newspaper-man-interviewing-the-sheriff so much as extended conversations between friends with Hank a full participant.

Hank had not betrayed Axel's confidence. He had been a friend. That's what Axel was looking for now.

After Ham left, Axel talked with Ange and laid out a ten-day plan for the reorganized sheriff's department. She had already called Arlyn and he was on his way in. Axel gave Ange Anne's cell number and the number for the emergency room at Billings Memorial. He asked her to call Anne and ask her to call in the late afternoon. He also asked her to call Hank at the *Courier* and ask him to come over about noon.

When Arlyn arrived, Axel was asleep in one of the cells. Arlyn wanted to talk to Axel, but Ange stood her ground. It helped her cause that Ham and three state troopers arrived and all but carried Arlyn out the door.

Arlyn walked back to his truck, parked across the street from the County Building. He got in and started it up, ready to drive away. Then he changed his mind. He got out, leaned against the door, and waited. When, ten minutes later, Ham left the office, Arlyn flagged him down. "Hey, I'm Arlyn Cooper, Axel's brother. What's up?"

Ham examined Arlyn in his rumpled, plaid flannel shirt, worn Levi's, and scuffed boots. Ham pursed his lips and looked away.

Then, turning back to Arlyn, he said with a slow, modulated tone, "I'm Ham Frazier, from Helena. Federal drug bust over in the Irish Kingdom. Meth lab. Coupla guys ran. Some shooting. One of 'em shot at Axe. He shot back. Two of 'em. Dead. We've got no problem with anybody but the Feds. One of the dead guys was undercover FBI. Never should have been there. Axel'll be all right. Needs some time to himself. Axel's a good man. Give him some space."

Arlyn, with his mouth open, stood motionless in front of Ham. Ham reached out and quickly shook Arlyn's hand and then turned on his heel to greet two approaching troopers who had just rolled in.

To the back of Ham's head, Arlyn finally said, "Holy Shit." Then he swung his head up and down the street and counted four MSP cruisers and two SUVs.

He walked back into the sheriff's office and up to Ange's desk. As Ange slowly stood and was opening her mouth to redirect Arlyn back out the door, Arlyn put his hands up. "Slow down, Ange. I just talked to Frazier, state trooper guy. He told me. So where's Axel? He's not under arrest?" He waited for Ange to reply, and after a moment when she didn't he said, "Well, goddamn it. Where the hell is he?"

Ange scanned the small room and said, "No, he's not under arrest. He's just staying away from the press and the busybodies. Frazier, who, if he didn't tell you, is not just an ordinary trooper from Helena but *the* Deputy Commissioner of the MSP. Anyway, he said it would be a good idea for Axel to stay here a couple days. 'Respite care,' he told me. Anyway, away from the public, away from the press. Give him time to sort things out."

Arlyn shrugged his shoulders in resignation and stuffed his hands in the rear pockets of his jeans. "Axel told me about the hike over Dead Horse Plateau at midnight. We talked about me coming along. Looks like I'm the smart one this time. Whole thing sounded like a damned stupid escapade, Alexander the Great, 'On to the Punjab.' Damned Feds probably wanted fucking war elephants and catapults." He stopped and let that settle in. When Ange said nothing he asked, "So where's Axel now? Back there?" He nodded his head to the door to Axel's office, the squad room, lockers, and cells.

"You bet. He's going to stay a couple days. Write up a report. He's cool with it. Actually, I think he's sleeping right now. I'll tell him to call you at home tonight, OK? You got a cell phone, maybe he can call you sooner. OK? We're all trying to protect and support him. One way or another, he'll call you, I'm sure."

Axel's nap was only thirty-seven minutes. He called Arlyn's cell phone when he woke up.

By early afternoon, Axel was physically exhausted but couldn't sleep anymore or even sit still in the jail. The shock had worn off. He had eaten two meals, talked to Hank Anderson and run out to the front desk to talk to Ange four times. He was pleased to see Ange when she pushed open the heavy cellblock door, and all the more pleased that Arlyn had arrived at the front desk wanting to see him.

Arlyn hugged him high across the shoulders and held him for a long time. Axel could feel the warmth of blood running to his face and said, "Thanks for coming."

Arlyn had brought a pair of loafers, blue jeans, a sweatshirt, a plaid flannel shirt, and a short stack of books, which he threw on the bunk. "Got these outta your room. Figure you're reading at least one of them."

Arlyn was there to hear the whole story and Axel knew that, but he didn't want to start right in. He would let Arlyn coax it out of him.

"So, what've you been doing then?" Arlyn said.

"You're looking at it. Sitting around. Wrote a few notes. Gonna write out the events of the day. Hank came in. Talked to him for a while. Off the record." Then he spread his fingers out and ran them through his hair. "I suppose the idea of staying back here's a good one, but it's still weird. Strange to think that this morning I was down in a creek bed, cold and thinking the raid was over for me. The raid and my *local liaison* service was over, and I'm back to working on next year's budget. Then 'bang, bang.' I shoot two guys dead—and then learn that one of em's an FBI guy. What the hell he's doing running outta the ranch house, I'll never know. Big change, real fast."

"But Axe, they're shooting at you, right? What else could you do? You can't tackle 'em both. Christ, they're shooting, you're shooting back. Swing at them with the stock of the shotgun? Run away? I don't think so. How long would you be alive if they got to you? Twenty seconds? What do ya figure they were thinking?"

Axel had sat back on the bunk, his elbows on his knees, and held his head. He stared at the floor and kept his eyes down as he answered. "Hell if I know. Escape, I guess. First I thought they were running to an old VW camper, 'bout a hundred yards out. Suppose they were just gonna drive away. Then they turned back away from it, toward me. I'm down in a creek bed with a fence behind that. Over the fence there's nothing, just the climb up to Dead Horse. Not much of a plan."

Axel looked up. Arlyn was standing, leaning against the door frame. From the tilt of his head, Axel knew he was trying to visualize the scene. "Couldn't they just run any which way to get away, and straighten it out later?"

"Suppose so. Nothing around the ranch. Sure, but they weren't thinking. They probably panicked. I figure the shooter, the lead runner who shot at me, recruited the FBI guy to make a run, and the guy was afraid of saying no for fear he'd blow his cover. The shooter, who knows why he asked, or why he didn't ask somebody else. Willy Ryan's the local kid. I gotta figure he knew the mountains pretty good. Maybe he felt more comfortable than he should have with nine lawmen surrounding the place. Didn't think too much. Seemed to change his mind every ten seconds. FBI guy just followed him."

Arlyn moved to sit next to Axel on the bunk. "So, how you handling it?"

"As for handling it, I suppose it's like a lot of shit. You work it over and over. Can't focus on anything else. Tomorrow'll be better than today. Day after that, who knows? One day at a time." Axel picked his head up, looked at Arlyn and smiled.

Then Arlyn said, "Sounds like AA to me, asshole."

Arlyn had flunked out of AA three times in the last ten years. He reported that he could not see surrendering himself to a "higher power," a keystone of the AA mantra, or even acknowledging that there was a higher power. But they both knew that his failure was not based on philosophical or religious grounds. In a sober, introspective moment Arlyn had once surmised that, "I like to get drunk. Being drunk's better'n being sober. I think I'm a better man when I drink. Otherwise I'm at odds with the world. Hell, you're about the only friend I got who's not a drunk. Guys like me, we like to drink and be stupid."

Axel knew it wasn't an all-or-nothing choice. It involved innumerable choices, like where you place your next step. Could be here, there or back the other way. Arlyn had once complained that the decision to have another drink was all consuming. Axel knew that Arlyn could argue that it wasn't a choice at all. It was a logical consequence of a physical condition. And as Arlyn had once told Axel, "Living hard is easy for me."

They both knew that, short a miracle, Arlyn was done with AA and would keep drinking. It was as though he had bought an unsightly tattoo and learned to live with it, but didn't want to have it acknowledged. The topic was off the table.

Axel smiled at Arlyn's pique. He said, "Hell, don't think I'll have to go to any meetings, do ya? I'm going to be on the offense. Damn right I did what I thought was the right thing at the time. No, I didn't interview the shooter to learn that he was just a punk without a clue.

No, can't say there was time. He's shooting, I'm shooting back. It's not a damned puzzle. It was a programmed response."

Axel paused and rubbed his chin. "What I can't really figure is the FBI guy. Like I told Hank, shouldn't we have known there's an undercover guy? Seems everybody would be a little more cautious." Axel shook his head. "Hilton, he knew. He knew and didn't tell us. He should've told us. Yesterday and day before he's talking about the terms of engagement—Langley Level 5, like it's some code. Can't shoot back unless you're about to die. Hell, he should've just told us, 'I think we got an FBI guy inside. Don't shoot him.' Did Ham give you the details on how it went down?"

"No, he just gave me the final score. When did the shooting start?"

"Damnedest thing. The whole time I'm thinking, Hilton, the U.S. Marshal, doesn't want me here. I'm just some checklist item—the local liaison. We get to the ranch, I'm done. I did my job. Hilton assigns positions around the ranch house. He pushes me back against the creek and puts guys in front of me. Not the plan at all, but I figure he's beefing up somebody else's role, squeezing me out. That's fine. I'm done working. Somebody else can handle the prisoners, load 'em up. Never good work. Shit happens."

"I guess it does."

"I've looked at it seventeen ways and the weakest link is this DEA guy. He's in front of me to the right, near the house. He's got a five foot high light pole with strobes. The two guys come out of the house. The lead guy has a .22. He runs a few steps, falls down, rifle goes off. Hits the metal barn. Thwack!! This DEA guy jumps up and shoots at the guy on the ground. DEA guy's got a new kinda thing, shoots tasers or electric jolts. 'Pop, pop, pop' All misses. So much for Langley's rules. Then both guys are up and running for some goddammed reason. They turn away from the barn toward the creek. They come straight at me. Lead guy shoots at me from five yards, here to there." He swung his arm from the far wall of his cell to the far wall of the next. "Missed by inches. Thought I was dead."

Arlyn jumped in, "Hell, that's self-defense, whatever the hell Langley says."

Just as he had thought, Axel found that talking to Arlyn had a calming, fortifying effect. Arlyn lived in a more rough-and-tumble, quick-response world than Axel. Arlyn looked to the future and, in spite of his frequent ups and downs, had few regrets or apologies. Arlyn summed up the morning's happenings as "a dumb-ass punk realizing how few clues he really had."

By late-afternoon, Ange had transcribed Ham's morning statement to the assembled deputies. She read Ham's statement to Anne when she returned Ange's morning phone call. Anne's response was quick and simple, "How's Axel?" Ange had made a twenty-year career of being straightforward, unemotional and uninvolved in the personal lives of the three sheriffs and thirty deputies she'd worked with. But she thought that this was a time for an exception.

She said, "I think he needs you. He's gonna stay here, back in the cells for a couple of days. Ham Frazier of the MSP, who's been super, like a mother hen, and Arlyn came by with some clothes. Then 'bout noon Hank Anderson came over. Axel had me call him. They talked, back in the cells for two hours. Arlyn came back and they talked for a while." Ange paused and then said, "But I think he really needs to see you. Can you come down tonight?"

Anne left the hospital immediately. In her car, she called the Grant Café to order two servings of barbequed ribs for carry-out. Arriving with the ribs, her first words to Axel were, "Sheriff, I'm mighty pleased you allow conjugal visits in your jail."

Anne left at 11:30 and made her way to Axel's work-in-progress house for the rest of the night.

CHAPTER 11

(Friday, October 21)

To his surprise, Axel was able to go right to sleep after Anne left. He slept for five hours before the thin mattress put him into a constant roll, searching for a soft spot.

He was at the work desk of the cell when Ange entered the cell-block. "Jack Hilton's here. Wants to talk to you. Very insistent."

Axel looked up. "Really, now? Here. Jack Hilton's here." He paused momentarily and continued, "'Bout had enough of Jack Hilton yesterday. Is he alone?"

"Yeah, he's alone."

Axel shuffled his stack of twelve pages of handwritten notes and said aloud, but not to Ange, "Hilton. We are done, Jack Hilton and me." He then turned toward Ange and said, "I'm not ready to talk to him. I want to get this organized. Tell him to come back in an hour. I gotta figure out what to do with him. I'm going to sort this out and get cleaned up." He looked at his watch, "Say nine o'clock. OK? Let me know when he arrives."

He then asked if any deputies or troopers saw Hilton come in. The answer was no. He asked her to call the morning patrols in for a meeting at nine. *Witnesses.*

Axel wasn't completely surprised by Hilton's unannounced visit—yesterday's exchange by the creek had been interrupted. Certainly showing up at the county sheriff's office without notice fit Hilton's profile. Axel knew that Hilton hadn't been straight with him. Hilton obviously had known for a while that there was an FBI undercover guy at the ranch, but, for one reason or another, he didn't want to tell anyone. Plus, there certainly had to be something to the way Hilton arranged the team around the house and pushed Axel back to the creek. Axel wanted to get answers, but at the same time considered how dangerous Hilton was. Axel got up from the desk and restacked the pages. Then he said aloud to no one, "Hell, probably here to serve another federal warrant. This time on me!"

Hilton arrived in the outer office at 8:52. Ange alerted Axel. But Axel had him wait in the outer lobby until 9:11, when Ange brought him back to his private office. Axel was pleased to hear that there were two deputies and two MSP troopers in the outer office. He sat behind his desk and had Hilton sit in an un-upholstered folding chair he'd brought in from the briefing room.

Axel stood as Ange brought Hinton in. Their quick, mechanical handshake evidenced their hostility. Hilton sought out eye contact with Axel and opened the conversation by saying, "Yesterday was a bad day in Black Rock."

Axel responded with, "Bad day, all round." So much for the preliminaries. This was Hilton's meeting. Axel waited.

Hilton stared at Axel and after a long pause, uncomfortable for both men, said, "The Department of Justice is all over Crestfallen. Any of them talk to you yet?"

Axel shook his head "no."

Hilton continued, "One of the guys was FBI undercover."

Axel's only reaction was to lean forward onto his desk, toward Hilton. He said nothing. Hilton waited. Axel waited. Finally Axel broke contact by taking a sip of coffee. He wasn't going to lose this sparring match. The burden of going further was all on Hilton.

Finally, Hilton said, "Story's going around that I told you yesterday that one of the dead guys was FBI. That's not right. I didn't tell you shit about an undercover guy. I didn't know myself. I didn't know for sure that he was there."

"That's strange, Jack." Axel spat it out. Hilton was no longer U.S. Marshall Jack Hilton—just Jack. "I seem to recall you knocking me to the ground and trying to beat the shit out of me. I think your words were, 'One of these guys is a federal undercover agent.' Something like that. Pretty close to it."

"You're right, I was really pissed. But it was because of the Langley Rules violation, I was … "

"Whoa! Violation? You think I violated the rules? Christ, that first guy shot at me from fifteen feet. Missed by inches. He wanted me dead."

"Sure it wasn't the other way around? Yesterday the county prosecutor told an FBI agent that you arrested Willy Ryan a couple years ago, and he got off with a suspended sentence. Could be you were gunning for him." Hilton turned in his chair and cocked his chin.

Axel swung his head in disbelief and said, "What the hell? How could anybody imagine I knew who those guys were? It wasn't even sunup. They were running at me. So you think I'm lying there in the creek bed saying, 'Oh great, here comes Willy Ryan. I've been hoping to blow him away to get even for the County Attorney's lame prosecution for an underaged DUI three years ago.' You are one sick chicken."

Hilton said nothing.

Axel started again, "How would I know anything about an undercover guy unless you told me? You never said boo about it beforehand. Hell, I told Ham Frazier about your new piece of information, not an hour later. That's certainly of some weight. What, you think I made it up?"

Axel looked at Hilton, who in spite of his size looked more comfortable in the small metal chair than anyone ever had.

Then Hilton scooted his chair up to the desk and put his forearms on it. Axel instinctively rolled his chair back, away from the desk. Hilton was ready to deal, playing cards or a proposition.

"Crestfallen is not an insignificant thing. This pissant county and your shooting those guys is big time DOJ—Minneapolis, Denver, Washington. I wanted to go out on a win. Can't blame me for that. And aggressive tactics always send a message. But this isn't a real war. Can't just call these guys collateral damage, set the occupation force and move on to the next engagement with the enemy. No, yesterday we had seven guys on a conference call on what we do now. My career's over. But I'm not going to jail. The way I see it you're the only player who's got much to lose."

Hilton stroked his chin. "You're the target—the rogue cop. The revenge-seeking, small-time operator who couldn't wait to even the score. I can easily see you in that role. You've got a lot to lose, and you're going down one way or the other. Only question is whether you take me down further. Sheriff, I aim to make sure that doesn't happen. If you know what's good for you, you'll find yourself a good criminal defense lawyer, one with experience in federal court."

Hilton stood, pushed his chair back and started for the door. "Now you have a good day, sheriff."

As Hilton reached the door, Axel asked, "One question, Commandant, why'd you put those guys in front of me around the house? That wasn't the plan."

Hilton turned and said, "Well, Axel, let's just call it the last break I'm going to be sending your way." He closed the office door behind him.

Axel waited two minutes and then walked out to the outer office and greeted the assembly waiting there. They brought him up to date on events around the county.

Ollie and one of the troopers had been out to the Bridal Veil mine. Ollie reported that, indeed, the brass lock on the gate had been drilled out, and that an ATV with well-worn tires had driven around the work yard and into the mouth of the mine, but they were unable to tell if anything had been stolen or tampered with. He noted several small piles of rocks at the far end of the mineshaft, but considered that it was the result of normal drilling operations. He reported that they saw no one, miners or otherwise, at the site or within a mile of it. Ollie had taken twenty photographs of the site, the lock, the ATV tracks and the mine itself. He handed Axel his written report. Axel noted Ange's handwritten footnote to the report that she had called the owner's security desk and read the entire report to them.

Axel looked at Ollie and Ange as if seeking counsel on what they should do with this report. They looked back at him with blank stares. Finally, he said to Ange, "Well, you already called the mining company. Ya know, the mine's on federal land, we could just send this to the FBI. But the only damage is the lock itself. Hell, let's not bring in the Feds quite yet. We've got extra staff. Ollie, have a look at their ten seconds of video. Let me know what you think. If they want us to push this further, we'll start looking for well-used, red ATVs driven by ranchers with a bad leg. I'd say we got 'bout two hundred of them in the county."

The group laughed, which cut the tension in the room.

Then Axel held up his hands in surrender and said, "That's all I got. I'm off duty. Ham and Ollie are calling the shots." He then walked over to the troopers to thank them for their efforts in Rankin County. He nodded to Ange and went back through the interoffice door.

At noon, the special agent in charge of the Denver office of the FBI called the sheriff's office to arrange a two-o'clock interview. He arrived promptly at two, and Axel met with him for an hour and one-half in his office. Axel was ready for him and told him his whole story, including Hilton's visit.

CHAPTER 12

(Sunday, October 23)

After two nights in the jail's spartan conditions, Axel found his bed at Arlyn's soft and welcoming. He immediately fell asleep but woke up six hours later with a cramp in his calf. He jumped out of bed and slowly walked it off, cruising from the bedroom to the kitchen and back again. Then he sat on the edge of the bed and looked at himself in the mirror above the now-neglected walnut bureau that Ivey had once cherished as "the most handsome piece of furniture a person could own."

He sat with his hands pushing down on the mattress with each elbow locked, releasing his neck and spine from the task of supporting his torso. His neck relaxed and his head swayed with his thoughts while his eyes remained fixed on the eyes of the man in the mirror.

After ten minutes, Axel realized that a return to sleep was not a possibility.

He slipped on his jeans, a sweatshirt, socks, and boots. He walked to the front door and out onto the porch, wondering what to do with himself—wide awake at five o'clock in the morning.

It was cold, but there was no wind. The front porch basked in moon glow from the southwest. He surveyed Arlyn's ranch. With a reflexive, decision-confirming nod, and a roll of his shoulders to stave off the cold, he struck out for McNally Creek.

In spite of the lack of wind, the few dry, delicate aspen leaves still in the trees spun on their thin stems.

Axel marveled at the strange ways time twisted and stretched. The dinner with Anne was less than a week ago. Everything then was so different—so slow-moving, light, easygoing, positive. Now life was different—cold, dark, and heavy and things were happening fast.

He straddled a huge downed cottonwood lying next to the creek. It had blown over in last summer's windstorm. His legs hung freely. He watched the creek and the reflected moonlight. He was captivated by the kaleidoscopic play of moonlight on the moving water. His thoughts strayed. In the winter, deep in the earth, the roots of trees keep them alive while above ground they look as dead as this cottonwood. He wondered if he had roots deep enough to sustain him in the coming wintry days.

He snapped a dry twig from the dead tree and tossed it upstream. The twig popped up to the surface and started downstream, back to Axel. This late in the season, the river had quieted down. No longer the roaring whitewater of June, or even the consistent flat-water flow of mid-summer. No, these days, the water was broken up by rocks. It was lower and slower; there were fewer places for the fish to hide but it was tough to lure them out of the deep pools. Arlyn called it "boney," as though it were a living thing that had lost weight.

Axel's twig floated listlessly—now hung up in an eddy, now plastered on a rock; then it zoomed through a short, fast run between two large rocks, finally getting stuck among the leaves of an overhanging branch. That's me. Drifting along, bouncing, responding, flipped over, pulled in, and pushed out. After years of law enforcement—coast guard, highway patrol, now sheriff, never once did I have to shoot to kill. Plenty of shots at far away targets. The blind innocence of dropping bombs from thirty thousand feet: anonymous shooter with anonymous targets. Not like Crestfallen. I saw their eyes. Their surprise. I saw them die.

As he climbed up the river bank to go back to the house, a pair of headlights turned off the gravel road to come up the long drive. It was an older truck, dark but faded. Chrome bumpers. Weak, yellowish, pulsating headlights. And there was another truck right behind it. A newer, white double-cab. Axel recognized neither and had a sudden, sinking feeling that these visitors weren't friends.

Axel stopped and moved back into the tree line, where he couldn't be seen. Both trucks had come to a halt with headlights on, casting their beams into the dense aspen grove ahead of Axel. The motors running, waiting.

Arlyn's dog, in her chair on the porch, pulled up her head and fixed a stare at the first truck.

Then Axel walked out of the trees, through the beams of the throbbing headlights and onto the porch. He heard the pop of a misaligned truck door being opened and from behind him, inside the house, the familiar creak of the floorboards by the front door

Arlyn's up. Axel scratched the dog behind her ear. He turned toward the trucks. The door on the driver's side of the first truck was half open.

"You guys lookin' for something?" Axel asked. There was no movement from the trucks. Axel braced his shoulders and walked off the porch up toward them. As he approached, the driver rolled out, pushing the truck door all the way open.

"You Cooper?" The driver stood tall without looking at Axel and then spat on the ground.

"Axel Cooper," Axel answered.

The driver looked like so many other strong young, but weathered, ranchers Axel had seen over the years: big shoulders of a steer-wrestler, square jaw coated with a black stubble. A faded ball cap shadowed his eyes from the light coming off the porch.

"You da sum-bitch kilt Willy J?" the driver asked as he tilted his head back and locked a piercing stare at Axel.

Axel said nothing.

He stared straight at the young man. "That'd be me," he said softly, standing tall. "And you'd be Frank, Willy J's big brother. Francis Xavier Ryan."

Frank glared back at Axel. "Get in the fuckin' truck. Grampa wants to have a little talk. Charlie Ryan." He flashed a malicious grin that revealed a missing front tooth.

"Tell him you found me. He's welcome anytime. Even in full daylight"

"He wants you now, dipshit. At his place."

Axel's mind was moving fast. "Can't say I planned on that this morning. What's he want to talk about? I imagine he's been doing a lot of talking to the FBI. Tell him to call my office. Set up an appointment.

He turned his back on Frank and started walking toward the porch.

Frank jumped forward and grabbed Axel's shoulder with one massive outstretched hand and squeezed, not to spin Axel around but to stop him.

"Hey, Grampa's waiting," he said.

Axel turned to face Frank. He took a step back and looked the younger man up and down. Each man subtly shifted his stance and weight distribution, ready for a fight. The gravel crunched with their footwork. But neither swung. As though announcing the stalemate, Axel turned away. Frank followed silently. From the second truck, a voice boomed, "Hey, Frank! Is he coming or not? You need help?"

Axel said, "I'm going in the house. I expect you boys to get the hell outta here. Right now."

"Can't do that."

"I think you very well can. Just turn around, get in your truck and drive the hell outta here." Axel pointed down the drive to the road.

"Grampa's dying. He's fixing on Willy. Hasn't got a lick of sleep since Thursday. He's wantin' some peace. Thinks you can help. Told us to bring you back or don't come back. 'Fraid, you're coming if it takes three guys to tie ya up."

Axel stopped and turned toward him. "I don't know your grampa, and I don't know how he thinks. Sure, I pulled the trigger, but Willy made some very bad decisions and they got him killed. Can't be shooting at folks and not expect 'em to shoot back. Everyone knows that."

"Tell it to Grampa."

Axel stood next to the porch and looked inside the house. He saw Arlyn moving around. "Frank, here's the best I can do. I'll go talk to Charlie Ryan. I'll go in *my* truck with my brother Arlyn. This is his place. He's up. We'll follow you. We can go now. I'll talk to your grandfather. Other than that, I think we got a problem, you being on our land without permission. This ranch being in Rankin County and me being the Rankin County Sheriff, I could probably do something about that."

Axel crossed the porch, opened the screen door and entered the house with the dog. Frank followed close behind, but stopped just inside the door.

Arlyn, wearing only his jockey shorts, stepped out of the kitchen and leveled a 12-gauge shotgun at Frank's chest. "Don't move," he commanded in a menacing stage whisper.

"Put that down," Axel said as he crossed the front room heading toward his bedroom.

Arlyn took the gun down from his shoulder but kept it pointed at Frank.

Axel stopped and said in an exaggerated slow, calming tone, "We're just talking here. Nobody's gonna get hurt. Arlyn, this here is Frank Ryan. He wants me to go to Charlie Ryan's ranch with him. Have a talk with his granddad. He's dying, I guess. I just told Frank we'd go out and talk with him. You and me. Now."

"What? Now? Why the hell … " Arlyn swung his head from Axel to Frank and back again.

"Arlyn, let's just go. I'm not ready for a standoff. Shot enough people this week. Get dressed; we're gonna just follow Frank out to their place. All right?"

"Sure."

As Arlyn dropped the muzzle to the floor, Frank silently backed out onto the porch as though retreating from an unpredictable grizzly bear. His head swung to take in the front room, its stuffed moose head, life-sized nude painting, and motorcycle missing a front fork. He stood there and held the screen door open behind him with his hip, eyes wide as they flitted from Arlyn to Axel to the moose head and back again.

Axel walked into the bedroom, leaving Frank and Arlyn in a faceoff. As Frank moved slowly out further onto the porch, Arlyn moved to his left, next to the motorcycle, to keep aligned with Frank. He took two steps forward. Then he slowly pulled the shotgun up to aim at Frank's chest. Arlyn pushed his chin out toward Frank and said, "You get back in your truck. We'll be out. You better watch your back." The cords in his neck stretched tight as he thrust his chin out further.

"Man," Arlyn said, and, on resecuring Frank's attention, he finished with, "Watch yourself."

Five minutes later, the three-truck caravan, led by Frank in the old pickup, left Arlyn's ranch.

They turned off Route 34 at milepost 31 and turned right, south toward the mountains. After three more turns from one narrow, unmarked gravel road to the next, they pulled up to a compound of ranch buildings. The setup didn't look much different from any Rankin County ranch. All the yard lights were on. Except for three large dogs, an ATV, and a hay truck, the scene looked deserted. Then, a tall, pot-bellied man with a stylized, black cowboy hat walked out of the white house on the left. He smoked a cigarette in a series of rapid, short inhalations. He yelled at Frank, "What the fuck? The old man's been waiting."

The third pickup pulled to a stop behind Arlyn's truck. Two thin teenagers got out and stood by it.

"Max, tell him we're here," Frank said coldly through the open window.

Axel had driven Arlyn's truck. They both got out and surveyed the buildings. The tall, black-hatted man walked up to Axel and introduced himself as Max McCreary, a son-in-law of Charlie Ryan.

Frank came up to the trio, looked at Arlyn, and said, "Gramps wants to talk to the sheriff, alone."

Arlyn looked to Axel, who said, "This won't be long. See if you can get some coffee."

Axel followed Frank away from the white frame house, behind the newer-looking pole barn to a low-slung log bunkhouse surrounded by hard-packed dirt, solid as concrete this cold morning. Axel figured the bunkhouse was a hundred years old or more. It was a settler's cabin built into a low-rise hill. Someone had cut a section out of the short side wall and put it on a long, strong hinge to swing up in fair weather. This morning, the place was dark, with everything lowered and latched to keep out the cold. They entered through a recent add-on: an unpainted plywood breezeway. In the breezeway, Axel could feel the moist heat coming from the next room.

"So, where the fuck is he?" a thin, gravelly male voice called through the door.

Frank walked in first and in answer tossed his head over his shoulder. Axel stepped into the low-ceilinged, cavelike room. The smell of cigars and coffee met him at the interior door. The room was smoky and had strange lighting, as though they'd used a red light bulb. It had the feel of a dank basement without ventilation. It was hard to distinguish shadows from dark surfaces. Axel momentarily lost his depth perception and shuffled his feet to keep his balance.

An old man was seated in a worn slat-back armchair in the corner. He was thin, almost gaunt, with a heavily lined face. He was hunched forward, drawing slowly and deeply on a strong-smelling cigar. He held his thin, boney chin in one hand and tilted it to the side, as though to straighten up would be painful.

Max McCreary had slipped in behind Frank and Axel. He covered the doorway and closed the door. He planted his feet a yard apart and folded his arms high on his chest. His hat almost reached the ceiling. Axel saw some movement through the narrow, smoke-grimed window on the side wall.

Axel sensed he was in the middle of a power struggle. Frank nodded to his grandfather and then all of them focused on Axel, as though he'd drawn a pistol. Something was going on in this room. Something Axel had nothing to do with—but he could sense that he was going to be the object over which they worked out their differences.

Charlie Ryan did not move to get up or raise a hand in greeting. He examined Axel for a long while, up and down without moving his head.

"You have kids, county man?" Charlie Ryan's breathy, rattling voice betrayed decades of cigars and cigarettes. Thin clouds of smoke swirled in front of his face as he spoke.

Axel briefly entertained the notion of lying, but then he said, "No sir, wife died of cancer before we could get it going."

"Sorry," Ryan said. "A man oughta have family. Settles him down. Gives a man a reason to keep on living. Keep on fighting, if that's what it takes. Nothing more important to a man than family." Ryan slurred his words, but he wasn't drunk.

Charlie Ryan called to Frank, "Got any coffee left? Give this man a cup of coffee. We're civil here." Frank obeyed and got a cup for Axel from the pot in the back corner. Axel drank deeply of the hot, strong brew while standing in front of Charlie.

The room was quiet as Axel took a second and third sip. He felt peculiar standing in the middle of the room drinking coffee while the three men watched. Axel flashed on Thursday morning at Crestfallen and the two young men running at him. He spurted out, "Sir … I … your grandson. I … " And then after a moment's pause, "I can't begin to say. He shot at me. Killing anybody was the last thing on my mind. I'm sorry your grandson is dead."

Ryan looked down at the floor and said, "Save it, county man. I'll ask the questions. Who cares what the fuck was on your mind! You blew him away. And if you really wanted to make a speech, you'd a been out here Thursday afternoon."

Charlie Ryan picked up his head and watched closely as Axel absorbed the verbal body-blow. Axel said nothing, acquiescing to Ryan's lead. "Like I say, family's important," Ryan continued. "Four days ago I had four grandsons. Now, I'm one short; I've got a son won't come out of his room, drugged up, moaning like a resurrected Jesus just left the earth without him. I've also got a herd of hotheads ready to set the county on fire."

The old man wanted to say more. Something in his scanning, watery eyes told Axel that Ryan didn't have a scripted list of questions but simply wanted to survey the man who had shot Willy.

After a moment of silence, Axel decided to override Ryan's directive, to lay his cards on the table. "That night was a disaster," Axel started. Ryan didn't stop him this time, so Axel went on, "A real fiasco. Sure as hell didn't go according to plan. I guess the U.S. Marshal figured all of us being there would be enough to get the guys inside to "come out with their hands up." Just like in the movies. The Feds were full of themselves and their new technology. The guy with your grandson was FBI—undercover. The whole deal was a bad idea." He watched carefully to see how his words struck the old man.

Charlie Ryan sat back and pulled a pint-sized Mason jar up to his lips and spit a brown slurry into it. He then took another deep draw on his cigar. He stared at the cigar for a moment and then said, "Justice, it's relative. The Feds, it was their gig. If anybody's responsible, it's them. But that'll never see the light of day. Feds'll blame anybody else. They're god's gift to the world. The rest of us are scum. They won't help me. You don't see too many of us in Montana, but you'll find we Irish, we're really good at gettin' even. Retribution. Revenge. Whatever ya call it. Yours wasn't the only finger on that trigger. Jack Hilton owns a big piece of this cow pie," the old man posited as though it were an irrefutable conclusion. Then, as if to highlight his pronouncement and allow Axel time to speculate as to his meaning, Ryan started coughing. He coughed steadily for a full minute. It sounded like his lungs were drying up. The room stiffened. Even big Max shifted his weight, waiting out the coughing spell. As his coughing subsided, Ryan waved his cigar in the direction of the door. "Frank, Max, go check on breakfast. Leave me the shotgun. Take out the shells and give 'em to me. I just might need something to beat this lawman to a bloody compost heap."

Max and Frank looked at each other in confusion. Axel wasn't worried about Charlie Ryan but wondered if Ryan knew Jack Hilton or had merely learned of him from the press.

Charlie Ryan waved the back of his hand toward the door, "Leave!! We're somewhat civilized. Give us ten minutes."

Frank picked up a short double-barreled shotgun from an open rack in the far corner of the room, cracked it open and removed the shells, handing them to Charlie. Frank then handed over the empty shotgun, which Charlie laid on the floor next to him. Then Frank and Max left. Axel stood alone in the middle of the aged log cabin. The face in the window disappeared.

"Sit down." Ryan motioned to a worn leather couch on the side wall. "More coffee?"

Axel sat on the sprung couch and shook his head "no."

Ryan started slowly as if laying the foundation for a long, complicated story: "Well, I got a real problem with Jack Hilton; he's got blood on his hands. He's the prime mover. We had an agreement. He just wasn't up to it. It's because of him my grandson's dead, and I'm taking him down, one way or another. You can help me out or get out of the way."

Axel was stunned. *What is he talking about? How would he even know Hilton?*

"I promise you, Jack Hilton's no friend of mine, but … I … I don't follow. You know Hilton?"

Ryan attempted to talk, but got caught up in a dry, hacking coughing fit again. He put down the cigar in a messy ashtray and picked up the jar and spit into it. He took a sip of coffee.

Finally, he started again. "Six months ago I got a call from the FBI. Seems they needed to see me. Wouldn't say about what. Said they'd stop by some time. So one day an agent walks in here—bold as brass. He's got all the credentials. Started out smooth enough talking about some irregularities, 'banking irregularities.' FBI got a call from a bank I did business with. A couple of years ago, I bought two small dozers and a dump truck. New ones. Borrowed some money to buy 'em. Bank in Billings. I had some earth-moving to do—back roads and shit—and thought I had a commercial gravel operation ready to go—down near the Wyoming line on some horse shit grazing land I got. Something to keep the boys busy. Make some cash." He paused to catch his breath. "Didn't work. Not enough gravel. Rocks too big. So I bailed out and sold the equipment to Willis Brothers—highway guys—down in Casper for cash. Billings dealer put me in touch with them. Sweet deal, closed in three days. Didn't say nothing 'bout a bank loan I had on the equipment. Figured I'd pay off the loan with the cash from Willis. Meanwhile, Willis had a lawyer. He checked at the court house. Guess the bank recorded the loan. Lawyer, anyway, he told the bank about the sale. Bank panicked and called the FBI. I never heard boo from the bank. I had the money. Coulda paid 'em in a minute. The FBI guy comes off like an accountant. White, button down shirt. Gray suit. Black tie. Probably got a haircut, 'specially for his trip to Rankin County. I told him that 'yes,' I sold the dozers and the truck and 'yes,' I still had the loan, so what's the fucking problem? I'm up to date on the loan. Bank's happy. He told me it didn't work that way. My deal with the bank said that I couldn't sell equipment unless they got paid first. Like a mortgage on a house. I told him, 'Well, hell, if that's the only problem I'd run up to Billings and pay off the bank.' He said that'd probably be a good thing, but I already did what I did and that was technically 'bank fraud': a federal offense. I gave him a long stare, through to his slimy backbone. He gathered himself. Kept calling me 'Sir" like he was being respectful, when I knew he was just a weasel-assed pencil pusher. I was cordial, didn't call him any names. Figured we were done. So I think nothing of it. My ten minutes with the FBI. I called the bank and paid off the loan the next week. Figure it's old news."

"Then last week a secretary from the U.S. Marshal's office called. She's all full of piss and vinegar. She's *very important*. Won't tell me what it's about. Calling for Hilton. We make an appointment for two o'clock the next day. He shows up all full of himself. His bald head gleaming. He's in shirt sleeves, khaki pants and boots. He is one big guy. Feels the need to tell me his life story. Wrong side of the tracks in Philadelphia. Marine Corps Worked himself up from private to major. Two years in Iraq. I guess I'm supposed to think he's a great American. Hilton says the FBI is ready to pounce on me, but if I cooperate now with him, he could hold them off. He's my champion, the U.S. Marshal, holding back the evil, bloodthirsty FBI. He gives me some shit about marshals being lowly peons of the Department of Justice. Serve warrants, guard prisoners, sweep the floor, shit like that. But the FBI's shorthanded and they enlist this underappreciated marshal to talk to me. Says he's looking to make a big play, show them that he too can make things happen, and then retire. Big buildup. I can't believe my bank deal is going to be his swan song"

Axel's mind was racing. Charlie Ryan's characterization of Hilton fit with everything he knew about him.

"Hilton's second piece of news was that I'm harboring a federal fugitive at Crestfallen, and Hilton's charged with bringing him in. Apparently, Willy hooked up with a smart-ass college kid out of Minnesota—been convicted on a meth charge there, parents made bail before sentencing, but he ran, went underground. Popped up here. Been hiding out at Crestfallen for a couple of weeks. According to Hilton, they were looking to set up a meth lab at the ranch."

"The bond jumper's Bob Johnson. Can you believe that? Name sounds like he should be an 'All-American.' Hilton wants to grab Johnson and close down the lab before it starts. Show up the FBI. Arrest any and all, including Willy. Wants me to keep Willy at home. That's all he wants and he will get the FBI to drop any charges against me for the bank deal and will go light on Willy—only go after him for possession of meth, if they find some—not manufacturing, apparently the difference between jaywalking and murder. If I tip off the boys at Crestfallen, Hilton says I'll wish I was dead. I'd be living in hell on earth. Timing's loose. Next two or three weeks. This guy, Hilton, I really can't figure. It's like he wants me to plan his raid for him. My mind's going a mile a minute. First, I really can't see bank fraud. I paid the bank. Second, does he really think I'm not going to talk to my grandson? Fuck, all I gotta do is drive up to Crestfallen and see what's going on. Any drug lab be collapsed in three minutes."

Axel nodded encouragingly and leaned forward, toward Charlie Ryan.

Ryan continued, "I'm trying to figure him out. Is it Johnson he wants? Is it to stop the lab? Why's he after Willy? I asked him a few questions. Hell, I told him the lab could be gone in ten minutes—I give the word. Where's he fit with the FBI—how good is his promise? I didn't like that he was here on his own, making promises for other people. Always seems to me you lawmen like to travel in groups, so you can support each other's stories when you get in trouble. Hilton seemed to have a vision of a big play to save the game, a Hail-Mary pass to the endzone. Midnight raid. I told him, if he wanted Johnson, I could deliver him bound hand and foot within ten minutes of the word. But, that didn't stick. Didn't fit his big picture. Strange guy. It was like he wasn't listening—all he wanted was for me to keep Willy home so that he could plan his raid."

Ryan twisted his face as though containing a bolt of pain. Then he bit into his cigar and chewed it in apparent relief.

"So, did ya talk to Willy?" Axel deadpanned.

Ryan looked at the floor and then brought his eyes up slowly and smiled. "Damn straight. 'Bout ten minutes after Hilton left. 'Bout ripped him a new one! Asked him if he knew Johnson—yes. Any meth production at Crestfallen—no. Meth sales—yes, he'd done some deals. Nothing since last trip to Denver in August. Anybody staying at Crestfallen? Here he got cagey. He said 'yeah' but there'd be nobody after midnight Wednesday. Shit, it all sounded like the truth to me. I didn't tell him 'bout Hilton. Just was vague: 'I'm hearing you got folks staying up to Crestfallen. People who don't want to be found.' We sorta talked around each other. No ultimatums. Coulda, shoulda cleared out the place there and then. Goddamn it! Can't say I made a bigger mistake in my life."

"When was this?"

"Friday, a week ago. Guess it was the fourteenth." Ryan went back to chewing his cigar.

"Hilton give you a timeframe? Did you talk to him again?"

"We didn't look at the calendar. Sort of like 'I'll be in touch.' Like I said, two or three weeks. I was planning a trip up to Crestfallen over that weekend. Make sure Johnson moved out. Close the place down for winter. Figured by the time Hilton comes by the place'd be sealed for winter. Quiet as a church on Monday morning. But with this cough and the roundup, I didn't go."

Axel leaned further forward in sympathy and, with his hands clasped between his knees, asked, "So what did you first think of Hilton's blackmail? 'You do what I want or the party's over?'"

Ryan chomped on his cigar and chewed it vigorously for a moment before responding, "Well, it was more like 'let's make a deal,' than straight-out blackmail. We never got to what would happen if I refused to cooperate. Other than he'd make my life hell. Fuck, I shoulda cleared out Crestfallen and called a lawyer—'Uncle Sam's squeezing me.' But I just can't hear myself saying that. Not the way I do business. We settle our own problems. Hilton wasn't in a hurry. I figured I could get Johnson to move on and handle whatever Hilton had as backlash."

"So why the raid? This whole thing was his idea!" Axel asked.

"Last Tuesday he calls me. The day before the raid. He told me that the FBI, out of Minneapolis, is also interested in Crestfallen. Apparently, they had started snooping around. Confirmed that Johnson was at Crestfallen. Also reported that somebody stole an ammonia trailer in South Dakota and hauled it to the ranch. South Dakota trooper trailed 'em back to the ranch. Hilton talked like he was afraid this plan of his could slip away from him, become public knowledge and the FBI would take the assignment back. He told me a vague story about the FBI wanting to squeeze in an undercover guy at Crestfallen, to make sure they got evidence on raw chemicals and manufacturing as well as the distribution angle. FBI's wanting to use Crestfallen to put a finger on a lotta bad folk. Capture three or four. Threaten to lock 'em up, throw the key away unless they talked. Learn about their networks. Squeeze two or three to get forty names. Hilton was vague, threatening. He just wanted me to know that there might be a raid soon. Not that there would be. Told me to 'behave myself.'"

"I straight out asked him why he's telling me this. 'You want me to help you? Or do you want me to blow the whistle and tell Willy so you can arrest me for interfering with you and the FBI?' I figured that if Willy threw everybody out—there's nothing left to deal with. Party's over."

Ryan shook his head, took a big draw on his cigar and said, "Hilton boiled over with the news of the trailer theft. Somehow, I figure, he thought he'd lose out on any credit for the operation. The FBI'd take it back away from him. Especially if they had an undercover guy at the ranch. Hilton seemed to be afraid that his secrets would be blown. That he'd lose his chance: this grab at the gold ring on the merry-go-round. The way he talked about it, I could tell that he didn't run our deal through channels. So Hilton jumps to beat the FBI and sets up a raid almost overnight, arms all you morons like it's D-day. Tells you nothing about what's really going on. 'Raids on.' Willy panics, FBI guy follows him. He trips—fires his rifle. Somebody shoots at them. Run away. You blow 'em away."

Axel leaned back onto the couch. He looked over his shoulder out the cobwebbed window, through which he saw the first light of day. Then he said, "Hilton thought he had all the answers. Everything was by the numbers. As though there was a Marine Corps field manual for midnight raids of seasonal ranches. Truth is, he was making it up as he went along. In a hurry. He didn't need to do this. This was some kind of swan-song shit. 'Remember the incredible Hilton.'"

Charlie coughed again and said with a small scratchy voice, "What do I tell Willy's dad? I set Willy up with a maniac?" Ryan sat back in his chair. The two men looked at each other, waiting for the other to say something. Ryan twisted his face muscles in pain. He chomped on his cigar, grinding his molars. Axel could see his jaw muscle tighten and then slowly relax. Ryan heaved a sigh of relief and turned in his chair toward Axel.

Then Charlie Ryan said, "You killed 'em. Hilton may be a loose-nut, but nobody got hurt until you pulled the trigger. You killed them both. You sealed the deal. I'll get Hilton, my way. But that doesn't get you off the hook. I got guys here that are fighting for the chance to nail your ass to the wall. Somehow they think that the winner will get my job. Like it's a contest. Can't say I can do much about it." He paused and stared at Axel, while chewing on his cigar. He then took the cigar out of his mouth and spat on the floor in affirmation and said, "I need some more coffee." He picked up the shotgun, leaned forward, and, using the gun for a cane, got up out of the chair.

Axel was surprised at what a short man he was. Small and crooked, Charlie Ryan leaned forward and to the left with his chin in the lead. He limped slowly past Axel, out of the room. Charlie was seized by another coughing fit as he left the vestibule.

Axel felt like he had been slammed in the chest with the back with a shovel. He stayed on the couch in the stuffy cabin trying to sort out the time line and what might have been going on in Hilton's mind.

Ten minutes later, a high school boy came in and reported that "Grampa told me to tell you to go home."

Axel walked out of the cabin to an assembly of men loitering in the big lot between the buildings. They stood in groups of two or three. Some leaned against their trucks. Frank sat astride a black ATV parked near the old bunkhouse. The group stopped talking. Those drinking coffee pulled their cups from their lips to focus on Axel. No one spoke. All eyes were on Axel.

Arlyn had stayed in his truck. No one had approached it or said a word to him. Arlyn slouched down and had fallen asleep.

Axel opened the passenger-side door. "Let's go. I've had enough of this."

Arlyn jerked awake and sat upright. He slid over the driver's side. He said, "Right," as he started the truck.

As the Cooper brothers left the Ryan ranch, Frank Ryan drove the ATV through the road dust their truck raised and followed them down the drive until they turned right onto the gravel county road.

Then Frank pulled out a rifle from a scabbard on the deck of the ATV and fired five shots toward Cooper's truck. He didn't want to hit the truck, just let the Cooper brothers know he was shooting at them.

To which Arlyn said, "Holy moley. Frank's shooting at us. What's this deal about?"

"Damned if I know. Old man's about dead."

"Yeah, I saw him walk across the yard. Took five minutes."

"Told me quite a story. Hilton was out here a coupla weeks ago, before the raid. Hilton had a story about the old man and bank fraud. Used that to get the old man to cooperate on the raid. Basically the message was 'keep Willy at home'. Feds would go easy on Willy. Old man bought it. Charlie knew about Bob Johnson, the Minnesota fugitive. Bank fraud case sounded pretty flakey. Old man bought some earth-moving equipment with a loan. Sold the equipment before paying off the loan. Bank had a lien or something on the equipment. Ryan paid off the bank late. Not supposed to sell goods without first paying the bank. Sounds pretty weak to me. Hell, bank didn't lose any money. Pretty flakey. Hilton told him there might have been an undercover guy. At least the FBI Minneapolis wanted to squeeze one in. Nothing positive."

As Arlyn turned onto Route 34, he asked, "So, what's the deal? The Feds would drop bank fraud if he cooperated on a drug raid? Christ, I don't see why anybody'd take that. Feds had to have something more on the old man."

As Axel turned to look back at the gravel road, he said, "Not anything Charlie Ryan wants to tell me about."

CHAPTER 13

(Sunday, October 23)

They got back to Arlyn's before ten. As they passed McNally Creek, Arlyn noticed the water level was up over yesterday—a good sign. As soon as he parked the truck, Arlyn ran into the house. Three minutes later, he ran out with his fishing gear. "I'll check it out. Come back to get you if it's good."

A half hour later, when Arlyn came back to the house, it was as if he'd totally forgotten about the early morning drama. Arlyn had seen a lot of fish and pressed Axel to join him for a session upstream from the house. While Axel wondered about Arlyn's motives, he also knew that the hours spent with Arlyn would be a recess from his thoughts about the shootings, his audience with Charlie Ryan and his attempts to understand Jack Hilton. As Arlyn had said, "A fish on the line captures the mind."

The trek from the house up to a long rocky run shook Axel into a better mood.

Axel wanted to fish but was still in something of a semi-coma, like he had a concussion from the clash of helmets in a high school football game. By tacit agreement, the brothers hadn't talked much on the walk out and would focus on their fishing.

As the men clambered down the embankment, careful of their long, delicate rods, the cooling moisture of the river engulfed them as though they'd entered an invisible igloo. It was time for the tactics, equipment, and technique.

Arlyn stood at the water's edge and looked upstream for insect action on the surface of the slower-moving water. Finding none he dug into a pouch in his vest in search of the right fly for the moment. On securing a plastic box the size of a cigarette pack, he quickly shot a glance to the opposite, eroded bank and its slow-moving water. Whatever knowledge he gained, it seemed not to change his objective—a small fly compared to the others in the box: an elegantly crafted, feathered arrangement on a tiny hook with a spherical bronze metal weight, intended to ride below the surface of the stream in a natural drift, imitating a larval mayfly. The fly was just over a quarter inch long, including the bronze bead.

Arlyn pinched the fly out of the box and handed it to Axel, who, upon receiving it, hooked it onto a patch of raw wool on his vest. Then Axel looked to his rod and his line. He pulled line off the large reel and pushed it through the rod's five line guides. Most of the line was pencil-lead thick, yellow plastic that would float, but the first ten feet was a clear leader tapered to the width of a hair. Then, carefully leaning the rod against a shore boulder, he gathered in the end of the leader and snatched the fly off his vest. He carefully threaded the line through the small hook's eyelet, wrapped it seven times around the lead stem of the line and then pushed it back through the V created by the twisted line. Then, with a drop of spit and a slow and controlled drawdown of the knot, he secured the fly. Axel's fingers didn't fumble the fly or drop the line, yet the process was slow and methodical. Twice the point of the hook stuck lightly into his fingers. With a clipper, he cut off the excess inch.

Meanwhile, Arlyn had tied a more elaborate rig to his line—two flies and three knots. The first fly in this assemblage had a fluffy wreath of feather encircling the hook to hold air and maintain its buoyancy—an imitation of a mature mayfly. To the curving lower shank of this first hook he tied one end of a two-foot-long piece of leader, and, at the other end of that, he tied a bronze fly.

The difference in the dexterity of the two men was noticeable. Arlyn's fingers moved with flowing muscle memory and purpose that went beyond conscious control. He was done with his compound assemblage before Axel tightened and trimmed his single knot—the expert and the novice.

Arlyn put down his rod and picked up Axel's. He inspected it with the brusque authority and efficiency of a drill sergeant scrutinizing the rifle of a new recruit. Then he pinched the fly and slowly tugged the line. The knot held. He returned the rod with a smile.

Arlyn turned down river and pointed to a spot on the near side of the midstream crease. Arlyn said, "Axe, you'll want to start there and work your way up." Then Arlyn moved his hand, palm down, higher in steps climbing up stream—further up the ripple and into the edge of the surging white water, and then all the way up to the half-submerged boulder itself.

"Got it," answered Axel.

Arlyn turned and pointed a hundred yards downstream to a smaller set up of half-submerged rocks and collected his gear. As he started walking downstream he signed off with, "I'll be down there. Go get 'em, Tiger!"

Axel flipped a "see-ya-later" nod and snatched up his rod. He hoisted up his waders and readjusted the suspenders. He took three deep breaths and suppressed a thought about Charlie Ryan's reaction to Hilton's phone call. *To anybody, that would have been a warning to close down Crestfallen. Why didn't he respond?* Axel took two steps into the river and faced upstream. He pulled line off the reel and held it in his left hand. There was some movement further upstream. It was in the brushes on the far side, the Custer National Forest side of the river. Perhaps a deer.

Axel exercised several whippy, short-line air casts, upstream, back and forth. With his free hand he fed more line to the rod with each cast. Then a flash of light from upstream. A mirror? A telescope? He slowed the rod and softly snapped the line back over his shoulders to stretch it out fully behind him and let it fall into the downstream flow. He stepped further into the river, up to his knees. He scanned the upstream bank. No movement.

Then raising his rod, he pulled the trailing line up out of the river and cast forward, not letting the fly and line fall down to the water before he pulled it into a back cast. By the third false cast, Axel had developed a feel for the weight of the rig, established a rhythm, and had the line and fly performing to his satisfaction. The line shot straight back behind him for forty feet to full extension, pulling the rod tip back with its momentum. Then, with the rotation of his lower right arm and an almost imperceptible, small snap of his wrist, the line moved forward out in front of him. This time he let the fly fall softly to the water just inside the chop line—a perfect placement.

The fly sank immediately beneath the rippled surface as the current caught the fly, the line and the leader.

Axel's hands were busy. With one, he held the rod, thumb on top of the round cork handle. The index finger pinched the yellow line against the bottom of the rod handle. With the other hand he pulled in the fast accumulating slack. He turned to follow the submerged fly as it drifted by and gathered in the line. As the line moved past him downstream, he followed it with the tip of his lowered rod. At the end of the drift, thirty feet downstream, the current tugged at the line and the fly fanned to the shore. Time for a second cast.

Axel slowly raised his rod behind him. With an arc of his lower arm and slight pop of his wrist, Axel took the line out of the water, added a bit of slack, and tossed it upstream. The fly sailed through the air and landed again on the cusp of the chop line. He nodded in satisfaction. On landing, the line was seized by the current, pushing it back toward Axel. Again he gathered in the slack. He tracked the assemblage through the chop, the ripple, and the ripple's dissolve, and into the slower flow of the lower, flat water downstream.

A hundred yards upstream on the County Forest Preserve side, a man stepped out from behind a tree and looked right at Axel. Axel saw him. The line flowed past Axel. *Who is that?*

The man moved behind the tree and Axel recast the line.

Wham!! A fish! The strike sent a startling, electric jolt up the taut line. It happened just as the fly landed on the outer edge of a heavy ripple. Axel's reflexes sent him half a step backwards while popping his right arm up, setting the hook. The feedback was telling. He hadn't pulled the fish forward. *This has to be a big one.*

A microsecond later, the second message was that this fish was pulling back and moving hard to the right and deeper water. *The game was on!!*

Axel slowly lifted his rod to vertical. The rod-tip bounced with each movement of the fish. Then, it stopped. The line went slack. *Had it spit the hook?* Before Axel could respond, the fish broke water in a leap right in front of him. Coming straight at him was a big-shouldered brown trout with bulging black eyes and a massive square tail. Axel pulled in line feverishly.

The fish, back in the stream, swirled and lurched to the right toward deeper water and the protection of the rocks.

Slowly, Axel fed out a little line, took a step back and reestablished the light pressure of his reel-hand index finger. The rod tip dipped and bobbed again, absorbing the constant movements of the fish. He coached himself, *let him move and take some line, but keep some pressure on.*

Arlyn was still far downstream but had stopped his casting to watch the performance, As he turned to go back to his own fishing, he yelled encouragingly, "Ride 'em, Cowboy!"

Axel smiled. The rod tip bent forward and stayed down, bobbing like a telegraph key. *More line, fish needs more line.* He could feel the line slide out above his index finger, which was warming with the friction.

Then the fish veered off to the left, toward the near shore in front of Axel. He cautiously walked further upstream, gathering in the developing slack line as he went.

Then, as though the fish saw Axel, it darted back toward midstream and deeper water. The fish caught the current and slid downstream past Axel.

Axel pressed on the line and with two hands raised his rod to vertical. The fish came to the surface, slowly gyrating in the current, facing upstream. Axel figured this as a turning point and lowered his rod and gathered in two feet of line. The rod tip was pointed at the downstream fish with the current further pressuring the line. Sensing the vulnerable situation, Axel took three steps forward and raised the rod tip to reestablish the rod as a shock absorber.

The fish responded with a slow move to deeper water. The fish turned sideways. The broadside of the fish was on display—a wide, tawny, olive-brown back flecked with black spots haloed in milky white. On the lower flank were orange and red spots scattered across its brownish white belly.

Axel eyed the stationary fish, as though facing off in a duel. He moved first, sidestepping toward the bank, dangerously putting lateral pressure on the fish. The fish shook its massive head left-right-left to dislodge the fly. Then left again, but this time the whole body followed and the fish seemed to slither like an eel over the rocks in the shallow water.

Axel cautiously closed in. He gathered line as he went—conscious that if the fish ran he'd need to instantly release his brake. The fish didn't move, but hung in the shallow water as if it were catching its breath. Axel held the rod high with one hand. With the other he snatched a small net from the back of his belt. At ten feet out, the pressure on the line pulled the broad, bug–eyed head out of the water. Axel stepped to his right toward shore. He gathered line. The fish saw him and lunged to his left, toward midstream. Axel swung the net with his left hand just as the fish jolted toward it. The fish hit the bottom of the net with full force and its momentum jarred the net and Axel's hand and arm. But the net held. The fish was done!

Axel marveled at the fish. Nose down in the small net, its tail stuck out a full foot.

In victory Axel threw up his heavy arms, holding the netted fish and rod aloft and stretching to the tiptoes of his wading boots. The big brown was his.

Only then did Axel see the black ATV and its rider on the high east bank, only forty yards upstream. As Axel lowered his arms, the rider—a tall, big-shouldered man in a baseball cap—put the vehicle in gear and moved away from the river.

CHAPTER 14

(Monday, October 24)

Over the weekend, the Salt Lake City security officer of the Huntington British Columbia Mining Company e-mailed Ange his ten seconds of video on the break-in at the Bridal Veil Mine. The quality of the picture was remarkably good, but it only showed the fenders and tires of the ATV and the bottom half of its rider. And it *was* only ten seconds long.

Early Monday, Ollie viewed it four times, rubbed his chin, and left the office. He told Ange he'd be back in a couple of hours.

He drove to Harlan Implements in South Billings, the closest Kawasaki dealer, to look at their ATVs and ask a few questions. He quickly learned that the last year Kawasaki made an ATV with ten-inch-diameter hubs was 1994. Then they changed to twelve-inch hubs supporting twenty-inch wheels.

He called Ange from the dealership to have her research how many 1994 and earlier Kawasakis were registered in the county.

An hour later, she handed him a computer printout as he walked back into the office. There was only one entry. She said nothing.

Ollie called Axel at Arlyn's. "Boss, need to talk to you. Think I got a line on the ATV at the mine."

"OK, Ollie. Shoot."

"Well, the video shows a pretty small-wheeled rig. First I figured they were 'bout nine, ten inches across the hub. Put a tire on that and you're at maybe sixteen, eighteen inches. They use bigger wheels and tires nowadays. The hub's got a K inside a hexagon—Kawasaki. So I went up to the dealer in South Billings. Harlan Implements. Didn't say why I was interested, but got some good answers. Kawasaki had ten-inch hubs back in the early nineties. Last year was '94. Since '95 they've used twelve-inch hubs. Twenty-inch wheels."

"Sounds like good material."

Ollie cut him off with, "Well, Boss, we got ourselves only one Kawasaki in the county that's old enough for such small tires: Thordahl. Sven Thordahl's got one he registers every year for road use. He's got brake lights, horn, mirrors. He's got tags and can drive it into town, just like a car. It's street-legal, but I can't remember when I last saw anybody's ATV in town."

"Wait a minute, Ollie. Thordahl's may be the only street-legal, old Kawasaki in the county, but there've got to be others. Folks never bothered to register. Use 'em on the ranch."

"Sure, but Thordahl's place is right below the mine. Easy access. Most folks would have to go on a paved road to get to the trail up to the mine, or trailer in their ATVs to the trailhead. Not too likely."

"I don't know about that. Can't say we're ticketing unlicensed ATVs running down the road. So, where you going with this? Is the mining company pushing?"

"Damned straight. They're excited and coming on Wednesday, and with all the troopers here, I got some time. Something happened. I'd like to figure it out. I'm going back up to the mine."

"Ollie, I don't know if there's a problem worth investigating. Why don't you do this, escort the mining guys up there. See if there's any damage. Who knows how they're going to react. They might just blow this off. Vandalism. I really can't see chasing down anybody if there hasn't been any real damage. Sound good?"

"OK, Boss. But the mine guys won't be here 'til Wednesday."

"Ollie, this can wait. Get 'em a new lock with a key and chain the gate closed. Do it today, then let 'em know that they'll need you on Wednesday to open it up. Let's see what they think before you go any further."

"Right, Boss."

At noon Wednesday, Ollie again called Axel at the ranch.

"Boss, I think we got a problem. I just got down from Bridal Veil.

The Canadians were really cool about the whole thing, until they went into the mine."

"What do you mean, 'until they went into the mine'?"

"Well someone blew four holes in the roof. All the way in, toward the back. The rubble on the floor wasn't from mining. One engineer was certain that the intruder was trying to collapse the roof. Cause a cave-in. There're four holes 'bout a foot deep."

Axel pictured the scene in the mine. "They're sure it wasn't just some loose rock or part of their own digging? Hell, I'd imagine that's pretty rough work with a lot of boulders and loose gravel making for a pretty rough finished product."

"You should see this, Boss. These walls are as smooth as concrete. One big cylinder, fifteen feet wide. Ceiling is smooth except for these four craters. The Canadians are positive and they're pissed. They're talking about posting a twenty-four-hour guard up there and starting back on their drilling early next week. Hell, one guy had a fistful of pictures of the ATV, wanting to know if we needed any assistance in our investigation."

"Are you serious? There really wasn't any damage, right? Couple of piles of loose rock. Where're they coming from?"

"They're into precision mining like the mine was a secure geology laboratory, and it's been violated. They started talking about how palladium could be used to build ignition switches for nuclear bombs. The boss, a guy from Vancouver, talked to the other guys about having the job transferred to an American firm in order to get some money for security from some U.S. anti-terrorist agency. The way they talked, they are just contract miners. Any ore is owned by a big defense contractor or the U.S. government itself. Anyway, they weren't used to having intruders at their mines."

"So, who's their client? The Feds? Hell, maybe they'll call the FBI. Custer is a national forest. I've had about enough of dealing with this big-government bullshit."

Then, in a shift of gears, Axel said softly, "So, what do you want to do?"

"Well, I didn't tell them anything 'bout the age of the ATV or about who might own it. So unless they call in the Feds, I'd just as well keep going."

"What do you mean?"

"Keep up our investigation. See if there are *other* old red ATVs around. Talk to Thordahl."

"So charge ahead as though it were a major event?"

"Sheriff, to those Canucks, this was a significant security breach. Like somebody had robbed a bank. They are not going to forget about it."

Axel paused. "So, you ready to go to Thordahl? Any chance of any more physical evidence? Bootprints? Tire marks? Tools?"

"Well maybe if we looked at Sven's Kawasaki we could get rock samples from the mine or something. Check the tires. Case is never going to be anything but circumstantial. Don't think Thordahl's going to admit to anything."

Axel wiped his mouth with the back of his hand. "Well, last thing we need is some more federal cops in town complaining 'bout how we do business. Call up Thordahl and tell him we need to talk to him about an explosion at the mine. Tell him we need to see him soon. Hell, better yet, let's go get a search warrant. We tell him we're interested in his ATV, he's going to spray it down with a hose, or repaint it. Thordahl, he's a pistol. He's gonna push back. We'd better do this by the book, like it was a murder investigation. Then we surprise him some morning with the warrant. 'Spose that's a better way."

"By the book. You bet, Boss," Ollie responded.

As Axel put down the phone and reached for his coffee cup, he was already thinking of alternatives. A warrant was certainly by the book, but was it really necessary? He walked out onto the front porch. How would he have handled this two weeks ago, before Crestfallen? After ten minutes, he walked down to the creek and sat on the trunk of the big cottonwood lying there.

At one o'clock, he called Ollie back.

"Ollie, this is Rankin County. Let's do this our way."

"What d'ya mean, Boss?"

"Drive out here and pick me up in a county car. Bring your camera.

We're going to the Thordahl Ranch. Just tell Ange you're meeting with me. Don't use the word Thordahl."

Axel couldn't remember the last time he talked to Sven Thordahl; could have been during the last election cycle two years ago.

It was late afternoon when Axel and Ollie drove into the barnyard at the Thordahl Ranch. There were several men working in the horse corral near the barn. Ollie parked the Cherokee away from the barn.

Axel spoke to one of the workers, "Need to talk to Sven. He around?"

The answer was yes, and two minutes later Sven came out from the back of the barn. As he approached, his prominent right-legged limp caused Axel and Ollie to look at each other in silent agreement.

Axel stepped forward and introduced himself and Ollie. Sven looked at both men head to toe and nodded his head. Axel flipped his head to the far side of the corral. Softly he said, "Mr. Thordahl, we need to talk to you. 'Bout the mine."

Sven looked back to the barn and the workers there and slowly led the trio in the other direction. Sven said nothing.

Once settled at the far corner of the corral with each of the men hanging on the fence, Axel said, "Seems someone on an old red ATV was up to the new mine last week and blew a few holes in the ceiling. Minor damage, but still it's a problem."

Sven said nothing.

"The miners outta Canada are pushing hard for an investigation."

Axel paused, and again Sven said nothing.

"They've got a tape. From a security camera. Ten seconds of tape which shows an old red Kawasaki ATV and the legs of a rider. A tall fellow with a gimpy right leg."

Sven said, "And I suppose you think their tape's got something to do with me?"

"We do."

"That all you got?"

"Seems that we got enough. Probably need to see what your ATV looks like."

Sven slowly drew up his arm toward the garage. "Have at it. Make your case."

Axel turned to Ollie and told him to go take a few pictures. Then as Ollie turned to go to the garage, Axel said to Sven, "You want to go with him?"

"No. You just do your business and be gone."

Sven turned back and looked across the corral to the rolling foothills.

After a minute of silence, Axel said, "I don't have a plan for this. I could take it to the county attorney and he could put together a pretty outrageous list of crimes. State police are in town. They could handle this. Hell, the mine's on federal property. I'm not going any of those places. But I've got to contain the miners. They're pissed. We'll keep a lid on this. If you wanna talk about it, that's fine. Can't see that there's any real damage, but I wouldn't be going within a mile of the mine if I were you. The mining's not gonna stop. Actually, they're pushing to make up for lost time."

"That it?"

"Guess so. Maybe we should let the miners stew a bit. Could blow over. But if you want to step up, then maybe we could close this investigation down right quick. Can't see we need to press charges, so long as there's nothing new coming out."

"Nothing new?"

"Yeah. Like you already did some other stuff we don't know about yet. Or you try again."

"Didn't say I tried the first time."

"Well *I* did, and I've seen nothing to convince me otherwise. Today Ollie could prove up this case all by himself in about five minutes. Don't kid yourself."

"So what you looking for?"

"A straight-up admission. Formal statement that you won't interfere with the operation and acknowledge their rights."

"That'd be hard."

Ollie walked out of the garage and approached Axel and Sven.

"I can see that," Axel said. He turned to leave.

"You have a good day, Sheriff," Sven said as Axel and Ollie walked away.

Axel stopped and turned back to face Sven. He said, "Sven, the next move's yours. Make it a good one."

As Axel and Ollie drove back to town, Axel considered what differences there were between Sven and Charlie Ryan. And what similarities the old, weathered, independent Montanans shared.

CHAPTER 15

(Thursday, October 27)

The phone at Arlyn's rang early. Axel answered it, "Yeah?" It was Ange calling from the office.

"Hey Boss, Charlie Ryan just called."

"What? Charlie Ryan called the county sheriff's office? What's wrong with him? Know what he wants?"

She said, "Well, Sheriff, what he said was that the U.S. Army's moving onto Crestfallen—buses, big trucks, and a bulldozer. He said he's trying to figure out what to do about it."

"Hello? The U.S. Army?"

"That's what he said."

"When did he call?"

"About a minute ago."

"What's his number?"

"He called from 234-5716. But he didn't offer it. The caller ID picked it up. He gave me his home number: 476-1237." Axel wrote down the numbers. Then he drew lines through them.

"Any of our guys in my neighborhood?"

"No, nobody really close. The only county car out is Ollie and he's up in Everhart. Out by where that pole barn blew apart in June."

"Everhart? Could be the first call in three years. Is he on his way back yet?

"No, we got a 5:25 call on a deer crash. No injuries. No alcohol. Sounded pretty routine."

Axel looked at his watch: 7:30. "Call him, would ya? Tell him to meet me at Stanley's on Route 34 at 8:15. About milepost 17. He knows it. Abandoned gas station. No siren, no light bar, within the speed limit. Tell him to wait if I'm not there. I'm going to get dressed and drive my truck to Stanley's. Do not broadcast your call to the MSP and don't be talking to anyone but Ollie. And don't tell him squat⊠but to meet me at Stanley's. I should be there before 8:15. Got it?"

"You bet. Call Ollie, one to one. He's to meet you at Stanley's 8:15, but no sights or sounds. He's in the dark as to why," Ange relayed. Axel smiled at her reiteration of his instructions.

"Right. Call Ryan and tell him I'm coming. Be there within an hour. I'll get back atcha when I know anything," Axel said as he hung up the phone.

While he got dressed, he thought of calling Ham and decided against it. Axel decided not to wear his uniform. He was still on leave and he wasn't ready to deal with Charlie Ryan officially as the County Sheriff. This was still personal.

Ollie was waiting at the abandoned gas station when Axel drove up in his pickup.

Axel was on edge—as though he'd drunk too much coffee. He needed to consider every movement and closely watch what he said and did. Certainly, he didn't need to say anything to Ollie. Ollie would be curious, but he'd have to live with it.

Approaching the county car, Axel opened the driver's side door and, with a impish grin, pushed Ollie over to the right. "I'll drive," was all he said. They drove east on 34 into the new morning sun.

The drive was short, shorter than Axel expected—a lot easier than slogging over Dead Horse Plateau. The side road didn't have a name, just a placard with a list of family names—Casey, Larkin, and Sullivan, and the word "Crestfallen."

Two hundred yards down the unpaved and dusty road, which paralleled an irrigation ditch, two men with rifles suddenly stepped out from behind a giant cottonwood. Axel braked hard and skidded on the gravel. He rolled down his window. Frank Ryan strolled up to Axel's window.

"Morning, Sheriff. Still with us? I hear Charlie's looking for ya. Go past the big ranch. 'Bout a mile past, then take the left fork. Then up the hill. 'Bout five miles, all told." Frank sounded like he was directing traffic at the county fair.

The left fork did indeed go up the hill. The rutted, rocky road climbed more than a thousand feet in its four-mile length. Axel remembered none of the route from last Thursday morning's ride with Ham and the trooper.

As Ollie and Axel crested the ridge they realized that this was only the first of two parallel ridges which eventually ran up onto Dead Horse Plateau. The road dipped sharply into a shadowed valley. Near the top of the second ridge were a small contingent of dusty pickups and a group of men carrying rifles. As they drove toward the group, Charlie Ryan broke away from a trio peering over the edge of the ridge in order to greet the new arrivals.

He walked up slowly to the car with a heavy limp but a welcoming grin as if Axel were a late arrival at a family picnic. He opened Axel's door. His greeting was, "Well, we got some action—invaders for you." Charlie didn't move his head but looked hard to the left side of his field of vision and caught Ollie getting out of the car. Ollie got out, closed the front door and stood next to the car.

"C'mere, Sheriff. Axel." Charlie commanded as he waved Axel up to peer over the top of the second ridge line.

Axel wondered on what basis he was now a friend of Charlie Ryan. Ollie stayed behind and lit a cigarette.

For Axel, who had expected to see the ranch appearing as it had on Thursday morning, the scene was startling. First of all, it was now full morning with the bright sunshine illuminating the entire enclave. While the colors were dusted over like all of Montana in October, the rich brown and red hues of the buildings and their roofs jumped out at Axel. The angles were all different. Axel hadn't realized how steep the hills on the left side of the Ryan Meadow were and how broad and beautiful the high mountain valley was.

He adjusted his sunglasses and looked to his right trying to trace the route down from the Plateau through the forest down to the ranch. He found the stream and its intersection with the fence. He followed the creek bed down to the point from which he had sprung up to meet the runners. He swallowed hard and looked away.

To anyone else, the most obvious features in the valley were the military equipment and the swarm of soldiers dressed in olive drab and flitting back and forth. A throbbing diesel engine masked all other sounds coming out of the valley.

Even from five hundred yards out, the vehicles were massive. There were two buses, two low-boy tractor-trailers, one bulldozer, a short but stocky dump truck, and a straight, open-bed truck. The last vehicle was a standard military two-and-one-half-ton truck with a canvas-covered bed.

As a soldier ran by the dump truck Axel noted that the wheels were as tall as the soldier. Axel scanned the scene side to side and simply said, "Unbelievable—Hilton's called out the Colorado National Guard."

Charlie pointed to the front door of the ranch house. It was Jack Hilton. Hilton in full uniform, hatless, with his bald head gleaming in the sun, standing with three smaller men in uniform.

Hilton stepped off the porch. He took four long strides out to the old hay truck. He waved his clipboard and directed each of the soldiers off in a different direction. He commanded the smaller men as if he belonged to a giant mutant species capable of crushing them if they didn't obey.

One soldier climbed up onto the nearby bulldozer. He started it up, worked through the controls, and increased the engine speed, creating billows of coal-black exhaust. He shifted into gear and began crawling his way around the house. Axel calculated that its target was the equipment shed, the shed that on Wednesday morning had covered the VW microbus. The bus was gone. The stolen tanker was gone.

As the dozer slowly worked its way around the ranch house to the shed, Axel considered that it was on the path of the lead runner, Willy Ryan—before he changed his mind.

A group of soldiers in fatigues ran alongside the lumbering bulldozer, like children prancing alongside the car of a local politician in the Fourth of July parade. Diesel smoke poured out of the dozer as the driver revved up the engine and shifted gears. The men of the Kingdom watched closely from their hilltop.

Charlie turned back to the assembly. "If we're gonna stop em, now's the time. Three minutes that shed'll be flat."

Axel looked at Charlie in amazement. "Stop him?"

Charlie turned away from Axel and looked back to the clutch of

Ryans, Sullivans and O'Neils behind him and said loud enough for all to hear, "We'll send Hilton a message from here."

Frank Ryan drove up in his old red pickup and parked next to the county car. He was carrying a rifle as he came up to Charlie and Axel. Axel noted that it was not a simple varmint gun, but a big bore elk rifle with a high-power telescope.

Charlie turned to Frank, "Taking down the shed. He's committed. Are we?"

"You bet." Frank replied. He looked at Axel and back at Charlie as though to ask if Axel knew the plan—if Charlie had just told Axel the plan. Charlie flipped his head, effectively saying, "Whatever, go on." Frank continued, "Going to go with Mike, Tommy and me. 'Fraid Pete might hit somebody. Three will do. I figure we'll get off twelve-fifteen shots a minute. Three minutes."

Charlie said, "Do it."

Frank moved on to pass the word to the other shooters. Axel looked at Charlie and put his hand on the shoulder of Charlie's jacket, "What're you doing? You're shooting at the Colorado National Guard? Targets? I hope to hell you're not aiming at people. Christ, Hilton's outta line, but you can talk to him. Let's go down the hill. Start honking the horn."

Charlie pulled away from Axel and jerked his jacket out of Axel's grip as though he hadn't heard anything Axel had said. Charlie painstakingly climbed to the edge of the crest. "I'm not afraid of Hilton. You said yourself he'll do what he wants. All I can figure is that he's trying to rewrite history. No evidence, no crime. His timing's screwed up. FBI was here for two days. 'Bout carted off half the furniture. He is just one screwed-up dude. All-round!!" He looked down at his feet.

"Hey, Charlie, this is stupid. Don't be shooting at anything. If you shoot at him you're as screwed up as he is. Hell, Hilton's liable to shoot back. If you're not going down there, I am."

Axel stepped in front of Charlie and started down the hill to the ranch. He got twenty feet before a young man came running after him. It was a crisp football tackle that swept Axel off his feet and put the two of them into a rolling heap on the rocky ground. When they stopped rolling Axel was under the young man, face down.

Ollie started to run down the hill but Frank grabbed his arm and stopped him. "Sheriff'll be all right," he said.

Charlie looked down at Axel and said with a snarl, "I think you'll stay right there, Sheriff." Then he turned back and said, "Frank, let's go."

Frank waved to the two middle-aged men standing by a new pickup truck. They picked up their rifles and small backpacks out of the truck bed and followed Frank as he climbed up to the crest of the ridge.

Frank said, "Three minutes. No targets within twenty feet of anybody."

Axel, still under the tackler, looked up at Charlie and said, "Charlie, this is dumb, the dumbest thing I've ever heard. Somebody's gonna get hurt. Hilton might shoot back. What, you want me to arrest you guys? I can do that."

"Well, lying where you are, that would be worth the price of admission. Hell, we're just going to blow out some tires. No blood. Frank, let's go."

Then, with a flip of his head, Charlie signaled the tackler to get off of Axel. Without a word, the tackler got up and walked up and over the ridge behind the Kingdom's trucks. Ollie walked down to Axel to help him up. Axel slowly got to his knees and then Ollie pulled him to full height. He stretched and stepped up to Charlie.

He asked, "Why'd you call me? You're planning to do this all along. What'd you want me to do? Try to stop you? Arrest you on assault—take you away? I don't think so. You're trying to rub my nose in your crap. I'm outta here. Calling the MSP. I'm not gonna get killed trying to settle a dispute between two wacked-out gangs who'd both love to see me caught in a firefight."

Charlie Ryan stood, and lost his balance and stumbled over the rock he'd been sitting on. He caught himself with one hand on the ground. The two closest men quickly shuffled forward to help Charlie stand.

Axel turned sharply away from Ryan. Walking tall with squared shoulders, Axel approached Ollie, now standing back by his squad car, and said, "Saddle up, we're outta here. You drive. I gotta call Ham." Axel never looked back.

Ryan waved away his men who had started following Axel.

As Ollie cautiously maneuvered the car through the first of the three switchbacks going down into the deeply shadowed valley, the first of the rifle shots cracked and reverberated behind them.

Axel called Ham on the overland radio and told him to send every MSP trooper who was within fifty miles of Crestfallen, the full Rankin County contingent. Axel called for sirens at full volume. Axel also told Ham to send a helicopter medical rescue unit.

The shooters were good. In the first two minutes they took eleven calculated shots and flattened nine tires. Two vehicles escaped their scrutiny altogether as soldiers were standing too near them. The bulldozer had knocked over two corner posts of the equipment shed before the operator turned it off, climbed down, and huddled against it as protection against the shots coming down on the ranch.

Hilton shuffled from the safety of the ranch house out to the rusting hay truck to scan the ridge. He leaned over the front fender with his binoculars. Frank Ryan, lying on the back slope of the ridge and using a large boulder as a gun rest, sighted the bus parked thirty feet away from Hilton's truck. He squeezed off the shot, and immediately feared that it would be short. His left hand supporting the rifle had slipped. The bullet hit the ground in front of the bus and jumped to the left.

It was a glancing blow across the left side of Hilton's chest, ripping open the skin and plowing through his chest muscle before caroming off a rib and exiting.

The wound was a ragged gouge. Hilton grabbed his chest with both hands as he slowly turned and sprawled face first onto the hood of the truck. The shooting stopped as he slowly slid to the ground. He spiraled to sit on the ground with the tire as a back rest. He faced the shooters. The truck's hood and his shirt were deep red.

Forty-three minutes later, the MSP medevac helicopter lifted up out of the Ryan Meadow carrying General Jack Hilton of the Colorado National Guard and the U.S. Marshal for the Eastern District of

Colorado. The MSP medical crew had strapped a mask on him, pressure bandaged his wound, and made radio contact with the emergency room at Billings Memorial Hospital.

The helicopter was met on the roof of the hospital by Dr. Anne Lynwood and two hospital technicians. The conversation between the two medical teams was clipped and professional. They all knew that they had a fragile patient and a prominent one. The story was simple: here he is, this is what we did and this is how we think he's reacting.

Hilton was conscious, lying with his right side propped up at an angle, so that his bandaged wound was easily accessible. Anne shot a malevolent, laser-beam glare at the head MSP paramedic. She declared, "This man can't breathe. Put him on his back."

Anne knew who Jack Hilton was. Regardless, she was resolved that he would get the best care that she and Billings Memorial had to offer. Now she needed to get him to the ER and stabilized. She called for pure oxygen to replace the mix and pressed a triangular button on her electronic lanyard to alert the cardiac unit.

Within minutes, she had achieved her initial goals and had determined that he needed to be sewn up quickly to prevent permanent muscle separation.

Anne performed the surgery, three layers of dissolving stitches at various depths within the muscle. Jack Hilton was under general anesthetic by 10:30 AM, into the operating room at 10:45, out by noon and out of the intensive care unit by 2:30. By 4 PM, several members of the Colorado National Guard had arrived looking for orders from Hilton. He was obviously in pain, but alert and intent on checking himself out of the hospital.

On Anne's third visit, Hilton was propped up in bed in a seated position. He was struggling to get out of bed and swearing under his breath. In response to her question as to what he thought he was doing, he told her that he wanted to do everything he could to "get out of Montana before somebody kills me." Then, ignoring Anne, he ordered one of his subordinates to get the home addresses and telephone numbers of Charlie Ryan, Ham Frazier and Axel Cooper, saying that "we got work to do."

Anne scowled at Hilton. He ignored her.

Hilton's feet hit the floor as she crossed the room to look at his chart hanging on the foot of the bed. After he secured his balance and realigned the IV trolley, he looked up at her and said, "And what the hell do you want?"

She continued reading his medical chart.

He looked her in the eye and said, "Get these fucking tubes outta my arm. I got shit to do. I'll sign whatever legal-ass form you want me to, so long as I'm long gone within the hour. You were great, honey, but I'm out of here. Seems you folks in Montana are out to get me."

She looked at him and the soldiers, and said, "I'll have the hospital administrator secure your release. For the record, you've done very well by this hospital and Montana. We could only wish that Montana had done as well by you."

CHAPTER 16

(Thursday, October 27)

Ollie dropped Axel off at Stanley's. Axel drove back to the ranch.

At noon, Ollie called at the ranch with an update he'd received from the MSP: Hilton was slightly wounded by a ricochet, off to Billings Memorial by MSP helicopter, no arrests. Axel left a message for Anne at the hospital.

Late afternoon, Jim Faraday called. Faraday, formerly of the MSP, was now out of the FBI's Denver office. Axel wanted to talk to him, for no reason other than to see just where Jim's loyalties lay—with the Feds in Denver or with his Montana connections. Axel would hear him out. He fleetingly wondered whether Faraday was tape recording the conversation. Axel knew that Faraday had a message to deliver.

"Hey Axel, finally got you. You're a man on the move. I got about two minutes. Can you talk?" He paused. He was breathing fast and shallow. Axel gave a short grunt in reply. Faraday continued, "Sorry to hear about the raid. Situation was tough. Sounds like self-defense to me. Our undercover guy never should have left the ranch house. Undercover's shitty work, 'specially when the bad guys are doing bad shit. If everybody else is shooting at the cops, you're gonna look mighty peculiar if you're not shooting too." Faraday paused.

Axel grunted a thank you.

Faraday started yet again, "Axel, here's a message you never heard from me. Hilton's trying to stir up a catfight. Story here is, he never told the DEA guys squat about Doug Burns, the undercover guy. I'm sure he didn't tell you. Burns worked out of Minneapolis. Never met him. On paper, he sounds like he's even more squeaky clean than the rest of us. Had to learn to smoke cigarettes to go undercover—almost backed out because of it. Marine Corps Captain, Annapolis. Early Iraq. Should've stuck with the military. So how you doing?"

Axel was warming up to Faraday and realized that he had called solely as a friend. Axel replied "Me, I'm doing okay. Ham's been super. I'm chillin' out at my brother's. A guy just can't shoot two folks dead, one of them an FBI agent, and say it's a good day for law enforcement and his soul." He paused and let his stream of consciousness flow. "This has rattled my cage. I know I shot in self-defense. Christ, I thought I was gonna be bayoneted or drilled at point-blank range. I couldn't tell one kid from the other. Burns was the follower, never used his rifle, but he was coming on strong. Christ, what do you tell his parents, his wife. He made one lethal mistake."

Faraday interjected, "No wife, no kids."

To which Axel said, "That's some consolation. I guess so. Still dead."

Faraday jumped back in, "Hey, Axe, I got to make this quick. Strange things are going on here. You heard about Hilton this morning?"

"Yeah, I was there 'til the shooting started. What the hell was Hilton up to? Guess he got hit by a ricochet. At Billings Memorial."

"Well not anymore. He checked out an hour ago. Ten minutes ago, the governor canned Hilton as a commander of the National Guard's First Division. Then the governor came to my boss to have us, the FBI, do fact-finding on the National Guard's trip to Montana. We're not going to take it. Fastest decision the FBI's ever made. But that's not public. We're not doing cleanup of Hilton's mess. Call it institutional self-interest. Story goes that Hilton's unit was scheduled for maneuvers west of Fort Collins. At 4:00 AM today, Hilton told half of them to go home and took the rest to Montana."

Faraday continued as if reading a script, "Yesterday Hilton was working the U.S. Attorney's office hard. He's got a new angle on Crestfallen. Hilton thinks there might be a second facility, one that's up and running. Trying to get the FBI and the U.S. Attorney to push you on the shooting and go after Charlie Ryan for the second plant. Nobody at FBI-Denver's doing anything, but we've got swarms of Minneapolis guys flying in. They got Autry, the U.S. Attorney, scheduled for tomorrow morning for three hours. I can't see John Autry moving without the FBI-Denver putting together a rock-solid case, that's the way it works—bottom up, not top down. He needs a client—he's not going to go freewheeling. Autry's political, but he's a pro. He's not going to do anything to help Hilton with damage control. Hilton wants an escape route. He's trying to get close to the Minneapolis guys. They've got Autry's ear and they're pissed. Hilton wants to have them pin the tail on *you* so he can walk away with a medal. It's good news, bad news. For you, it might be worse if Autry doesn't do anything. Hilton may go freelance again. I think he's losing it."

Axel interrupted, "I'm not holding my breath for anybody to do anything. Nothing from Hilton would surprise me. Hey, what's up with Samuelson, the DEA guy? Have they taken him out of the padded cell yet? Can't figure why he started shooting when the runner tripped. He must have been juiced up. When the guy tripped, his rifle fired, but the shot didn't come close to Samuelson. Hell, it hit the barn eighty yards the other way."

Faraday replied, "DEA swallowed him up; probably the best thing that could happen to him. I think his future includes inspecting poppy fields in Afghanistan. Hilton wants to draw and quarter him. Axel, hey, I gotta go. You take care. Keep the faith. I'll let you know if either the FBI or the U.S. Attorney starts anything formal. Watch your back, partner. These are angry days in Denver. Hilton's a loose cannon."

The two men were silent for a moment. Then Jim Faraday said, "You take care. Gotta go," and hung up.

Then Axel left his self-imposed exile at Arlyn's to "check on things" at the sheriff's office. He wanted to get off the ranch.

The call came in through Axel's private, unlisted telephone line at the sheriff's office; Montana Bell's caller-identification system was baffled by its origin. The LED panel on the phone on Axel's desk read only: "6:13 PM—unknown caller." He lifted the receiver.

She didn't have an introduction. Her message was straightforward and compelling: "My name is Delores. You're at profound personal risk. Meet me at 2:00 PM, tomorrow, in the Rainbow Warrior Tap in East Billings."

They both knew that Delores wasn't her real name. Something about the tone in her voice told him that she knew that Axel knew. Axel's immediate questions were met with non-responsive sounds of steady, but shallow, breathing. The caller waited. She did not repeat her statement or acknowledge even having heard his questions. Then Axel calmly answered the only pending question, "Will you or won't you?" He said "Okay. Two o'clock tomorrow."

Then, the voice called Delores hung up without a word of good-bye. The duration of the call recorded on the LED display was thirty-seven seconds.

Over his career, he'd received numerous requests for secret meetings with unknown or mysterious people. He had routinely turned them down, basically on the premise that Rankin County law enforcement was a top-of-the-table business with employees that wore easily identifiable uniforms, drove around in well-marked cars and had an open-door policy at a large building on Broadway in Grant. The Rankin County Sheriff was easy to find and wasn't interested in undercover intrigue.

"So why did I agree?" he asked himself. His answer was slow in coming and complex. He certainly agreed with the caller that he was, in fact, in peril. Between the threats of Charlie Ryan and warning from Jim Faraday, Axel felt as exposed as if he was taking rifle fire while riding a horse down Broadway in the Fourth of July parade. Any volunteer that agreed with him would receive a warm reception. *Support local law enforcement.*

He sat at his desk with his feet up on it, staring at the wall. Then Ange suddenly was at the open door, startling Axel so that he pulled his legs off the desk and stood up.

She came to ask if he wanted anything from the restaurant. Axel listened to Ange's mid-range, mature female voice and only then realized that a further reason he had agreed to meet Delores was that he recognized her voice on the phone. Recognized, but could not identify. *Where have I heard that voice before?* So Delores was someone he knew who didn't want him to know who she was. Unless, of course, he agreed to meet with her. And if he didn't agree to meet her, he'd never solve the riddle. Her tone and implied authority impressed Axel. She spoke with certainty, as though she had a rock-solid foundation for her statement. She had selected her few words with care, like a poet sounding out each syllable and nuance of interpretation to combine the sound and meaning to create the full experience. Nobody in Rankin County used the word *profound.*

Regardless, his response had been almost reflexive.

In his last analysis Axel also realized that another consideration was that he simply wanted to meet her and find out just who Delores was.

CHAPTER 17

(Friday, October 28)

Late Friday morning, Axel jumped into the driver's seat of his pickup with a bounce. Today, he was Axel Cooper—everyman, off the ranch and out of Rankin County.

En route to Billings, he made a point of paying attention to the landscape, the animals, and the weather. He needed a break. It was one of the best times of the year in Montana, mid-autumn, fewer drunken tourists, no punk skiers, fewer troubles among the locals who were busy getting ready for winter, yet it was warm enough to leave the jacket in the truck. Every day he would check for early snow in the upper reaches of the Harlan Range. The lush green color of June and early July had been dusted over by the dry heat of August and September. The spring's crop of Angus calves was being rounded up to begin the next phase of their short lives. Their thrill at life was apparent in every step they took.

As the river wound its way down the valley to its juncture with the Yellowstone, it supported a long string of tall, sprawling cottonwoods on its banks. Axel slowed at two or three spots to check for eagles' nests in the tops of dead trees. At Washington's Crossing, he spotted a clutch of wild turkeys feeding near the river.

Axel couldn't take a complete vacation. Route 176 in Rankin County posted more deaths per mile than any two-lane in the state. The Rankin County Sheriff's department spent half their time patrolling Route 176. Personal memorials were staked along the road at the sites of deadly accidents: on the right, two white wooden crosses within fifty yards of each other followed by a cluster of smaller, foot-high crosses and then, on the left, a small collection of weathered teddy bears, baby dolls and dust-encrusted plastic roses. If pressed, Axel could recite the names of the victims. The road was a problem. It could have wider lanes: ten feet wide with flat shoulders. Better yet, it could be a lane wider or at least have periodic passing lanes, but at five hundred thousand dollars a mile, that was not going to happen. The immediate problem was the drivers and the speed limit. Axel's latest effort was an educational one: "It's ninety minutes to Billings at forty miles per hour, not sixty minutes at sixty."

Axel looked at the clear road ahead, checked his speedometer, the rearview mirror, and his watch. He shook his head and smiled. He was off duty driving his own truck, but there were six observant citizens of Rankin County in a disciplined parade behind him at thirty yard intervals at forty-two mph. They recognized his truck and were actively paying respect to the beleaguered county sheriff.

If there had been a lunch crowd, it was gone by 1:45 when Axel first walked into the bar and inhaled the once-familiar, sweet-musty odor of stale beer. In spite of the seventy-eight degree temperature and bright, full sun outdoors, the Rainbow Warrior Tap was cool and dark. It was a working man's tavern: a one-brand tap, seventy-five cents for seven ounces of Rainier.

Axel ordered a beer at the bar and took a seat in the far corner away from the blacked-out window. As he sat down, he casually flipped his head over his shoulder to catch a possible audience. There was none: all four patrons were busy with their own troubles and solutions. *Good for them.* Axel hunched over his beer, inhaled the aroma, and was seized by a memory of the beer halls of Key West after three solid weeks of Coast Guard narcotics patrol covering Florida's west coast. That sortic had set a record: seventeen boardings, seventy-two arrests, twenty-four tons of marijuana and one thousand pounds of Columbian cocaine—all without setting foot on land for twenty-two days. While the hunting was good, the tension and lost sleep took their toll. Axel's memory of the three-day shore leave in Key West included only the first three beer halls of the first day. The fourth and fifth, and the Shore Patrol escort, were lost to the ages.

Axel surveyed the inside of the bar to complement his external appraisal: one story, no attic, no basement, two johns, small kitchen and two exits—front to the parking lot and back through the kitchen and storeroom. Some budget hard liquor but the mainstay was beer, which meant fewer late-night drunks. The simple truth is, more folks get full on beer before they get fighting drunk. Key West was the exception.

He knew she was Delores before she even opened the door. At the doorsill, the owner of the small midday shadow stopped to scan the room. Middle of the day, lone woman. Had to be her. As she opened the door and took her first steps into the building, she squinted to see in the dim light and then hitched her shoulders back, as though to readjust her brassiere or, perhaps, a shoulder holster. On her third step, she spotted Axel, nodded her head, and redirected herself mid-stride, revealing her profile for the first time. The other patrons looked up to assess the new arrival.

Axel allowed himself a full examination of the turning silhouette with the conclusion she was a small, solid, well-proportioned, athletic woman. She was well-bottomed but had a muscularity that was readily apparent. Short, low-maintenance hair. Maybe a rider; graduate of the barrel-racing circuit. He guessed she was strong willed and outspoken—a western outdoor girl. Her figure and posture were important to her and she was trying to be as tall and wide as she could. She had a command-presence about her, maybe ex-military or law enforcement. She strode across the room like President Bush, the younger, approaching a lectern at a White House press conference; head high, shoulders back, spine straight.

Axel, ready to have his instant profiling tested, pushed back from the table to greet his mystery guest. He stood as she approached.

As he stepped to the side of the small table, she strode up to him, toe to toe. He smiled as he shuffled back. Her introductory greeting was crisp and louder than necessary, "Glad you're here." Axel reflected that she was wound up and was prepared for a major delivery—of what, he had few clues.

Right off, he knew that if this event was going to be satisfactory, he'd need to slow this cowgirl down; otherwise, it would be her speech and her exit, with the possibility that he'd be left with more questions then he had yesterday.

She did not offer to shake hands, but grabbed the back of the chair facing Axel and started to sit down. Axel stayed standing and asked if she wanted a beer. She declined, but Axel, wanting a few more important seconds to pass, grabbed his glass and walked to the bar for a refill.

As a state trooper and a county sheriff, Axel was used to leading the conversation and pushing for answers until he captured them or came to the recognition that they simply weren't to be had. As Ivey often told him, he wasn't a good listener unless someone was answering his questions. He certainly had questions for Delores, but he wondered if the answers were going to be available. He asked his first question while still three feet from the table, balancing two beers and a small bowl of peanuts. He wondered if it would be his last. "I'm not sitting down, 'til you tell me who you are."

To Axel's surprise she responded immediately, "My name is Kris Bradford. Kris with a "K." I'm the Senior Assistant U.S. Attorney for the state of Wyoming. I am here as a private citizen today." She paused to let that sink in and then continued, "I live and usually work in Cheyenne, but I have been seconded to the Denver office to work on a federal murder case, six week trial, and a backlog of drug cases coming out of the ski resorts. Clancy Ellis, the Wyoming U.S. Attorney hired me six years ago. Been down in Denver for six months. Ten years of private practice in Denver and Cheyenne. Wills and trusts—some small family-owned corporate stuff. Real estate deals. Clancy sent me to Denver. I aim to make federal prosecution my career, but I just can't handle what's going on in Denver."

She stopped, took a dry, hard swallow, and turned her head up toward Axel. He nodded slowly as though silently responding to her unspoken question. Then, she smiled and cracked, "Sit down, Sheriff."

He placed a beer in front of her. He settled into his chair and looked at her for the first time at eye level. He was struck by her bright, moist eyes under natural dark, thick eyebrows and long lashes. They were magnetic ,and as he quickly moved his gaze to her short auburn hair, tanned cheeks, small nose and patterned blouse, he was drawn back to her eyes, as though seeking permission for further review. She lifted her chin, sat still for the process, as though under a pre-parade inspection by the base commander. As she reverted to looking at the far wall, her only reaction was to flash her lashes repeatedly. She had been scrutinized at close-quarters before and was not flinching.

Axel caught himself staring at her chest, and slightly embarrassed, dropped his gaze, kicked his leg outside from under the table, and brought his hand to his mouth as through to suppress a cough. "Well, you know who I am. I think we've met. That right? Call me Axel."

Kris exhaled and said, "Never met. But we talked a couple times last year about a domestic murder in the park. Wife shot the old man and left him three miles off the road. They had stayed a couple nights in Grant before driving over the pass to the park. You checked out local motels for me. She's doing twenty-five at Menard." She paused, but Axel had no reply. She started in again. "Well, first off, today's problem is Jack Hilton. He's trying to get John Autry to go to a grand jury with a Section 257 action against you and DEA agent Derrick Samuelson. Autry's the U.S. Attorney for Colorado. A 257's a federal criminal indictment based on a deprivation of civil rights under color of law. Basically, federal felony by a law enforcement officer. Looks to be adding manslaughter and negligent homicide. He's also got Hamilton Frazier lined up for some conspiracy after the fact, obstruction of justice. I'm not on the case. I've got no conflict and a clear conscience. Hilton's been in Autry's office four times in two days. He's trying to railroad you. Just not fair. And won't help anybody."

"Hilton's trying every way he can to squeeze Autry. The Colorado governor. Both U.S. senators. The vice president's lawyer called, for Christ's sake. The man's a maniac, flying in four directions at once. But Autry hasn't thrown him out yet. Or told him to go away, take a hike. Hilton is the U.S. Marshal, appointed by the president. Even a U.S. Attorney can't dismiss him out of hand. I'm sure Hilton's got pictures of somebody, somewhere. Autry's looking to run for Colorado's open U.S. Senate seat in '08. This might just be the horse to ride. Camden's retiring. But Autry's not doing anything political without calling a focus group. The good news is that everybody in Autry's office is arguing that this is Hilton's baby and the worst domestic federal law enforcement mess since Waco in the early days of Janet Reno. Maybe as bad as Ruby Ridge. Can you believe Hilton brought up the Colorado National Guard? Is this Honduras? To a man, the assistants are telling Autry to run away from this. But somebody somewhere has got to get to the bottom of this. "

Axel leaned back in his chair. Sure, he knew that he would eventually hear from the federal government again. Faraday's call had not allowed him to breathe any easier. Certainly Hilton, singlehandedly, could not push the FBI into face-saving indictments against him. But with help from the FBI from Minneapolis, the U.S. Attorney could probably be persuaded to launch an inquiry.

In the jail, Axel had written thirty pages of raw notes and then redrafted them to twenty, neatly hand-written pages, divided into eight chronological segments starting with the governor's call. He burned the original notes. He was ready to testify what happened when, what he felt, what he said, what he meant, what he did and why he did it. What he wasn't ready for was to be indicted for murder or go *mano a mano* with Hilton.

While his mind raced to catch up with the Senior Assistant U.S. Attorney, Axel's only physical reaction was to lower his gaze to the far corner of the room and nod his head as though physically digesting the news.

Then, without looking up or turning back, he said, "Federal murder. Federal murder. Federal murder." Then he turned to Kris and said, "Why Derrick Samuelson? Sure, he shot first, but I was the guy who hit 'em."

Quickly Kris jumped in. "Conspiracy. Section 351. Basically conspiracy to commit murder. Not an unusual approach: manslaughter, insubordination, reckless endangerment, violation of the terms of engagement. Pile up the allegations, broaden the range of suspects; somebody'll cop a plea to something and be extremely cooperative in burying the others. Can't say it's the best way to get at the truth, but it works to improve the U.S. Attorney's hit ratio, indictments versus convictions. We usually use it on the bad guys, not DEA agents. Hilton's going six directions at once." She paused. "I've thought long and hard about how to say this. Here it is, bold as brass. He's out to get you in order to save himself. He failed to control the operation and cannot handle the blame. If he can't lay this on you and Samuelson, I think he'll go after the FBI, arguing that the rest of the Justice Department, basically the FBI and the U.S. Attorney's office, had knowledge of an ongoing crime, the meth ranch, and it should have been their operation rather than his. Argue that the U.S. Marshal is just a go-for service. No rough stuff. Argue that he's just a delivery boy, a custodian. This was more than he could ever be expected to handle. He'll argue this wasn't a job for a U.S. Marshal, but the FBI. I think he's schizoid. He'll stop at nothing. He'll contradict himself mid-sentence. You probably don't want my advice, but I'm giving it to you."

"That's so unlike Hilton. He'd have to argue that he was incompetent. Can't see it."

"Yeah, but it works. Same as 'I'm innocent. I didn't do it. But if I did, I was insane.' We see that once a month."

Axel looked at the floor then let his head float up slowly to the bar's front door. He focused on the small window in the door. "That might work in a court of law, but Hilton's ego won't let him say he's incompetent. So why's he going to Colorado's U.S. Attorney? Doesn't Henry Otto, here in Montana, have jurisdiction?"

She shot back, "End of the day, you're right, but if Hilton can convince Autry to want it, Otto won't stop him. Professional privilege. Basically, the Feds in Colorado have been offended in Montana and Feds in Montana will let them pursue revenge."

Axel responded, "But it would be easy for Autry to duck this entirely and tell Hilton that he was talking to the wrong guy and that he should be talking to Otto in Billings."

"That's a possible outcome, but if Autry thinks this is an easy win, he may jump on it and only give Otto a quick 'by your leave.' Autry could also try to get Washington in the picture. While the local U.S. Attorneys aren't beholden to the Attorney General, they will not want to openly oppose her wishes. I could see the AG choosing one office to handle this."

While she spoke, Axel had started chewing the skin on the inside of his cheek. "You know Otto?" he asked.

"Met him a few times. Had a couple of bank robbery cases with his office. He's only been in office about fifteen months. I think he's a Montana native, always a good thing. Local boy. Do you know him?"

Axel straightened up in his chair and pulled his feet together, ready to stand up. "No, can't say as I do. I'm pretty much willing to let them do their business and I'll do mine." Then he cocked his head and looked intently at the far, upper corner of the room, "Maybe it's time I get to know the man." Then he stood up and looked down at Kris.

"'Preciate your doing this, Delores." He smiled. "Looks like I've got work to do. I don't think we need to tell anybody about this discussion, do we Kris?" He reached out to shake her hand, which he gripped in both of his.

While still holding hands, she looked up at Axel and said, "I'd rather not."

At that, Axel started for the door.

She called after him, "Good luck, Axel."

CHAPTER 18

(Friday, October 28)

Axel sat in his truck in the parking lot of the Rainbow Warrior Tap and contemplated his next move. He stared at his cell phone. *How things change,* Axel thought to himself as he punched in Ham Frazier's now familiar private, direct-access cell number. *Up until a week ago Ham had been high on my short-list of those who could fly off the earth and I wouldn't miss them a bit. And now, he's, what, my godfather?* He shrugged his tight right shoulder, waiting for Ham to answer. *Maybe Charlie Ryan's not the only one who is blaming the wrong guy.*

Ham's voice on the other end of the line interrupted his thoughts, "Frazier," he barked.

"Hey, it's Axel, Can you talk?"

"Uh … yeah, What do you have? Wait, hold on." Axel heard Ham talking to someone else. Ham then covered the phone with his hand, and Axel heard muffled noises and a door closing.

"Back now. You go." Ham said, with the brusque enthusiasm of a high school athletic coach.

"Ham, well, first of all, sounds like you saved Hilton's life. Anne said he could have bled out if he'd arrived at Memorial any later than he did. Can't believe he checked himself out the same day. Fits his profile, I guess."

"I think that's a stretch. More than just a surface wound, but it was a glancing blow. Pretty bloody though. I hear he flew in muttering to himself about Charlie Ryan and that he never should have tried to work with him. Kept saying 'fuckin' idiot' over and over."

Axel hadn't told Ham about his abduction to the Kingdom and wasn't ready to yet. "Can't imagine there's much love lost between those two." He wasn't ready to explain to Ham how Ryan and Hilton had talked before the raid.

Axel squirmed in his seat in the pickup and looked to change the topic. He started with, "I gotta thank you for taking care of me this last week. Good advice and super support. Haven't heard word-one of complaint from any of my guys or any of the fine citizens of Rankin County. Everybody's curious about exactly what went down at Crestfallen, Wednesday and then again on Monday, but I can handle that." Axel's voice dried and cracked. "You're a real godsend. Without you, I'd still be over in the corner drooling. No way I'd have worked myself out of the hole I dug, especially with Hilton trying to bury me deeper. Lord knows … "

"Don't mention it, friend," Ham interrupted.

"Well, all the same. You're a good man, Frazier. Not half the bastard I was telling everybody about." Both men laughed.

"We're not out of this yet, though," Ham cut in. "I've got the feeling we're gonna have to work fast—keep pushing."

"You could say that again. I'm getting signals Hilton and his friends in Colorado are cooking up something nasty to blame this whole mess on me, and maybe you too, brother."

"I've felt that coming, after Hilton's first news release and his interview two days later. But there's good news: I haven't seen anything about *Crestfallen II—the Kingdom Fights Back*. Have you?" Ham chortled at his billing of the second event at the ranch as though it was a Hollywood movie.

Axel didn't want to get Anne any further into this maze and slid over Ham's comment to the purpose of his call. "Well, I've got reliable folks telling me Hilton is all over his U.S. Attorney in Colorado to bring me up on federal murder charges before the current sitting grand jury down in Denver."

"How reliable?" Ham asked.

"People—inside—who don't want their names in print. People I'm inclined to trust. You probably know one or two." Axel figured that Ham had already heard something from the extended family of former MSP personnel now in federal law enforcement, one place or another.

But he doubted that Ham knew Kris Bradford. Axel was certainly not going to reveal her.

"Federal murder, that's a stretch. Can't see much use in the Colorado U.S. Attorney chasing you, unless it's to turn the spotlight away from Hilton, the DEA and, who knows, maybe the FBI. Folks are dead. Somebody's going to start looking at the back story and the motives behind Crestfallen. Christ, we got drafted."

"My thoughts exactly. As for assigning the blame—story from Denver is that Colorado's U.S. Attorney, John Autry, is looking at a U.S. Senate run. Wants his name in the news. Hilton's priming him on how it is that I'm such an easy target, open-and-shut case, easy victory, big headlines. And I'm thinking these two have a lot of reasons to support each other: Department of Justice—Colorado's U.S. Attorney bailing out the Colorado's U.S. Marshal. Sounds reasonable. With Hilton a steady source of front page news, Autry can get all the coverage he wants. Autry doesn't sound like a gambler. But we'll never know what Hilton's telling him."

"Think Hilton's got anything on Autry? Has he got the negatives?" Ham asked with a laugh.

This was the second time that someone had suggested that Hilton had incriminating evidence against high-placed officials. *Hmm, maybe* . . .

"My people didn't go there. Autry appears to be sharp and squeaking clean. Can't see him making anything—any kind of deal—with Hilton. Recently he's turned down a couple of high-profile cases that the FBI wanted to push. Didn't think he could make the case with admissible evidence. Thinks for himself."

"Let's hope Autry plays hardball with Hilton. I don't think they could get an indictment against you for this, not in a million years! And if Autry gets the facts, he'll know that. He'd be throwing his career away, not stepping up to the U.S. Senate." Ham got quiet for a moment. "Just what makes your *people* think this is strong enough to get worried about?"

"All they report is that Hilton's chasing Autry. And nobody's heard a response from Autry."

"You seen or heard from Hilton lately?"

Ham replied, "No, he's been quiet—convalescing in Denver. Anne patched him up pretty good. Christ, just imagine the magnum crappola had he been killed out at the Kingdom. We'd all be in jail. I'll bet he's livid. This deal sure didn't go down the way he expected. Not by a long shot."

Ham paused and then said, "Hey, you do your homework?"

"What, write the report? Hell yes! It was the only thing I did. Kept me sane those two days in the jail."

"You got it down? You gotta have your story down cold. No equivocations. You gotta be rock solid."

"I'm telling you, every word is the gospel truth: twenty handwritten pages, single spaced. I'm not confused about what I know. I'm just trying to figure out what the hell was going through Jack Hilton's mind. One thing's for sure, he wants to pin it all on us."

Ham breathed deeply and then said, "Well, I guess we'll have to stir up a circus of our own if we're gonna have any chance at getting out of this. You go see if you can talk to Ryan. I'll assign one of the troopers to find Samuelson. He's got to know something. I'll work on the governor."

"Good. I'll talk to Ryan, take care."

Axel hung up the phone, glad to have Ham on his side.

CHAPTER 19

(Monday, October 31)

Halloween had always been quiet in Grant and throughout Rankin County. In town, the grade school kids trick-or-treated each other's houses with no real malicious tricks. A smashed pumpkin in the middle of Broadway was noteworthy. This year was typical. The bars were busier than usual for a Monday night, but there were no adult masqueraders. The county was quiet. By eleven, the town was back to normal and Axel's late-afternoon shift at the sheriff's office was winding down.

It was his second day back at work since the shootings at Crestfallen. It had been a long day and he was pleased that no one had asked him any questions about Crestfallen the entire day. Axel was looking forward to a cold beer and a good night's sleep out at Arlyn's. But first he had to stop off at his town house to collect his tool box, which he would need tomorrow to replace a water pump on an old hay truck at Arlyn's. He had forgotten to take it with him after this morning's work to level the floor. As he turned off Broadway, he passed an old red pickup truck with dim headlights coming the other way.

Axel heard the explosion and felt its concussion almost simultaneously. The fireball blossomed a moment later. His house, his work-in-progress, simply blew up before his eyes. He checked his watch: 11:23. As he rolled to a stop, debris was raining down. He saw the last of the new blue siding consumed by the flames. The roof was gone. A billowing cloud of black smoke towered over the house. Flames shot upward as though propelled by a giant bellows. Neighbors came out of their houses. There was never a question of saving the small frame house. It was gone in a single wave of fire that now swept over the top of the chimney. The neighboring house had several windows blown out, but didn't look to be at risk from the fire.

Axel jumped out of the Jeep and ran toward the burning house. The intense heat stopped him at the far curb. He stepped back and with his hands on his hips silently scanned the fire. *Who did this? Who in the hell did this?*

Neighbors were pleased to see Axel. Pleased to see that he was not inside. They gathered in front of the Cherokee and together in silence watched the leaping flames.

At 11:42, the first Grant fire truck turned off Broadway and lumbered down the side street. It was the fully loaded tanker, great for grass fires and an effective first responder, capable of a solid twenty minutes of a steady four-inch stream of water until the other trucks could hook up to the hydrants.

Axel alerted the driver to the fact that no one was inside. Otherwise, he couldn't talk or take his eyes off the bonfire that was his house. In wide-eyed amazement, he walked up and down the street in front of it and the gathering crowd. The whole house was in flames. The scene through each window was the same. Fire was everywhere, all at once.

Axel waved at each of the town's volunteer firefighters as they arrived, assuring them that he knew of no one inside. More than ten turned out. To each Axel cautioned, "The house is lost, don't get hurt." Ten minutes later the chief sidled up to Axel to say the fire marshal would be investigating.

Axel figured that for the house to go up all at once like it did, either propane or natural gas had to be in the air throughout the house and then ignited. This wasn't a leaking gas line, a bad connection or a faulty stove. This wasn't any kind of accident. This was deliberate arson, if not attempted murder. This morning, the natural gas heating system was fully functional. No one had been working with the gas piping, the furnace, or the range.

The driver of the tanker in full gear waddled up to Axel, who was now by himself, leaning against his car.

"Sheriff, got a message on the radio: call Ollie."

Axel nodded, walked back to the Jeep and reached in for the CB. "Hey, Ollie. What's up?"

"Hell, Boss, what's with the house?"

"Explosion. Total loss. What's your news?"

"Came back from a cigarette break and there's a big envelope taped to the outer door. Addressed 'Personal Cooper'."

"Before or after the explosion?"

"After."

"I'll be over when the fire's out."

At 2:20, the house was a smoldering, waterlogged pile of charred lumber. Two volunteers were to stand guard overnight.

Ollie, upon seeing Axel through the glass of the door, greeted him in the inner lobby with the large envelope. He hung near Axel as he opened the envelope. The envelope held one piece of paper, plain white, full size:

> THE HOUSE IS JUST THE DOWN PAYMENT.
> REGULAR INSTALLMENTS TO FOLLOW.
> ACCOUNT TO BE SETTLED SOON.

Axel looked up at Ollie, who had read the note over Axel's shoulder, and angrily spun the paper onto Ange's desk.

He then walked up to the door leading to the back hall and slammed it open with his shoulder.

CHAPTER 20

(Wednesday, November 2)

"Governor, we've got a problem," Ham started. It was after 6:00 PM—a time when Governor Boyd Jefferson was notoriously impatient and prone to be argumentative.

Ham was also hoping for a short meeting. They met in the governor's reception room, more than sixty feet long, with one long wall of windows. Both men were standing looking out at Helena's lights in front of the low, shadowy mountains. "We've got to do something. The Feds are blaming Montana for the Crestfallen debacle," Ham said without turning away from his window. "Jack Hilton, the U.S. Marshal, is on a tear. He's claiming that Axel Cooper and I were rogues, independent operators, unwilling to be team players. I don't have to tell you what he could do to the reputation of Montana law enforcement. Hell, we're still recovering from the black eye Kaczynski gave us ten years ago. And he just *lived* here."

The governor didn't have to be told that the amorphous institution called *Montana Law Enforcement* was still smarting from the spring of 1996; first, the eighty-one-day standoff with the Christian Patriots over in Jordan, and then Kaczynski—the world-famous Unabomber—was discovered to be mailing out explosives from a cabin up in Lewis and Clark County.

"Dammit, Hamilton! How did this happen?" The governor turned toward Ham with his hands out, ready to grab an answer.

"This is all we need. The national news made it sound like *Montana's 'Righteous Avenger' Rides Again*. Shoot first, ask questions later." Then he held up his right hand with his thumb and index finger an inch apart. "I'm this close to stringing up your man Axel Cooper myself!

Why are you here? Did you see this drivel from Denver?" The governor walked to the table and slid a single sheet of paper toward Ham. It was Jack Hilton's October 31 press release.

> For Immediate Release
> October 31
> U.S. Marshal's Service, Department of Justice
> Denver, Colorado
>
> Today's statement is a follow-up to the information released by this office on October 20.
>
> Further investigation has confirmed that on October 20 the Rankin County Sheriff, Axel Cooper, shot and killed two individuals. The site of the shooting was a ranch house in Rankin County, Montana. One of the individuals was an undercover FBI agent, attached to the drug enforcement contingent of the FBI's Minneapolis office. Identification of this individual has been delayed, pending the location and notification of next of kin. The second individual was William J. Ryan, 20, Rankin County, MT, a suspect in the U.S. Marshal's investigation of a $100 million methamphetamine production facility being established at the seasonal Ryan family ranch, the site of the shootings. The two were shot while fleeing the ranch house. A directive from U.S. Marshal Jack Hilton to surrender to federal authorities had been issued in the early morning interdiction. The Rankin County Sheriff, Axel Cooper, was a member of a joint federal-local law enforcement task force.
>
> Three suspects were taken into federal custody, including Robert W. Johnson, 22, a federal fugitive who had failed to appear at an August 8 sentencing hearing in Minneapolis. Mr. Johnson had previously been

> found guilty of illegal drug manufacture and distribution.
>
> The shooting is under investigation by the FBI, U.S. Attorney's office/Denver and the U.S. Marshal service.
>
> Cooperating in the initial effort were the Federal Drug Enforcement Agency and South Dakota State Police. The Montana State Police provided logistical support.
>
> Further information will be made available as it is developed.

Ham quickly scanned the document and looked up at Jefferson, "Hilton can really spin it. This makes it sound like an execution, certainly a crime. Bullshit, how about Cooper shot only in response to being shot at. And at close range. Where is the description of that?" Ham heard himself shouting. But he knew that wasn't going to do any good with the governor.

Ham wanted to focus the governor back on Montana law enforcement and away from Hilton. "Governor, suppose you heard about Axel's house? Down in Grant?"

The governor shook his head no, and Ham continued, "Well, Halloween night, 'bout 11:30, it blew up. One big explosion. Nobody home, no one hurt. But there's nobody who thinks it's an accident. Found an empty, burned-out, forty-pound propane tank in the basement. Folks figure some kind of remote-controlled trigger was used to ignite the gas after it was out of the tank. Three minutes later, Axel would've been inside and dead, dead, dead. He got an anonymous letter at his office saying this was just the first installment. Something about settling the account soon. We sent the arson squad down to pick through the rubble."

The governor pursed his lips and acted not the least surprised. Then he shook his head as though to come out of a trance and said, "So where are we?"

Ham knew he had to get the governor engaged in a rational, tactical response and that the way to do that was to be cold, calculating, and not too argumentative. "Sir, word on the street is that Hilton's courting John Autry—Colorado's U.S. Attorney. Hilton's looking to bring Axel and probably Samuelson, the DEA guy, up on federal charges. Argue that they went way overboard. Reporter called me yesterday with one storyline that you encouraged Cooper to act independently of the Feds. Wanted me to corroborate something Hilton told him about you. There's no telling who Hilton's out to bury or where he'll stop. We have to take counter measures. Pronto."

"I encouraged what? Hell, I told Axel Cooper to cooperate, 'make Montana proud.' I'm not into cloak-and-dagger bullshit, but I'm sure as hell not going to condone any cover-ups. Including one by the federal government. It sounds like you've got a plan, let's hear it. I am going to need the full story before I'll sign off on anything. Whatever you got, I hope you talked to Johnnie about it." The governor was reluctant to do anything. He had learned the hard way that the response to a possible short-coming held more potential for foul-ups, bad press, and legal problems than the initial event itself. Johnnie Walker, the thirty-year veteran leader of the MSP and Ham's boss, was one of Governor Boyd Jefferson's closest confidantes.

"Course Johnnie's with me. You think I'd be here if he wasn't? In a nutshell, we've got to go public: stage a big hearing. In Billings. All kinds of press. Call it a 'preemptive' strike against the Feds. I see a lot of elements of a range war here—a fight for our integrity."

"Ham, don't overplay your hand." Governor Jefferson interrupted, "My integrity and that of this administration isn't on the line and you haven't and aren't going to put it in a vulnerable position. Overstimulated law enforcement is everyday news. Whether it's Hilton or Cooper or cops in L.A. I'm the innocent cooperator here. And I don't find a good fight all that exhilarating. Eats up time and wastes money."

"Governor, hear me out. I'm talking big picture. We've got to get our story out. If we hold back and let the Feds formally accuse any of us, including Axel, they've won the whole ballgame—ten runs in one inning. Game's all but over. If what I hear about this Autry character is correct, he could get Montana's statehood revoked. Very smart. Very political. Very ambitious. I don't know about you, but I'm not interested in being accused of anything by some Colorado hotshot who has

Potomac fever. If he wants to use his office to get elected senator, he can damned well do it by prosecuting crime in Colorado." Ham stopped and fixed on the governor to make sure he was still paying attention.

The governor paused to consider Ham's statement.

"Frankly, Ham, are you sure there's a game to be won? Is it really us versus them? I can't see any western lawman going after a county sheriff who's been shot at. I don't care who you are, if somebody's running at you shooting a rifle, there is no response that can be fairly labeled 'excessive force.' Deadly force *is* the reasonable response." He emphasized the word "is" as though he was lecturing in a large hall.

Ham could tell that the governor was drawing on his days as the county prosecutor in Billings, Yellowstone County, Montana's biggest. He'd held that position for twelve years, been reelected twice on a law-and-order ticket, before using his solid Billings base to launch a bid for Attorney General of Montana and from there to the governor's mansion.

After a moment of silent reflection, the governor continued, "Ham, has anybody looked at crimes committed by federal agents in Montana and what we could do about them? Federal officers have no immunity from state law. Can't say you often hear about state criminal actions against federal employees—Feds usually take care of their own problems—but it's had to have happened. Especially if you can establish that they acted outside their authority—whatever protection they've got disappears altogether. The preemption clause in the Constitution doesn't apply. Crestfallen II or whatever the hell we're going to call it, looks like a classic case. Here we've got a U.S. Marshal trying to wear a second coat of protection—the Colorado National Guard—all the while he's beyond the righteous realm of either. Talk about outrageous!!"

Ham looked at the table and without looking up, slowly said, "No."

This wasn't anything he'd considered. He gave the governor credit for the approach. Ham wasn't ready to talk legal theory with the governor but felt that whatever case might be made some day against Jack Hilton, today Hilton was leading a very public, and so far successful, crusade against Axel Cooper and Hamilton Frazier. *Today we have to stop this parade—a rush to judgment.* Ham also knew that the immodest governor would have to come to that conclusion by himself, or he had to put in the last piece of the puzzle, in order to claim it as his and use his authority to implement a plan. A board of inquiry led by the MSP and initiated by Ham and Johnnie Walker wouldn't make it out of Helena.

Ham wanted to be as persuasive as he'd ever been, but not appear that way to the governor. *This needs to be his idea.*

"Who runs a pursuit like that?" Ham asked, picking up the governor's inquiry into crimes in Montana and playing him out.

"Montana law—the Montana Attorney General or the county prosecutor. U.S. law—U.S. Attorney," the governor quickly flipped back to him as though he'd already considered the issue "Can overlap. See that in death penalty states. McVey down in Oklahoma. I think he coulda been executed three or four times by different jurisdictions."

"Any prosecutors owe you any special favors? How do we get one of them to drop everything and jump all over this?" Ham had three in mind: Montana's Attorney General, the U.S. Attorney for Montana, Henry Otto, and the Rankin County prosecutor.

Jefferson shook his head, "Christ, don't pretend to be so naive. Andover, our Montana Attorney General, wants my job. Think she's gonna step up and bail us out? Not in this new century. Can't imagine that she'd ever even publicly consider it. Make her look committed. Then if she didn't go after it, she's going to look like she's going soft on crime or wasn't a Montana team player. Lord knows what she'd do if I made a public referral to her. No, nothing personal, but we'd probably get farther with an MSP referral from you. I'm without positive influence on the woman." He held his hands up palms out in resignation.

After a moment he continued, "I don't know boo about the Rankin County guy, Cuzman. Seems to be another good-ole'-boy who doesn't want to make waves. Support the party and the tourist trade. Can't see him making a serious run at the federal government."

Two down, one to go. Ham calculated.

Ham, wanting to clear the slate, said, "You got a bead on Henry Otto? I haven't see him very active at all, 'cept bank robberies, EPA enforcement and going to Republican rallies."

Officially, Ham and the entire MSP, including the Johnnie Walker, Ham's boss, were apolitical, but they were under the statutory authority of the MSP Board—a very political nine-member panel with revolving three-year terms. Every year, three new members were appointed by the celestial troika of Montana constitutional office holders: the governor, the attorney general, and the treasurer. On January 1, the board was paid its $1,000-a-calendar-year stipend. On January 2, there were usually one or two resignations leading the troika to search for a candidate who would attend the board's six meetings a year without any pay. Effectively, junior politicians earned their way in. At one time or another, every state-wide politician had served and become an expert on the MSP and almost all were supporters of Ham and Johnnie Walker. The board kept Ham and Johnnie Walker interested in Montana politics.

"Watch yourself, Ham. You might be guilty of knowing too much about too much. Is Otto really a Republican? I guess the president can pretty much appoint whoever he chooses. Didn't know we had any Republicans at the University. Ya know he was the provost there. At the law school. What the hell does a provost do? Sounds military. This case has enough military. You know him?"

"No, not really. Coupla years ago, before he was appointed, he gave a presentation on RICO violations, federal white-collar crime, to a bunch of us. Talked to us like we were a pack of mules. Let's just say he had problems finding a middle ground between constitutional lawyers and kindergarteners. Whatta ya think his take on Crestfallen is going to be? Couldn't he just initiate his own investigation?"

"Well, if he's got any sense he'll avoid a fight with Denver. Prosecutors have a lot of discretion, but I just can't see him starting his own investigation. Can't see a foundation. What would he gain by chasing this? Also, if Denver has already taken two steps forward and opened a file, our boy, Otto, would have to talk them into closing their file before he could do anything. It would take a month to get any traction."

Governor Jefferson got up from the table and paced across the wall of windows. When he reached the far end he spun around quickly. He was forty feet from Ham, who was still seated at the table. As he walked toward Ham the governor threw his hands in the air and said in resignation, "Okay, we need fast action. We need it very public. A legal counter-offensive, while possible, would take too long and involve too many independent, non-political thinkers. A hearing it is!" He stopped and put both hands, palms flat, on the table. As he leaned forward, he said, "Public hearing, downtown Billings, next week. We gotta fight fire with fire, federal with federal. We've got three guys in Washington. Who could pull off a Congressional Committee hearing right quick? What's the big, tall, hotel on Twenty-seventh in Billings called now? Sheraton? Hyatt? The Crowne Plaza? They could hold a coupla hundred in the ballroom."

Bingo!

Of the two Montana senators and one congressman, the governor had his pick. It was common knowledge that Senator Alvin Johnsrud, a former governor, and Ham had been friends since their Montana National Guard duty in the seventies. Johnsrud and his son, who owned the Montana Coors Beer distributorship, were often Ham's guests, fly fishing the upper Yellowstone above Livington—Paradise Valley. They already had plans for next July to fish the Smith River—a source of local humor. Float permits for the Smith were severely restricted to protect the stream, and under the exclusive control of the state government. Montana Fish and Wildlife regulators played no favorites. The senior U.S. senator and the number-two man at the MSP were just two more names in the annual lottery. Every year their names weren't drawn gave them cause to reflect that this was actually a good thing and demonstrated a lack of political corruption. In Montana, everything was public. Finally last month, after six years in the draw, Ham's name got pulled for a three-man boat for a five-day Smith River float next July. Ham wanted Governor Jefferson to choose Johnsrud to lead the hearing. But, again, this had to be Jefferson's decision. Ham stood up and turned to the window.

The governor finally spoke up, "I don't know Washington politics or who's got a higher profile with the Department of Justice, but Johnsrud's my man. He had my job long enough back in the nineties. He knows what we're up against, and he's not gonna take this lying down. He'll appreciate our vulnerability. Isn't he on the judiciary committee?"

Ham smiled broadly, but stayed facing out the window to hide his reaction and then slowly turned to the governor and softly said, "I think he'll take care of us."

The governor had turned back to the long table and put his hands on his hips. Slowly he turned back to Ham. "Johnsrud will love this. He likes to show off in front of the home folks. I'm not certain, but I think he's on the Senate Judiciary Committee. Least he was. They usually get first crack at the Department of Justice and new appointments—both, judges and prosecutors. Gotta have some clout. I'll make the call. I can feel the excitement building already. Anything else I need to do to make you happy?"

"Sooner the better. Just play it straight with him. He's gotta see the alternatives as unacceptable. We need to take this on here at home."

"I'll call him tomorrow, first thing. I'm on the run after that—water rights to the Big Horn. Wyoming wants to keep more for their ranchers, kill our number two Blue Ribbon trout destination. We'll get back to you."

"Can't lose that one," Ham replied. Ham swiveled his lower right arm forward as though fly casting.

Jefferson escorted Ham to the door, feeling a tiny bit like Ham should be showing him out. He recognized that he was a puppet whose strings were being pulled. It was a feeling he was unaccustomed to. Still, if Ham was right and Hilton was angling to bring federal indictments, it was time to move.

First thing the next morning, Governor Boyd Jefferson dialed a private, unpublished telephone number.

"Senator Johnsrud's office, Blake Markham speaking," the voice said.

"Blake, this is Governor Boyd Jefferson. I need to speak with the senator right away, this morning."

"Yes, governor. He's on the Senate floor at a vote right now, and has a break at eleven. He can call you back then."

"Can you page him?"

"Um, sir. I … "

"Page the senator, son. Now. Tell him Governor Jefferson has an *urgent* matter to discuss with him and is waiting on the line." Every time he had to deal with Washington, he came away angry. *Just imagine the run around an average citizen gets.* Things were so much simpler in Helena. He rarely reflected on the notion that it may have had something to do with the fact that in Helena, Boyd Jefferson was the superior executive officer.

Blake Markham had never paged the senator. But calculated that if ever he were to do it, now would be a good time. "Yes—yes sir. Let me put you on hold," he said.

Governor Jefferson punched the speaker-phone button and cradled the headset. It could be a long wait. Meanwhile, he went back to leafing through the Crestfallen press clippings. He had two stacks—national media and Montana state press, including Internet sites. The new articles this morning including one from the *Seattle Times*. He scanned the *USA Today* article, which read like the latest press DOJ release. It included a quote from an unnamed senior official of the Department of Justice—*probably the same person who wrote the original press release,* thought Jefferson. *"Yes, I agree wholeheartedly with what I said." Can't see how they could ever complain about the fairness of the media—Christ, they control it!*

"Governor, Senator Johnsrud is available now. Let me transfer you."

"Thank you, son."

"Boyd, good morning!" The senator boomed through the speaker phone.

Boyd Jefferson snatched the phone out of the cradle and responded with "Indeed, it is."

The senator went on, "So you met the intern, Blake. Jack Markham's son from Miles City. Runs 800 pair on the Tongue River. Must have 20,000 acres."

"I don't know Markham, but it seems to me that eighteen-year-olds aren't getting any smarter than we were. Guess if I don't sign his paycheck, I'm just another brick in the wall."

"Well, governor, join the club—seems the only folks that acknowledge my position are people on my payroll or higher on the totem pole. And they're only doing it to put me in my place, my lowly place. Abraham Lincoln used to sign his letters with, 'Your obedient servant.' That's 'bout right. How can I serve the interests of Montana today?"

"Thanks for taking the call. I'm sure you planned on something else. Have you been hearing about the Crestfallen raids?" He paused a moment and then continued, "No? Well, we've got a damn mess out here, and it could get a whole lot messier. We worked with the U.S. Marshal's office on a raid of a meth lab and it's come a cropper. Your good buddy, Ham Frazier, and the Rankin County Sheriff, Cooper, Axel Cooper, are under the Colorado U.S. Attorney's microscope. The raid was at a seasonal ranch outside Grant, halfway up Mt. Elliott. U.S. Marshal out of Denver's out to serve an old warrant. Our guys along for the ride. Everything goes haywire. Cooper got shot at. He shoots two guys dead. One of 'em an undercover FBI guy out of Minneapolis. Federals are all over the media blaming Montana law enforcement. So far, Ham and the sheriff have yet to go public. Then, two days later, the U.S. Marshal, who also happens to be a one-star general in the Colorado National Guard, brings up ten guys in uniform and a bunch of vehicles, and starts dismantling the ranch. Here's the topper. The rancher, Charlie Ryan of the Irish Kingdom, has a bunch of his boys blasting the tires of the Guard's trucks and buses. Ricochet hits the U.S. Marshal. Medevaced to Billings. Guess he'll be ok. He checked himself out of Billings Memorial the same day. Can you believe all this? The story's out that the U.S. Attorney out of Denver is looking to cover the U.S. Marshal by blaming our boys—Cooper and Ham. Christ, Ham called in the MSP's helicopter. Jack Hilton, the U.S. Marshal, could have died at the ranch without it."

The senator groaned and said, "Wow, that's the wildest story I've heard in weeks. How could I have missed all this? I've heard nothing from anybody, including Colorado's senators. You really think that the U.S. Attorney for Colorado is going to indict Ham and the county sheriff? Can he really do that? Isn't his jurisdiction restricted to Colorado? Those guys are as slimy as salamanders. Put my wallet in my inside coat pocket when I meet with 'em."

Jefferson continued, "Nothing public from John Autry, he's the U.S. Attorney in Denver, but the U.S. Marshal Jack Hilton's working overtime on influencing the press. More spin than I've see in thirty years. He's issuing his own press releases. Getting some solid national press. I'd imagine anybody just reading *USA Today* would have Montana law enforcement screwed, blued, and tattooed. The closer you get to Grant, the more objective the press gets. Hell, I don't have to tell you 'bout the stuff that gets publicized. We've got to turn this around, take control of what the public knows right away, or it won't matter what really happened. This could set back Montana law enforcement fifty years." The governor realized that he now sounded as plaintive as Ham did last night.

The senator responded quickly, "Okay, so what are you thinking? So what can we do? You have to know, there's a limit to what I can do here. I can't exactly be giving get-out-of-jail-free cards. Can't say I know the Attorney General to say 'hello' to her on the street."

The governor was focused. He wanted to close the deal. He decided to jump to a conclusion, "Look, Al, I know you're busy, what I need right now is for you to call a Senate hearing here in Montana. How about Billings next week? Steal the march on them. Preempt anything they might be planning, solidify the incidents as Montana's business. Christ, if this thing goes to Denver, Montana'll look like a vassal state, under the heel of the lords of Denver. I can't see the U.S. Attorney General closing down an active file of the Denver office. Too political. Hell, all this is political! This is a case of a good Montana soldier shooting in self-defense. But that story will never get told out of Denver. The whole U.S. Marshal service—not just Hilton, the Denver guy—has got to be leaning hard on Autry to find and label a scapegoat."

"I see. And you say they're after Frazier and the Rankin County Sheriff?"

"Frazier didn't shoot anybody. But he's standing tall behind Cooper, the sheriff. The way it sits is the sheriff, Ham, and the MSP against the U.S. Marshal's office, the FBI, and possibly the rest of the Department of Justice, including the U.S. Attorney from Denver. Goliath about to trample David."

"Okay. Okay. Okay. I got it. I've seen this DOJ steamroller do its work before. They do protect their own. This certainly would not be the first time the FBI, U.S. Marshal and the rest of the Department of Justice have teamed up to squash a little guy in order to deflect the blame away from their more-than-obvious shortcomings. In fact, I'm surprised they haven't already pushed the Patriot Act button to clamp down on public information. Get their story out and then stop anyone else from talking. DOJ doesn't like to talk on the record, unless they've got a conviction to put up on the marquee or a sure thing and they're ready to pounce." The senator paused and then said, "Hell, Boyd, you're the prosecutor. You know that things are often not what they appear. Maybe there's not as much a united front in Denver as we might imagine. This U.S. Marshal might be DOJ's loose cannon. You gonna talk to Henry Otto? He's a good kid. Sailed through our committee in less than half an hour."

Governor Boyd considered the idea. "No, haven't talked to him yet, but we will. It could be that this media show of Hilton's is all for Autry's sake. Autry could be just another leader chasing public opinion. If Autry is, in fact, thinking of higher office, he's going to want to be convinced this is worthy of his efforts."

Johnsrud responded quickly, "I should talk to the boy. Being a senator's not as fun as being governor. You should keep that in mind. And let me tell you, these U.S. Attorneys are about as wild as billy goats. They don't answer to nobody. Their number one priority is always about serving their own prerogatives. Once appointed, they wander off on their merry way. Federal prosecutors are strong people. Don't know they're there until they are all over you. With them, you're guilty unless proven innocent. Anything could be the grounds for a future indictment. The last one I had a run-in with was over banking allegations in Eastern Pennsylvania. Banker accused of defrauding his own bank. Martin Laidlaw, I believe, was the attorney's name. I swear, he would indict his wife, if it furthered his career. After three years of investigations, discovery and pretrial, and a six-month jury trial, the banker was exonerated after an hour in the jury room. Our Judiciary Committee held a hearing in Scranton, Kaplan called it. He was pushed by every banker in Pennsylvania. Laidlaw fought us all the way. Then,"

Boyd Jefferson was getting impatient. He didn't need to be told about strange behavior of prosecutors; he'd been one for twelve years. He jumped in, "Senator, at the rate this is moving, even if this is all for show, an indictment may not be far off."

"Okay, I'm hearing you loud and clear. Today's what … Thursday? I'm coming back to Montana next Wednesday. Going up to Havre—whose idea was that? I think I could round up Casey and a couple of guys that owe me favors. Best thing would be to have Judiciary Committee authority—special subcommittee blah, blah, blah. I'll see about that tomorrow. I gotta be back for the following Wednesday's roll-call vote on the budget. How 'bout Tuesday morning, the sixteenth, in … Billings, I suppose. Go back to Washington from Billings. That oughta give the witnesses some time. Don't like issuing subpoenas for an immediate appearance. Serve 'em subpoenas late next week to appear the next Tuesday. Not too bad. Billings is close to the action. Grant's too small to handle this. Won't be the thinnest window. Hell, back in '04, I personally served a three-star general at the Pentagon for an appearance the next day. He was dumbstruck. Can you handle the logistics? Ham can ID the witnesses. The Judiciary Committee staff'll handle the hearing itself. Witnesses, videotape, opening statements, couple of guys to ask the right questions. I gotta find somebody here who can put this together. Somebody'll call you, but you call my office if anything unexpected comes up, and keep an eye on Hilton's friends. DOJ is going to squirm like hell, but we got a few arrows in our quiver." Senator Alvin Johnsrud was about to hang up.

Then he said, "Wait a sec." He hummed into the phone for five seconds of uninterrupted thought. "Ya, know, I think I just got the right guy to quarterback this. He's another wayward Montanan. Bet he'd love to spend a week or two reacquainting himself with the high plains. Yeah, let me talk to him. He's got an east coast education and an attitude to go with it. He's made for this endeavor! Well, I'd better ask him first. But he'd be foolish not to jump on this like a crow on a June bug. Political dynasties have been founded on a lot less."

Governor Jefferson was ready to move on, but Senator Johnsrud started up again. "OK. Billings. I'll set up the panel and all the Washington ass kicking and kissing. First, though, Ham has to give us a list of witnesses. You can do the building, set, lighting, security. I'm gung-ho!!! Let's grip it and rip it. I'll have somebody give your office updates three times a day. I'll let you know when we've got a critical mass. We should handle the media. That's what this is all about, right? OK? Don't tell anybody at DOJ, right? Not until we're ready to go public. Could take a coupla days." The senator paused again, "If DOJ calls me, I'll send them back to Denver. I wasn't born yesterday. I'm trusting that we're not going to look any worse after this than we do now."

"Right," said Jefferson and the whirlwind conversation was over.

Hanging up the phone, Governor Jefferson wasn't exactly feeling better, but at least it wasn't worse. Johnsrud was cooperative, but he'd dumped the responsibility for the outcome right back on Jefferson and Ham Frazier. As strongly as Jefferson believed in Ham's argument and Axel Cooper's innocence, there were always unknowns. He'd seen too many criminal trials go sideways with surprise wacko testimony. And with all these independent players, there were lots of opportunities for this train to be derailed. *So much for 'elegant simplicity.'*

The next three days were a blur for Ham. He received a voice mail from Blake Markham that Johnsrud secured commitments from four other senators to appear at the hearing in Billings on the sixteenth. It was a "go." Time to put the word out and do the logistics. Ham worked his contacts with Montana's daily newspapers and Hank Anderson at the weekly Rankin County Courier. Also, the local NBC, CBS, ABC affiliates fell into line. They all wanted a scoop, no matter how small, on the Crestfallen II scenario. Ham doled out tidbits as though they were gold doubloons. But he was at a bit of a loss as to how he was going to get CNN and Fox News involved. He called Johnsrud's office to ask Blake what he would do on that front. The young man said he'd do what he could. Almost immediately, Ham's office started getting calls from CNN producers. *Okay, "Operation: Media Circus" is under way. Now we've just got to get through the hearing.*

By Monday, the eighth, the Senate Judiciary Committee hearing was a living thing—a juggernaut which rearranged schedules, rerouted airplanes, demanded personal appearances, cancelled fact finding trips to Baghdad, preempted the Council of Montana Mayors annual meeting, commandeered resources from stage lighting and risers from MSU-Billings, and requisitioned luxury top-floor suites at the Crown Sheraton for the five U.S. senators set to arrive on Monday the fifteenth.

While Ham did his job with local logistics, the Washington focus had swung from Senator Johnsrud to Cole Morris, a Billings native, Columbia educated, former Assistant U.S. Attorney in Billings.

For the last eighteen months, Cole Morris had worked for Senator Johnsrud and the Senate Judiciary Committee on federal legislative matters, spending considerable time on military tribunals, enemy combatants at Guantanamo, and the erosion of the rights of individuals at the hands of the federal government. While he felt the work was important, it lacked the intensity of trial preparation and the focused spotlight of a federal criminal trial. He had come to agree with the common description of the U.S. Senate as the world's longest standing debate society. The hearing was a step back into the bloody world of face-to-face confrontation. He was raring to go and jumped into the project with youthful enthusiasm.

After working with Ham on the list of witnesses, Cole Morris flew to Billings to confirm the arrangements and to interview Ham Frazier and Axel Cooper. Of the six or seven names on his subpoena list, they were the most important ones to get the facts out. As Cole counseled Ham, "Let's build our case first. Make the FBI, DEA, and U.S. Marshal have to fight back the initial impressions left by the Montana contingent."

CHAPTER 21

(Friday, November 11)

Even after almost fifteen years in Montana, Axel continued to marvel at the vast differences between the towns of Evanston, Illinois and Grant. On some levels, Grant was quiet and reserved; on others, it was bold and outrageous.

It was the bold and outrageous that Axel saw when he'd first arrived. His second day in town was the day Oktoberfest began. Axel and Arlyn were welcomed at every bar and the free beer flowed. One drunk cowboy, kicked out of a saloon, came back on horseback to argue his case. He rode his horse right up to the bar and then they both fell onto the floor. Axel half expected a shootout on Broadway. The beer bash ran right up to Veterans Day—again a major celebration that was almost extinct back East. Every year on November 11, regardless of the weather, the town turned out for a Broadway parade, a speech held in the high school gymnasium and a pig roast. Over the years, Axel came to view it as the town's last public party before the long winter set in.

The local Elks' Club chapter organized the event. Sven Thordahl had been recruited to give the afternoon's address—after the parade, flag raising, and the local pastor's solemn reading of the "War Dead List" at the outdoor memorial in the park by the river.

Axel was looking forward to listening to Sven's speech, entitled "What Price Freedom," according to the posters.

After their last conversation, Axel wondered what Sven would have to say about local law enforcement. As an elected sheriff, he viewed the event as a must-attend event. After the shootings, the explosion of his house, and the news of next week's hearing in Billings, he wanted to be seen in an ordinary venue, as though nothing had happened.

Anne had known Sven Thordahl her whole life. Sven's son, Chester, had been a one-time boyfriend and the two had shared the scholastic honors at Grant High School.

Twenty minutes before the speech's start time, Anne and Axel filed into the high school gymnasium, shaking hands and waving hello to friends as they found their reserved seats in the second row. Axel was pleased to feel the support of the community. News of the pending senate hearing had spread. He had steeled himself for a few rough words and strange looks. *But, so far—so good.*

He turned to watch the crowd settle itself in and acknowledged and waved at a number of supporters. But he couldn't help but notice that there were several folks who looked at him from a distance and then turned away.

A screech of feedback over the new sound system brought all eyes to the stage, where Mayor Buster Jenkins—local merchant, small-time rancher, and a longtime power at the Elks' Club—was attempting to begin the evening's program. He was a casual speaker and had a long list of preliminaries, from on-street parking to no beer tonight in the lodge, but two kegs in the Elks' garage. He introduced Sven as a "true local hero" and "pillar of the community."

Sven stood up in the audience where he was sitting with Megan and Chester and walked up the aisle, wearing his wide-brimmed hat, swinging his right leg and sorting a short stack of index cards. As Sven slowly climbed the side stairs, Axel took a deep, but anxious, breath and wondered just what kind of unusual evening was ahead. Sven took off his hat and stood tall behind the podium, his summer tan still evident on his cheeks.

"Thank you, folks. Thank you, Buster." Sven laid out his note cards and adjusted his reading glasses. Clearing his throat, he started in, "Well, when Buster came out to the ranch last August, I thought he was going to offer to lend a hand with the calf roundup. But then I thought, with his riding skills, that wasn't too likely. Then I figured he must be looking for a couple good bulls, a chance to put another five to ten pounds on his next crop of calves. Good rancher's always looking for an edge."

The crowd chuckled. Good-natured Buster Jenkins ran a small

heard of Angus at a tiny ranch that bordered Route 176. Everybody driving north out of town got a good look. The herd was known as the thinnest stock in the county.

Sven smiled. He was off to a good start. "Instead, the bugger was asking me to give y'all this speech here today! It's impossible to say 'no' to Buster. I almost wished he was looking for a good bull. He sure could use one."

"Friends," he continued, after the laughter in the room subsided, "I've put a lot of thought to the topic of this here speech. Got some help from my granddaughter to sort things out. Don't mean to fire-hose you with wild ideas, but I want you to know this is a subject that burns dear to my heart. On Veterans Day, my mind is drawn back to the oath I swore when I entered the Army: to *'support and defend the Constitution of the United States against all enemies, foreign and domestic.'* I first swore that oath as a young man and find myself still in the defense of our own Constitution sixty years later. I say, friends, that this is something we cannot afford to be lax about. There is a cost to securing the rights and freedoms we enjoy. And we must constantly have our eyes open to efforts to impair our freedoms and be willing to pay the price to eliminate them. Today's celebration is in honor of those who have secured them on our behalf on the battlefields of the world."

Anne squirmed in her seat and sighed. Axel patted her hand, as if to say "hang in there, sweetie, what did you expect?"

Sven continued, with one hand raised over his head, punctuating every third word, "Today, we're at war on many battlefields. We cannot allow our lives to be dominated by foreign influences any more than we can allow an attack on our sacred soil. For when our economy—the lifeblood of this great nation—comes under foreign domination, our very way of life is no longer ours to command. The war for our independence is not a thing that began and ended two hundred years ago, my friends; it is a thing we must vigilantly secure. The cruel and bloodthirsty attack on New York's Twin Towers was no more of a threat to our independence than our staggering trade imbalance or the self-imposed loss of our civil liberties."

At this, several members of the audience shifted in their seats and the general noise level in the room rose as if they were asking each other for an explanation. *Trade imbalance?*

"For I ask you, my friends and neighbors," Thordahl continued as he pounded his fist on the podium, "what will become of our ranchland and farms when Canadian and South American beef producers make it impossible for us to sell in our own markets? Today our country is a net *importer* of beef. As I stand here today, two cases of Mad Cow in the last year have cost us over a million and a half tons of export. We're certainly not masters of our destiny. How will we be able to send our children and grandchildren to school, when we can no longer make a living off of this land that has sustained us for so many generations? If you'll open your eyes to the realities of the situation, you'll see as clearly as I do that these things are already happening. Restrictions on exporting our beef, higher tariffs in foreïgn markets, the abomination of this grand 'NAFTA Highway,' which makes it all but impossible to compete with Argentina and Brazil—these are but the first steps in squeezing out the hardworking American rancher and farmer."

As Sven paused to get a look at his notes, Axel realized that the tension in the room has changed. *He's got the audience now—Rankin County will support its ranchers.*

"Some of you will be surprised to hear me say this, but we must strengthen our local and state governments. They are ours. But the federal government isn't ours and we need local government to stand up for us and protect us from the federal bullies. Too many local issues are being taken over by federal agencies—EPA, BLM, FDA, the list goes on and on. I say that only Montanans clearly know how to handle Montana's resources. What can some yahoo in Washington know about my water rights?" A spattering of applause broke out from the left rear of the audience. Sven looked to the corner and, spying an old friend standing in the back near the fire doors, he said, "Thought you'd like that Jake." He looked down at his notes and flipped a card on the floor. Sven then went on to criticize the Bureau of Land Management, the U.S. Forest Service, the Park Service and the EPA.

Axel was staring straight ahead, fearful of where Sven was going next.

"As for the raid out in the Irish Kingdom, I don't pass judgment on our county sheriff, the Montana State Police, the FBI, the DEA, the Forest Service or even the federal marshal from Denver—600 miles from Grant. But I raise the point to ask, 'Why in hell did the federal government invade our county in the first place?'

"My answer is that we have given too much authority and responsibility to Washington and become the victims of its overreaching tyrants. I wish I could call the government 'ours,' but if Montanans were to design a federal government, it would look one heck of a lot different from the one we got."

A round of applause broke out from the corner.

Sven smiled in acknowledgement and went on, encouraged, "It's as though Montana's been declared incompetent and some desk-riding East Coast intellectuals appointed as our guardians. Continuing to view more government as the solution to problems will only make matters worse. It is a slippery slope best avoided. When ya draw a bad hand at the poker table, it's wise not to overinvest."

The audience interrupted with a loud, widespread applause. Axel sat stock still in apprehension of Sven's next statement.

"How many thousands of dollars in livestock have been lost to Yellowstone wolves over the past ten years? I have to wonder if those bureaucrats, who brought back the wolves, have ever been off the pavement in Yellowstone Park—if they've even visited the Park! Do they realize Yellowstone is not the Brooklyn Zoo? Did they even stop to consider, once, before restoring the earth's most potent predator into the heart of our nation's great beef-producing country, that wolves respect no boundaries? That they'll travel hundreds of miles for easy prey, and that newborn cattle are about as easy as it gets? No! Of course they didn't think about this. I say if more wolves represent the desired 'way it used to be,' then let's bring back the $50 bounty." Two young men sitting together stood in applause, but a collective sigh could be heard above their clapping.

"Central planning out of Washington is an issue for Montanans. The tyranny of democracy is not freedom and is not all that different from the tyranny of totalitarianism. As for representatives in Washington, we've got three out of 535, less than one percent. The entire state of Montana is nothing but a playground for the rest of them. They control our land, water, and air, and our right to sell cattle to the world."

"What on earth is he talking about?" Anne squeaked to Axel under her breath. "Where's this coming from? Half this county's on one federal payroll or another."

Sven suddenly glared down at Axel and Anne. He knew Axel and recognized Anne, from somewhere he couldn't recall. Under Sven's harsh gaze, Axel said, "Shhhh, hon. Everyone can see us."

Sven held his stare and several people in the back of the audience stood up to see who Sven was drilling.

Sven looked up and silently gazed across the crowd, which collectively held its breath. "And so how many more idiotic initiatives will we put up with before we've had enough of all this blundering? What percentage, do you suppose, of our cattle will have to test for brucellosis before we are allowed to shoot sick buffalo that wander out of the Park? How about this? Keep the animals in the zoo!"

Sven paused, took a drink of water and looked down at Anne. Then he continued, "Every day, we see the erosion of our freedoms under the guise of democracy. We need vigilance and, dare I say, *vigilantes* to protect our property, our investments, our opportunities and our rights. No one will take care of us if we don't do what we can to take care of ourselves."

Sven cast a cold, menacing look over the front rows, as though to engrave his words on the county's elected officials. The audience was abuzz. Axel couldn't tell if it was agitation or support. *Vigilantes. The last thing we need.* Axel shook his head and hoped that Sven was done and that his tirade would not return to the topic of vigilantes.

Sven's gaze fixed on Axel while he was shaking his head. "What I'm saying is that our own federal government has proven again and again that they do not have our best interests in mind. Montana looks big on the map, but it weighs little in the minds of federal bureaucrats. If we are to continue to enjoy our way of life, we must speak out against stronger federal government, and make changes to bring those powers back home to Helena, to our own people. I know that what I've had to say may be a little unsettling to some of you. But we have to ask: What price are we prepared to pay for our freedom? Thank you."

As he gathered up his notes, Sven shot a final glare at Axel and Anne and stepped back to a chair on the dais. The stunned audience remained silent for one uncomfortably long moment. Finally, an applause broke out, more than a minimum, polite applause, but not a rolling appreciation either.

Axel found himself applauding lightly.

Mayor Jenkins quickly stepped up to offer closing comments. "Well, thank you, Sven, for those fine remarks. I think it gives us all something to chew on, though I can say for myself, I don't believe I'm ready to see the days of vigilantes return. The last of the Rankin County Irregulars, my uncle Calvin, was buried ten years ago." He was referring to a vigilante group from the thirties that had sought to protect ranchers and their cattle, and was known for swift verdicts rather than justice, resulting in the deaths of a number of innocent men. The audience relaxed and laughed, supporting Jenkins. The presentation was over.

Anne leaned over to Axel and said, "My God, what a narrow view of the world. You ready for a beer?"

"Hon, you can go on now if you like. This is my coming-out party. I gotta touch base with twenty different people. Make sure I still got a job left. You know how this town can get once it's stirred up. And I gotta make sure there's nothing to this vigilante business. That's a direction I really don't want things to go at this point. How 'bout we meet up at the garage in an hour?"

"You bet," was her answer as she waved to a friend down the row.

The hubbub continued as the crowd got up from their seats and started milling about. Many had dazed looks on their faces. One loud teenaged voice asked if "that old rancher was for real." Axel scanned the moving crowd. He saw Ange clustered with a group of women. He caught her eye and waved. Axel noticed that the audience had split—basically ranchers and townsfolk—and that while several of the older ranchers were congratulating Sven on his speech, the majority of the townspeople were edging away from him.

He met up with Ange in the hallway. She blurted out, "Vigilantes?"

"Can't argue with him about the Feds, but we sure don't need any vigilantes."

She replied, "For sure." Then, lightening her tone, she asked, "You up for the roast pig? I brought a German potato salad—Grandma's recipe. Look for the one with black olives and paprika."

"You bet," Axel said as he walked back into the room, trying to put Sven's speech behind him.

Sven had gone into town with Randy, his wife, and two of their children. They drove home about an hour after his speech. On the drive home, he was tired and discouraged, lost in thought. Except for a few old friends, no one had approached him at the pig roast. He did manage to find out who the small woman with Axel Cooper was: Anne Lynwood, Clyde Lynwood's daughter, now an MD in Billings. He remembered her as a bright, outspoken girl, a friend of Chester's from high school. As they traveled beyond the lights of town, he considered that he had little in common with the people he spoke to tonight. Even the young ranchers weren't interested in changing the system, only in working it to their advantage. They couldn't possibly appreciate the importance of his opinions. Certainly Randy and his wife were clueless to what he was talking about. They would not understand exploding the mine. They were too easygoing. They were short-term thinkers who didn't care about solving long-term problems. They didn't respect him for who he was or value the legacy of the Thordahl Ranch.

He hadn't become the respected elder. Or even a wise man among dry-land farmers, ski-bums, tourist merchants, cattlemen, motel operators, and hot-tub purveyors. To them he was just another old, sunbaked cowboy who'd been out on the range too long. He might as well have been reciting cowboy poetry for their amusement. As he slumped his shoulder against the door, he considered that he was bone-weary and needed to do something soon, before he got any more tired and totally lost his edge. He needed to do something different, an event to prove his point, an event that would command attention and focus

Montanans on the need to take their destiny into their own hands and loose this foolishness about the federal government taking care of them. *Seize the day, make an impact.*

The short trip home was quiet. Sven figured that Randy and his wife didn't want to talk about the speech and the kids were exhausted.

Once in the yard, Sven jumped out of the truck and, with a quick wave, left his sister's son's family behind.

The respite had energized him. He entered his house intent on making plans.

Sven sat at the kitchen table to sort things out. He gazed around the room as though he was seeing it for the first time. In spite of the hour he was alert, even more than alert. He was vibrant, pulsating, and hypersensitive. His skin was tingling. But a sudden turn of his head to the kitchen window to spot a cat crossing the yard prompted an instant throbbing in his temples, and then his sight became blurred by a red mist. The barn light was now circled in a pink cloud that gyrated like the surface of the sun. He stood and tried to pierce through the fog with a focused stare, only to magnify the pressure in his temples, and the frequency of the throbbing gyrations. He closed his eyes to ease the pressure.

The sudden pain was intense, and he sat back down at the kitchen table with his head in his hands. He breathed deeply and explored possible causes of his headache. The two beers he had in the Elks' Club garage? An uncooked piece of pork? No, that was hours ago. Maybe the speech triggered something. But if so, why didn't he react sooner? Now it's over, time to relax.

Still sitting at the table, he turned toward the white refrigerator. The red cloud followed. His thoughts careened from the heat generated by the light bulb, to the noisy compressor in his refrigerator, to the good price Randy got at the calf auction, and then to Bridal Veil Creek and the scuffs on his boots that he'd just polished today, and to the fact that he couldn't remember ever polishing them before. The pain was leaving.

The picture of the county sheriff whispering to that smart-aleck Lynwood girl at the hall came to Sven as an evil image. They were beyond discourteous and rude, they were ridiculing him in his home and plotting against him. Sven figured that the sheriff already knew that he had blown up the mine. But the sheriff couldn't prove it. He also wondered whether he was tracked by electronic signals from the ATV.

Sven suddenly was uncomfortable in the kitchen; particularly, he felt a tightness in his upper back and shoulders. He was warm. He slowly stood up, favoring his tight right knee. He stretched and stood tall. He heard the abrasive grating of his realigned spine as it straightened. The pain was gone, but he just couldn't stay still. He had to move.

He swung his arms over his head and recalled the choreographed jumping jacks of his army days. He knew his knee wasn't up to jumping off the ground, so he slowly went through the motions of swinging his arms over his head while sliding one foot out, widening his stance. He then pulled his arms down and drew his feet together. One. He counted out ten repetitions and then put his hands on his hips. He rolled his shoulders and hips. He felt better but he still couldn't sit down. He had to keep moving, go somewhere. But where? Where on the ranch could he go at this hour?

He walked out to the horse barn and its attached corral. The cool night air was refreshing. His red fog faded as he passed the barn. He lit a cigar and watched the smoke intently. Several of the older horses came out to greet him and lick his hand. Sven talked to the horses in soft, bass tones, soothing the animals and himself. He walked to the end of the barnyard beyond the range of the yard lights and then turned around and headed back to his little house. The red fog was almost gone now.

Back at home, he sat at his computer table in the corner of the kitchen and looked for another distraction.

After an hour of internet research at his kitchen table on topics ranging from Dr. Anne Lynwood's page on the Billings Memorial's website to the market value of used Kawasaki ATVs, the pain in his head had diminished to a dull ache. Sven began to feel the small, dark kitchen was closing in on him and his brain was being squeezed into a cube—a small cube, like a child's alphabet block. When he looked away from the computer screen, he focused on the bent-hickory coat rack on the wall by the back door. Then the refrigerator door and its daisy-shaped yellow magnets securing a copy of the Elks' Club flyer announcing his Veterans Day speech, then out the window to the shaded yard light attached to the horse barn. The red cloud was gone but he felt that tunnel vision was coming. *Am I losing control?* It was then that he came to the belief that his angst, the headache, the red cloud, and the tunnel vision were all telling him that he needed an action plan, something to happen, to change things. He was to be the catalyst for change. He was the one who would make a difference.

The tightness in his head eased as he developed his plan. He picked up the cold cigar butt and began to chew it as though it was fuel for his new initiative. He took out a pen and a pad of paper. He put together a list of the events of the last few months; and with a complex, convoluted and impenetrable logic concluded that Axel Cooper, the sheriff from Illinois who had drawn the federal government into Montana and who had laughed at him as he gave his speech, was the crux of the problem. The sheriff was not a sympathetic figure but the instigator, the plotter, the portal for the federal advance. Axel Cooper was an invader, a mole sent to infiltrate the Montana society. Without Cooper, Rankin County would be a different place. Without Cooper, it would regain its independence and assert itself as a bastion of freedom. Axel Cooper was the door through which evil entered Rankin County and it was time to close that door.

At midnight, Sven nodded his head in support of his conclusion, put the mangled cigar butt back in the ashtray, looked out the window at the bright white barn light fluttering in the Montana wind, and went to bed.

CHAPTER 22

(Tuesday, November 16)

Tuesday morning, the sixteenth of November, the streets in Billings were alive like never before. Traffic was bumper to bumper from the rimrocks to the interstate with media vans, limousines, and semitrailers. A helicopter hovered over the Crowne Plaza. City police had cordoned off two blocks around the hotel in all directions. Pedestrians were funneling into the hotel through every door.

Ham had arranged for an MSP trooper to drive Axel, Anne, and him to the hotel. The men were in full uniform. They circled the building, searching for a door directly into the ballroom. Axel shook his head and said, "Man alive, Ham, it looks like all we're missing is that guy who ties balloons into giraffes. We should be collecting extra hazard pay, just walking into this crowd."

Ham chuckled and smiled back at Axel. He said nothing.

Axel swung his head side to side. He'd never seen this kind of media display in his life. Technical crews wheeled large tripods holding bulky cameras, pushing them up service ramps into the building. Meanwhile, others with shoulder-held video cameras with attached spotlights were recording the opening statements of heavily made-up, daintily dressed on-camera staff.

Axel wondered what the media thought about this "Circus on Twenty-seventh Street"; perhaps it was just another day on the job. Perhaps Axel and Ham were today's gladiators, soon to be devoured by the media lions.

Anne reached across the top of the bench seat in the MSP SUV and squeezed Axel's shoulder.

She said, "You're okay, babe. These are the good guys. They're going to spread your story. Ham's story. Remember, they may be terrifying, but they're on our team. We like them. They like you. I won't let them eat you." She smiled and squeezed Axel's shoulder again.

He smiled with her, but only for a second.

They pulled up to the ballroom entrance and a Billings policeman opened the doors for them. "It's now or never, I guess," Axel announced, and stepped out into the fray.

Inside the ballroom, things were even more intense. Ham had scheduled the largest room available. It was already standing-room-only. Even at 9:00 AM, with the windows just under the high ceiling cracked open, it was getting warm.

Axel and Ham had spent all of the previous afternoon with Cole Morris in an empty courtroom in the Yellowstone County Building. Morris quickly stepped back into his role as an antagonistic prosecutor. Much too easily for Ham and Axel. Ten minutes into the session, they had begun to wonder if the hearing, intended to be a preemptive strike at the Feds out of Denver, was such a good idea after all. In spite of their age and experience, they were disarmed by the intense young man with question after question attacking their experience, courage, and integrity.

Morris's questions were pointed, leading, belittling, and impossible to deflect. "So, Sheriff Cooper, if, as you say, you questioned Marshal Hilton's experience at the POB—the day before any shots were fired—when did you first bring this to anyone's attention?"

"Deputy Commissioner, in your thirty-two years with the Montana State Police, on how many occasions have you approached a building, inhabited by armed hostiles, with the intent of securing their arrest."

"Sheriff, isn't it true that, in spite of your years of experience with the U.S. Coast Guard, MSP, and as County Sheriff, you had never been shot at before—at least shot at by anyone within half a mile of you?"

"The county sheriff is an elected position, is it not? And are there any prerequisites for the job, other than qualifying for the ballot?"

"Sheriff, can you outline for me the previous cooperative efforts involving your office and the MSP?"

"Sheriff, I understand that you voluntarily resigned from the MSP in 1999. Can you tell us why you did so and the degree, if any, that Commissioner Frazier was involved in your quick exit?"

Initially, Axel and Ham answered the questions as they would in the actual hearing under oath; as though their answers were essential and being etched in stone. They all knew that today the answers weren't being recorded. But Axel slowly came to the opinion that Cole Morris had better not ask these absurd questions tomorrow at the hearing. *So why ask them now?*

After twenty minutes, Axel and Ham looked at each other in amazement: *Who is this guy?* Axel also noted that Morris seemed to enjoy the Montanans' anguish, and reveled in their responses. *He's the man. We're scum.*

After being asked to describe the last mountain ranch assault led by the MSP, Ham did not reply. All three knew there had never been one. Ham got up and left the courtroom without a word. His briefcase stayed at the end of the table, leading Axel to wonder if he was coming back or had forgotten it altogether.

Axel called for a break, leaving Cole Morris alone in the courtroom. Axel went out to the hallway but Ham was gone. Axel went to find a soda machine. Ham called Senator Johnsrud at the Crowne Plaza only to learn that he had yet to check in.

Twenty minutes later, when Morris and Axel were huddled over Axel's written description of the raid, Ham returned to the table without a word.

After the break, Morris changed to a softer approach. Earlier in the week, he had talked to each of them for more than an hour on the telephone from Washington, and he now was reviewing his notes. He asked simple fill-in-the-blank questions, which lacked the sting of his earlier ones: "Since you became sheriff, has anyone in the Kingdom ever been arrested on any drug charges, including possession? Charlie Ryan is how old? Is he credible? Whose idea was the early-morning raid? Could you have stopped the Irish Kingdom shooters during Crestfallen II? If Hilton denies ever having that first meeting with Charlie Ryan, why would we believe Ryan? Do you have any evidence as to who bombed your house in Grant?"

And of Ham he asked, "Why did you participate in the raid? Couldn't you have assigned a subordinate, a regional commander? You haven't done a field operation in how long?"

Axel and Ham did not rebel. They answered the questions. Axel again wondered just what was in store for them at the hearing.

After ten minutes of inquiry, Cole Morris shifted gears again and started coaching Axel and Ham on how he planned to run the next day's hearing. Axel considered that perhaps Morris thought that he had beaten the witnesses sufficiently and convinced himself that there would be no surprise answers tomorrow. Morris made the point that while this wasn't a criminal proceeding, all witnesses would be under oath and that it was a valid subcommittee of the U.S. Senate's Judiciary Committee. And then, as though he were their personal attorney, he outlined that this was no small thing and occasionally such hearings were the basis for subsequent prosecution for contempt of Congress, perjury, conspiracy to suborn perjury and witness tampering. Furthermore, the next day's testimony under oath might be used in any subsequent federal or local criminal trial to impeach any other statements by the witnesses, which again would raise the question of perjury at this hearing. *Are you lying now or were you lying then?* He further explained that they could be sued for money damages for their participation in the raid in a private federal action for the violation of one's civil rights "under color of law." The testimony at tomorrow's hearing could be the foundation for just such a lawsuit.

Ham swung his head violently and pushed himself up from the table. He thrust his chin toward Morris and said, "Young man, when are you going to read us our Miranda Rights? I'd have thought you knew who you were dealing with here. We're not two snot-nosed rookies out to test our manliness. We're career law enforcers at the top of our game. And our game is a hell of a lot different from what you've seen on the East Coast, since you left Billings West High School twelve years ago. But then the crime rate in Montana is less than a quarter of what you live with in D.C. and we've got twice the population. We are who we are—and we're damn proud of it. No, I'm not General Eisenhower, U.S. Grant or the Green Hornet. We cooperated on the U.S. Marshal's raid of a Montana ranch. He asked, we answered. Guilty as charged.

We're certainly not criminals. I think you'd better be saving your tough questions for the power-engorged U.S. Marshal, the Brigadier General John T. Hilton of the Colorado National Guard, or if you wish Major Jack Hilton, USMC (retired). That guy's got so many unresolved interpersonal conflicts I hope he brings his psychoanalyst to help us sort out his multiple personalities and the multitudinous entanglements."

Axel knew Ham well enough to know that he was enjoying this minute of role-playing—Elmer Fudd with a list of high school vocabulary words, but he could feel his own tension ebb—*Yes, this young sharpie was pushing it, but better today than tomorrow.*

Morris stayed in his seat, as though to absorb Ham's blow and then started nodding his head, as though agreeing with Ham. Finally, he said, "You want to know how I think it will go? You might be surprised."

The tone of the session changed again as Cole Morris became more of a guide than an inquisitor. Axel left after another thirty minutes for Anne's, leaving the two to review Ham's map of the ranch and the positioning of the personnel around it.

Before Axel left, the young former prosecutor sternly delivered his final admonishment. "Whatever happens tomorrow, remember three things. Don't lie. Answer the questions and no grandstanding. You're not here to give us your personal perspective, just the facts. Like Joe Friday of 'Dragnet,' 'Just the facts, ma'am, just the facts.' Hearings are frustrating because there's no resolution, no verdict. But, I'm confident that the facts will speak for themselves. You'll both do fine."

Axel shook hands with Cole Morris as he left him with the statement, "I'm just glad you're on our side." Ham nodded his support and confirmed plans for the morning's logistics.

Today Axel was awestruck by the scene that greeted him as he turned into the ballroom from the entry hall. It was almost theatrical. At the far end, a riser had been installed, creating a stage three feet above the floor. The stage was backed by a deeply pleated, wall-to-wall, floor-to-ceiling maroon drapery. A curved bench thirty feet long was set with microphones, brass goose-neck lamps and crystal water pitchers. The bench was varnished hardwood that reflected the glare of the overhead spotlights. Five high-backed leather chairs were arranged along the arc of the long bench, facing out to the audience and, more immediately, to a shorter rectangular table on the floor with its own set of goose-necked lamps and three smaller upholstered chairs. The witness chair was angled to face stage left, allowing most of the audience a profile of the witness. To the left, close to the outer wall, were two work tables with a jumble of equipment, computers, telephones, and TV monitors. Nearby, a staff of technicians was working on two full-size television cameras integrated into three-legged dollies. Spotlights on motorized tripods careened left and right between the tables, under no apparent human control. They reminded Axel of small unmanned submarines sent to the ocean bottom. Technicians whirled left and right.

"My God, what have they done?" Anne exclaimed on entering the ballroom.

"Cole told me that we wouldn't recognize the place. Boy, was he right," Axel responded. "I didn't realize how much the room sets the tone. This looks like serious business. God, we're really going through with this. This is like the Supreme Court."

Ham slowly took it all in, including the bevy of local media notables coming their way. "Axe, look at this parade of Montana's media moguls. Don't say anything now. Save it for the hearing. I'll steer these guys into the wall." He stepped out to greet the leader of the small pack of journalists.

Anne turned to Axel and said, "You're the man. Isn't that what I always tell ya? You'll do great." She squeezed his hand as they stood against the wall.

"Hilton going to show?" Anne asked of Ham when he returned.

Ham answered Anne's question, "Well, he's here. I was hoping he'd wear his Colorado National Guard suit—that'd goose up the Colorado versus Montana angle. But today he's in his Marine Corps uniform, chest full of ribbons. One of the troopers saw him. Whether he's talking is another question."

Then Ham reached out and held Anne's hand and said, "I'm really glad you're here. It means the world to Axel."

Axel looked down on Ham, holding Anne's hand, and said, "What the hell. You find your own girl. This one's mine and I can speak for myself, you bird dog."

All three burst out in nervous laughter.

Axel stretched, yawned, and gave a slow, controlled nod of friendly recognition to Hank Anderson, who was coaching a photographer. Today Hank was wearing a herringbone sport coat over his signature starched white shirt. Axel knew that Hank wouldn't look for anything more today than the full drama of the public hearing. Axel certainly wasn't up for any prehearing exclusive interviews. Axel figured that Hank already knew everything that Axel would say, at least about Crestfallen I.

The hearing was set for three hours. Morris told them that after one o'clock—three hours—there was the risk of senators actually leaving the hearing to return to Washington. Even the commitments of senators to senators had their limits.

Cole Morris wanted Ham to be the lead-off witness. But Ham didn't want to go first. There were few, from MSP patrol officers to governors, who had tried to change Ham's mind and succeeded. Morris argued that Ham was the most credible witness to set the stage for the raid and describe the action. Ham wanted to go after Hilton to rebut anything he had said. But having experienced Cole's ability to destroy a witness, Ham and Axel finally agreed on the order of the witnesses. Ham was to go first, followed by Axel.

Ham was to establish the timeline, describe the POB and the hike, and detail the layout of Crestfallen, including the group's route down to the ranch, the fences, the creek, sheds, access roads, and the final placement of all the members of the troop and the light stands.

By design, Axel's testimony was to be brief and limited to his interactions with Hilton, his placement by Hilton at the ranch and the shootings themselves. After dealing with Morris yesterday, Axel had lost his enthusiasm for burying Hilton and was now focused on simply getting the hearing behind him. He just wanted to answer the questions and tell the truth. And go home.

After Axel, the lineup was Derrick Samuelson, the DEA agent, Susan St. John, the South Dakota trooper posted to Axel's left at Crestfallen, then Jack Hilton followed by Charlie Ryan.

Axel had also been concerned that Charlie Ryan would lie convincingly and confuse everyone. But this morning, Axel's focus narrowed, so that his sole concern was his own testimony.

The "Montana gospel according to Ham and Axel" was the standard by which others were to be judged. Any witness who strayed from the gospel would be destroyed.

The hall was filling as the heavy cameras were rolled into position and the bright lights focused on Senator Alvin Johnsrud, who gaveled the noisy, nervous crowd to order.

As Morris had explained to Axel, none of the senators, including Johnsrud, wanted to commit themselves beforehand. They hadn't climbed to their lofty political perches by taking unnecessary risks. They'd come to Billings at Johnsrud's request. They'd stay awake and log this favor for future reciprocity. The senators certainly did not expect any follow-up inquiries or legislative initiatives to be launched by today's gathering.

Senator Johnsrud's opening statement was simple: "This hearing has been convened to better understand the happenings of October 20 and 27 at the Crestfallen Ranch, Rankin County, Montana." Axel felt that he made the hearing sound like an everyday event.

Axel and Ham sat in the first row, while Cole Morris sat at the witness table and Anne in the fourth row with some friends. Axel wanted solitude: to be alone in the crowd. He rebuffed several conversations with Ham and had few words for well-wishers who came by to support the Montana duo. Axel pursed his lips and slowly rocked in his chair, ignoring the pomp and pageantry.

He succeeded in isolating himself to the point that he lost perspective of the event. Later, he explained that he felt that he was an actor in a complex movie and had little sense of his role carrying forward the plot.

Axel watched Ham as he methodically answered Cole's straightforward questions. Axel wondered if he would have the confidence and authenticity that Ham projected. Ham's map of the ranch captured everyone's interest and even generated specific questions from the senators.

When called as a witness, Axel did exactly as Morris had told him.

He breathed deeply and answered the questions truthfully, without conclusions or grandstanding. He had a sense that there was so much to say, but his time in the leather witness chair was short, the questions simple, and the answers brief, and he was back in his folding chair next to Ham before he realized it was over. Afterward, he swore he couldn't remember walking away from the witness table. He could not remember the audience, which had been virtually silent, hanging on his every word.

Back in his chair, Axel wasn't ready to listen to the next two witnesses. His brain was pulsing with reworking his own time in the leather chair. His focus drowned out the outer world.

Derrick Samuelson, the DEA agent, who started the shooting with his electronic stun gun, was not ready for Cole Morris. He admitted that this was his first drug raid, in spite of four years at the DEA, and that the reason he initiated the shooting was that he believed his life was at risk. "Yes," he had heard the explanation, of the Langley Rules of Engagement, Level 5 and "yes," no one was actually shooting at him yet. He saw no conflict between his two statements. He described his rifle as a 'charge-unit' which shot bolts of electricity fifty feet. Since his shots couldn't kill anyone, he figured that the terms of engagement didn't apply to him. He also reported that, effective November 1, he had been reassigned to the DEA headquarters-Washington, as a control officer for property confiscated in drug raids and arrests.

The South Dakota trooper's testimony was brief. Axel was just starting to pay attention when Cole Morris thanked her and she stood up from her chair and took the long walk to the back of the crowd.

Hilton was next. Axel watched him closely. He felt that today Hilton had more of a theatrical aura about him than usual. He held his head high and still, shoulders back, and smoothly strode the length of the room when his name was called. As he walked by, Axel was again struck by his size. Hilton was definitely a force to deal with.

Morris shuffled his notes, surveyed the panel of senators, and scanned the room before starting his questioning. From Axel's perspective, Cole Morris was informal, to the point of casual, in his role and didn't appear to be particularly impressed by Major Jack Hilton. Hilton's green Marine Corps uniform struck the crowd by surprise and led Morris to open the questioning with his military record. Hilton's bald head glistened in the television lights. His chest full of colorful campaign ribbons beamed, making them impossible to ignore.

As Hilton ran through routine answers about his military background, Axel began to get nervous. Jack Hilton was an experienced and credible witness. Axel started thinking that this hearing was not going to exonerate him at all; it was going to indict him for an over-response. If Jack Hilton was the model of a reasonable man, then Sheriff Axel Cooper could come off as the unreasonable one, the over-responsive, hypersensitive one—the one that makes his own rules and doesn't respect authority.

During Hilton's testimony, Axel's mind fogged repeatedly, as he framed his own answers to the questions. Then he lost track of Hilton's answers. He didn't hear the answers. He noted that Ham, sitting next to him, had started squirming in his seat. Then the crowd gasped, and suddenly Hilton's testimony was over. He marched the length of the ballroom. The crowd was silent for his entire journey, as though in shock.

Next came Charlie Ryan and Axel was back in the moment. Charlie took a long time to walk up to the witness table. He was hunched over forward and shuffled slowly, wrestling with a four-legged aluminum walker. It was soon obvious that he had not prepared for questions today, but that he was intent on blaming Jack Hilton for the death of his grandson. While Axel found that somewhat comforting, Charlie Ryan's testimony was disorganized and argumentative. When he wasn't attacking the questions posed, he was intermingling the preraid conversations he had with Hilton or confusing the original raid with Crestfallen II. His voice cracked with a gravelly harshness and was at times inaudible. He balked at Morris' attempts to clarify his answers. On three distinct occasions he stated, "Son, I already told you all 'bout that."

Axel thought that this morning Charlie lacked the candor he had shown back in the musty cabin. Today, Charlie had an agenda and wasn't willing to accept any responsibility for the death of his grandson.

Cole Morris thanked Charlie Ryan, ending his testimony. Charlie stayed in the chair looking for his walker. He swung his head in a deep loop toward the corner of the room. Then he fell forward onto the floor. He fell head first and did not put up his hands to break the fall. The sound of his head hitting the hollow floor reverberated throughout the ballroom. The crowd gasped.

As though it had been rehearsed, a team of EMTs from the Billings Fire Department ran up the center aisle pushing a gurney. Charlie didn't move. The EMTs loaded his inert body onto a flat board and then up and onto the gurney with drill-team precision. The ambulance was on its way to Billings Memorial within five minutes of Charlie's fall.

The hearing ended quickly. As Morris had warned, there was no summation, no inquiry by the senators themselves, no conclusion and no judgment.

Ham enthusiastically congratulated Axel. Anne checked in with a statement of "great job" and a peck on the cheek, but she had to run to the hospital. Arlyn and an AA friend who had driven in from Grant this morning reported to Axel that "Hilton proved himself to be the weasel they knew he was."

Somehow Axel had missed the most significant piece of the hearing. Arlyn reported that he had counted seven times that Jack Hilton refused to answer tough questions and that he thought Hilton was afraid of incriminating himself. After dropping that bombshell, Arlyn split to pick up electrical supplies, leaving Axel alone in the crowd at the Crowne Plaza.

In a state of confusion, Axel was surrounded by a crowd of supporters from Grant. He smiled broadly. He saw no one from the Kingdom and no one knew of Charlie Ryan's condition.

Charlie Ryan was dead on arrival at Billings Memorial.

Friday's *Rankin County Courier* carried the banner headline: "KINGDOM SHOOTINGS: FED FIASCO." Except for the weather report and the first three paragraphs of an obituary of Charles W. Ryan, the entire front page was coverage of the hearing. The lead article, bylined by Hank Anderson, read like this:

Tuesday, November 16

Today in Billings the U.S. Senate rescued two prominent Montana lawmen from pursuit by the U.S. Marshal from Denver. The result of a standing-room-only hearing at the Crowne Plaza was an exoneration of Montana's finest in the shooting deaths at Rankin County's Crestfallen Ranch in mid-October.

Charlie Ryan, a native of Rankin County and owner of Crestfallen Ranch, was the last witness of the day. Mr. Ryan collapsed at the end of his testimony and died prior to arriving at Billings Memorial Hospital. (See Mr. Ryan's obituary above.)

Montana Senator Alvin Johnsrud convened a panel of the U.S. Senate Judiciary Committee to take testimony on the U.S. Marshal's October raid. The raid led to the deaths of two individuals, one of whom was an undercover FBI agent. The other was a twenty-year-old Rankin County resident, William J. Ryan. In three hours of testimony by five witnesses, the raid led by Jack Hilton, U.S. Marshal, and its aftermath was dissected in front of Johnsrud's panel, four hundred onlookers, and the national media. Joining Johnsrud's panel were Senators Andrew Norby (MN), Henry Levator (AK), Judith Belt (DE), and Alexander Camden (CO). The inquiry was orchestrated by Cole Morris, a legislative aid to Senator Johnsrud and a former Assistant U.S. Attorney in Billings.

The preliminary facts had been previously established through several provocative press releases and interviews from the U.S. Marshal's office. The raid, organized by the U.S. Marshal out of Denver, Jack Hilton, occurred during the early morning of October 20 on the high-altitude, seasonal ranch in the Harlan Range, believed to be a methamphetamine plant. The raid was initiated to apprehend Robert Johnson, a federal fugitive previously convicted in Minnesota of the manufacture and distribution of illegal drugs. Johnson failed to appear at an October sentencing hearing in Minneapolis. The timing of the raid was accelerated by the group's theft of an anhydrous ammonia trailer in South Dakota and their return with the trailer to the Montana ranch.

In the early October morning, two men, attempting to escape the surrounded ranch house, ran at Sheriff Axel Cooper of Rankin County. Willy Ryan shot at the sheriff at close range. Sheriff Cooper fired in self-defense, killing both men.

The October events at the ranch in Rankin County have been the subject of an Eastern Slope controversy as various elements of the federal Department of Justice have sought to establish responsibility for the shootings that took place there. Conflicting perspectives had been characterized as a feud between Colorado and Montana.

If that was the case, then yesterday's hearing clearly gave Montana a resounding verdict.

Close followers of this controversy found themselves somewhat disappointed in the straightforward testimony of Hamilton Frazier, the Deputy Commissioner of the Montana State Police and Rankin County Sheriff, Axel Cooper. Frazier's testimony painted the background to the raid, the involvement of Governor Boyd Jefferson to recruit local law enforcement, the midnight hike through Ajax Pass, across the 9,000-foot Dead Horse Plateau and the descent to the ranch before sunup. With high-tech graphics, he mapped out the ranch site and the positioning of the nine members of the rapid-response task force.

The raid was on the ranch house of Crestfallen Ranch, a seasonal cattle ranch north-northeast of Mt. Elliott. The ranch is in the so-called "Irish Kingdom," a portion of Rankin County long owned and controlled by several related Irish families. At various times over the past century, the Irish Kingdom has been alleged to be the home of cattle thieves, rum runners, and other criminals.

Sheriff Axel Cooper's testimony lasted less than ten minutes. He has been the target of a steady stream of criticism from the U.S. Marshal, Jack Hilton. Cooper responded to the detailed questioning by Morris with short, straightforward answers, which established that, contrary to implications of press releases of the U.S. Marshal, Cooper had no personal agenda in the raid and no personal animosity toward Hilton or members of the Irish Kingdom. Cooper's report on the shooting was that "two guys came running at me. One of them fired at me from less than fifteen feet away. I feared for my life and I shot back." He reported that he knew neither individual.

When called to testify, Hilton brought the crowd to silence as he marched the length of the room in his U.S. Marine Corps uniform. Hilton, a large man, is a retired Major, having last served in Iraq. In his testimony, he repeatedly blamed Cooper for the shootings, but was unable to present a clear reason as to why Cooper should be held accountable. Hilton recited the terms of engagement, the so-called Langley Rules, four times during the course of testimony. His descriptions of the rules required the responding individual to be under fire and be at risk of loss of life. Hilton implied that Cooper was not at risk and therefore he over-responded. Attorney Morris repeatedly probed as to the assessment of risk, particularly in light of Sheriff Cooper's sworn testimony that he was shot at by one of the runners at the range of less than fifteen feet. Hilton stated that he believed DEA agent Derrick Samuelson violated the terms of engagement, as well as Sherriff Cooper.

As to his own knowledge, opinions and actions, Hilton was less forthcoming. He repeatedly plead the Fifth Amendment to deflect questions about his discussions with Charlie Ryan prior to the raid, his behavior during the raid, and to repeated grilling as to his knowledge of the FBI undercover agent and his failure to communicate that to others in the raiding party. Further, he refused to answer any questions about events surrounding the so-called Crestfallen II, an occupation of the ranch by the Colorado National Guard, seven days after the shootings and three arrests of the first raid.

The mysterious follow-up episode occurred on October 27, when Hilton, who in addition to being a retired Marine Corps Major and U.S. Marshal is also a General in the Colorado National Guard, led a party of ten Colorado National Guard troops to the Crestfallen Ranch and prepared to dismantle several buildings. Their equipment included a dump truck and a bulldozer. Their efforts were interrupted by rifle shots at their vehicles. The shooting came from a ridge near the ranch. Hilton was injured in the shooting and was subsequently flown to Billings in an MSP helicopter and received treatment at Billings Memorial Hospital. In spite of his injuries, he checked himself out of BMH "against medical advice" and returned to Colorado with his men.

The next witness was Susan St. John of the South Dakota State Police. Prior to the raid, the SDSP had tracked a wheeled tank of anhydrous ammonia to the Montana ranch. The tank was stolen in Lowther, South Dakota.

The day's last witness was Charlie Ryan, the leader of the so-called Irish Kingdom in southeast Rankin County and owner of the Crestfallen Ranch. He testified that he organized the shooters to stop the destruction of his ranch by the Colorado National Guard.

Ryan repeatedly stated that the shooters were out to disable the Guard's vehicles and that it was his belief that Hilton was hit by a ricocheted bullet.

Ryan appeared to be in great pain, often wincing as though he had an injury to his left side. A number of his supporters in the audience cheered as he repeatedly laid the blame for the death of his grandson and the FBI agent on Jack Hilton. Senator Johnsrud gaveled the crowd to order on four separate occasions during Ryan's testimony.

Ryan generated a surprise reaction from the entire crowd with his report of two preraid discussions he had had with Hilton. Ryan stated that Hilton had told him that the FBI's Minneapolis office wanted to place an undercover agent at

Crestfallen. After his testimony, Mr. Ryan appeared to suffer a stroke and collapsed, falling out of the witness chair.

The intense, three hour hearing concluded with short statements from the panel of senators.

U.S. Marshal Jack Hilton, as though acknowledging defeat, left the building immediately after his limited testimony and was not available to respond to the assertions of Charlie Ryan.

Sheriff Cooper and Deputy Commissioner Frazier were all but carried from the room by a contingent of supporters.

The week's edition of *The Rankin County Courier* was sold out in three hours.

CHAPTER 23

(Monday, November 21)

Axel read and reread Hank Anderson's article on the hearing. He could feel Hank's supportive words slowly eroding the granite of his consternation. As usual, Hank Anderson couldn't keep his personal perspective out of the *Courier*. But Axel couldn't relax completely. While the media coverage of the hearing was universally favorable, Axel was still concerned about Hilton, his unpredictability, and a possible indictment by Colorado's U.S. Attorney, John Autry.

Ham's call early Sunday caught Axel off guard. According to Ham, Senator Johnsrud and Montana's U.S. Attorney had been talking since the hearing. Senator Johnsrud had implored Henry Otto to "step into the ring" and "get these Coloradans off our backs." By Thursday evening, Otto had been convinced to open an inquiry into the October events at Crestfallen. Since nothing official had come out of Denver, the field was clear. Otto was ready to jump into the ring and wanted to talk to Axel Monday afternoon.

Anne worked the Sunday afternoon shift and Axel tracked her down at the hospital to tell her the good news and line up Monday dinner in Billings. She invited Axel to dinner at her house, a rare event.

Axel drove the Cherokee to the Federal Building in Billings. He parked in the public lot and met with Henry Otto and a staff lawyer in a small conference room on the fifth floor. The washed out, creamy lime décor and the metal furniture reminded Axel of the Coast Guard and his youthful innocence. They had a transcript of the entire hearing and had pasted the four-inch think volume with yellow and green Post-It notes to highlight conflicts in the testimony. Otto sat in the corner of the room listening while the younger lawyer dissected Axel's testimony in front of him.

Axel uniformly supported his statements. As to how others could hold different opinions, he was not judgmental. More than once he said, "Well, that might be his position, but I saw it just like I said I did."

The female staff attorney asked him a list of newly prepared questions, some of which were simple restatements of Axel's testimony at the hearing. Her delivery was cold and exacting. She moved mechanically from one to the next. She avoided eye contact to the point that, when she lifted her eyes off the page, she looked over Axel's shoulder to the picture of the Iwo Jima Memorial statue at Arlington Cemetery on the far wall. She had several complex questions, which reminded Axel of Cole Morris's prep session. Maybe they were taught by the same teacher. Axel asked her to repeat several of the questions. She would repeat her question in the same chilling, slow monotone, as though a tape recording had been replayed. He actually wrote out three of the questions in order to solidify his understanding. On one question, he actually wrote out his answer and read it back to her. The attorney was patient and took verbatim notes of all Axel's answers.

Otto had left the conference room before the new questions began.

When, after forty minutes, the attorney had exhausted her list, she quickly read Axel's answers back to him and then piled up her papers and the transcript, ready to leave the room. She told Axel she had to get his answers typed up. She asked him to stay to sign an affidavit affirming his answers to the new questions. The process was wearing and Axel's high spirits of the early morning were slowly ebbing away.

Axel went back to the lobby and waited. He hadn't anything to read to take his mind off of Crestfallen, Hilton, the hearing and the new questions. He wasn't prepared to sit in the stark room. He reworked all of today's questions and his answers, wondering what they might add to the story. He wanted this chapter of his life to be over and done. The new questions might just breathe new life into the inquiry. After forty-five minutes, he was restless. He was worried that the longer it took, the greater was the chance that Henry Otto would change his mind and bow out of the case. *Maybe he had called Denver to tell them what he was doing and they talked him out of it.*

After sixty-five minutes, the staff attorney came out to the lobby with a typed affidavit. She offered no explanations as to why it had taken so long. After signing four originals of the document, Axel was escorted back to Henry Otto's corner office. Axel was aware that the young staff attorney was watching his every move. He tried to convince himself that it was nothing personal, that this was simply routine, and that federal prosecutors were a different breed who viewed the world as a universe of wrongdoers who had yet to be caught. This escorted walk struck Axel as similar to the walk from the booking desk to the cell block in the sheriff's office. Only this time he was the suspect.

She opened the door to Otto's office for Axel to enter first. She stood by the door, as though she would block his escape. Axel had hardly sat down when Otto, seated across the desk, started. "Sheriff, I think that there's a real risk of malfeasance here." He paused. Axel was confused and it showed on his face. Seeing that, Otto explained, "Malfeasance by federal law enforcement. I can't speak for the U.S. Marshal from Colorado, but I think he owes you an apology. Seems to me what you did was absolutely in self-defense."

Axel breathed a full sigh of relief.

He started up again, "Seems our man Hilton was operating under everybody's radar screen. He dreamed this up by himself. He recruited friends from the DEA and told nobody in the FBI or the U.S. Attorney's office in Denver. He's put the DOJ in a tailspin. Minneapolis FBI is all over Denver. Apparently, FBI-Denver gave Hilton a green light to talk to Charlie Ryan. FBI-Minneapolis had given notice to Denver that they had an undercover agent at Crestfallen. I've got no info on what Hilton knew about that. But I can't believe that FBI-Denver wouldn't tell him what they knew. They are now pushing back—arguing that they gave Hilton very limited authority—they were ready to toss the bank fraud allegation, but Hilton wanted to keep it in the mix, give him some leverage with Charlie Ryan. I don't feel a whole lot of support for Hilton coming from John Autry, the U.S. Attorney down there. From here, it looks like a real free-for-all. Everybody's out to cover their ass." Henry Otto looked up at Axel as though his use of the word "ass" was a bonding agent, putting the two of them in the men-of-the-world fraternity. Axel slowly nodded his head in support. *Internal conflict in Denver was certainly to be expected.*

"I've been encouraged to take a look at this. Can't say I would have without a few phone calls from elected officials. In this job, you learn to make very few moves and make damn sure you don't screw them up. Hell, Johnsrud called me before he left Billings the day of the hearing. I tell you, I don't get to do this very often, but today I'm going public with a statement." He looked across the desk at Axel for his reaction. Axel could tell that Otto was excited about the statement and felt it would be supportive, but what exactly would it say?

Otto responded to the curious look at Axel's face, "Let me read the latest draft." He coughed twice and picked up a sheet of paper from the corner of the desk. "My office has investigated the October 20 raid in Rankin County, Montana and we have determined that there is no factual or legal foundation for any federal criminal proceeding against two Montana law enforcement officers. The individuals are Axel Cooper, Sheriff of Rankin County, and Hamilton Frazier, Deputy Commissioner of the Montana State Police.

We have interviewed witnesses of the raid, scrutinized the testimony of the U.S. Senate Judiciary Committee hearing in Billings on November 16, and taken sworn affidavits. Should new facts surface, they will be examined to the fullest extent. However, I am of the opinion that it is highly unlikely that new relevant facts will be presented in the situation. At this point we have not examined the activities of other law enforcement officers but recognize that a federal law enforcement badge does not place its holder above the law."

Otto scratched his head and said, "I don't know about that last line. It's a little provocative. I'm not looking to prosecute Jack Hilton at this point. This will stir things up in Denver a little but it won't close down any internal DOJ inquiries. Anyway, the final will be out to the papers and TV folks before five."

Axel's reply was, "Super."

Axel was down the elevator and driving out of the parking lot before he knew it. He was operating on automatic pilot fueled by euphoria. Only when he arrived at the stop light at Twenty-seventh Street just west of the Crowne Plaza did he stop to consider where he was and where he was going. He smiled at himself and turned left toward Anne's. He would be early. Early with good news!

The row of single-story houses was built in the last two years. They had no landscaping. The houses had little to distinguish themselves from one another. Axel cruised slowly down the west-side block, looking on every porch for Anne's two-foot-high maroon statue of a Chinese temple dog. He parked the Cherokee on the barren street and crossed her front yard. He could hear loud rhythmic music coming from the house. He rang the door bell. He could hear the door chimes over the music, but doubted that she could.

Axel looked through the small side window and saw Anne in a black, skin-tight leotard in the living room moving to the music in a barefoot, aerobic dance routine. She was facing the sparsely furnished living room's fireplace, away from the front door.

Axel smiled as he watched her workout. She was good. She rhythmically twisted, turned, bobbed and weaved to the pounding music. She lifted her knees high and bent over low, stretching her hamstrings and back muscles. She then lunged with her right leg forward as if she was advancing in a sword fight but she pointed her arms to the room's upper corners. Then she bent over again and slapped the wooden floors with a heavy beat. She spun away from the fireplace, giving Axel a frontal view of the performance. She stared at the wall and bent over at the waist. Her breasts pushed forward, molded by the stretched spandex of her low-cut leotard. As she stood and spun again, Axel rapped with his knuckles hard and loud on the storm door.

She heard him this time and waved to him. She stopped her routine and stood flat-footed, hands on hips as though considering what to do. Then she nodded toward the door and walked toward the music, an iPod in a white speaker box, and turned down the volume. She grabbed a large bath towel and draped it over her shoulders. She opened the door and invited him in, but she told him that she had to finish her workout. She toweled herself off, breathing hard, then she punched her timer, started the music, and went back to her athletic dance. Axel sat on the sofa and watched. He took off his overcoat and shoes.

He was less at home in her place than she was in his, but after ten minutes, he walked past her into the kitchen to examine the good-smelling dinner in the oven. Axel pulled a beer out of the refrigerator and returned to the living room and *the show*. He hadn't told her anything about his meeting with Henry Otto. He watched Anne's workout, beer in hand. The Fleetwood Mac vocals were over and the slow rhythm of "Bolero" began. Anne started a slow sultry dance to the changing tempo of the music, swinging her shoulders, arms, and hips to the pulsing beat. Anne, with her green eyes wide open, her long auburn hair a flurry, wouldn't look at Axel. The tempo increased and she responded. She kept moving as though to stop would solidify her joints and wouldn't allow her to ever move again.

Her hypnotic writhing and flowing hair reminded Axel of Arabic belly dancers, Olympic gymnasts, and naked pole-dancers at the Bada Bing on "The Sopranos," all at once. Her flashing eyes radiated mischief. As the beat increased Axel's attitude changed from interest, to amazement, to intrigue.

With his eyes focused on Anne, he leaned back in the leather lounge chair, took a deep swig of the cold beer, and beamed a Mona Lisa smile of arousal. Anne danced in front of him just beyond arm's length. She aligned herself right in front of him. He reached out to put a hand on her hip, but she playfully took a step back. He scooted to the edge of the chair, as if to get a better position to catch her. Still she refused to look at him, but shot a piercing look over his head. She smiled wider as the tempo increased and she swung her arms and twirled a complete rotation just out of Axel's reach. Then as the music crescendoed, she threw herself backward over her right shoulder in a cartwheel toward the fireplace. Then she somersaulted forward and pushed herself up to a standing position in front of Axel.

He stood as though to catch her. His shouts of bravo were drowned out by the music and he felt that he too had a role in Anne's pantomime. *Was he the toreador to her raging bull or the male lead in Swan Lake?*

Regardless, he put his arm out to hold her and she reached for him. She infused him into her continuing dance. One hand clutched his midriff, pushing him to her left, while the other grabbed his forearm, pulling it out to the right with a tango stride. He was off balance until she pulled him back to her. Suddenly, the iPod moved to the next piece, a slow waltz, and she pressed her moist warmth to Axel's torso. Axel did not pull away as she pulled his shirt out of his trousers and slid her warm hand onto his bare back. He freed his left hand from her grasp and slid it along the underside of her sheathed arm, down to caress the outside of her breast and then to rest on her hip.

CHAPTER 24

(Friday, November 25)

Longbow Creek flows through the Custer National Forest in Rankin County. Fed by underground glacial melt-water, it holds the distinction as the spring creek at the highest elevation on the eastern slope of the Rockies. Arlyn Cooper spoke of Longbow and its spring-fed cousins as a higher order of moving water, while creeks fed by surface snowmelt were of a lower class. Most of the high-altitude, heavy surface snowmelt from this sector of Mt. Elliott avoids Longbow and is funneled into nearby Bridal Veil Creek.

The result was that Longbow ran steady, clear and cold year round, while Bridal Veil was often a muddy torrent in April and lukewarm in August. Longbow was a bountiful trout fishery while Bridal Veil was a quixotic rager. Arlyn had long ago identified Longbow, in spite of its altitude, inaccessibility, and modest flow, as a great all-season destination for brawny browns and feisty rainbows. Longbow required a skilled, patient, wade-fisherman who was willing to brave the colder air and hike extra miles through boulder fields to get to the best spots.

Over the centuries, the creek had its way with the limestone overlaying the mountain's granite core to create four, stair-stepped pools two thousand feet above the junction of Longbow with Vermillion Creek. They were spread over two miles of the river's arc after it tumbled out of a lodgepole pine forest.

Arlyn and Axel parked Arlyn's vintage Chevy pickup at the trailhead. The pickup was the only vehicle in the lot.

The outing had been Axel's idea—part of his continuing convalesance. They hadn't gone fishing since just after Crestfallen. Axel well remembered the big brown. In spite of that, Axel would always be the novice, the junior partner, the younger brother and client. When the brothers fished, Arlyn took charge in picking the spots, selecting the flies, choosing the time of day, and determining the length and diameter of the leader needed for the day's outing. Axel's every move was subject to Arlyn's close scrutiny. Even after Axel's landing of a significant fish, Arlyn would sidle up to him to check on the fish, the winning fly and the residual strength of knots.

Regardless, Axel knew what to expect. He had learned to keep his mouth shut and enjoy the attention. He always relished an outing with his older brother, especially when Arlyn was at peace with the world. On occasion, Axel had considered these outings as gifts that the brothers gave to each other. Axel worked hard at fishing, with the added benefit that his whole mind was occupied and today had no room for thoughts of Crestfallen, Hilton or Sven Thordahl. A further bonus today was that they were on federal land.

They were within the county but out of Rankin County jurisdiction. Another feature was that such off-road, high-altitude fishing reduced the chance of running into some of the Rankin County electorate, who persisted in believing that their sheriff should be working twenty-four hours a day, seven days a week.

By tradition, the men set up their strategy, tactics, and tackle in the parking lot and then together walked up the main trail, which zigzagged through a field of random boulders for two miles before it met the creek and followed its contours up into the forest.

Yesterday afternoon, after finishing the rough electrical work on a new vacation home and before finding the bar, Arlyn had driven up and scouted the creek. He was pleased to report a late-season three o'clock caddis hatch in the slack water with bigger fish active in the deeper pools. No ant or grasshopper activity. But then, there hardly ever was at this altitude.

Arlyn flipped down the tailgate, pulled out his mammoth tackle box, opened it, and started sorting small plastic boxes of flies. He flipped one open, closed it, and tossed it aside. Then he worked the same process with the next. He shuffled the boxes with mechanical precision.

After assessing his resources, Arlyn looked up and turned to Axel and said, "For you, young man, I'd go with a yellow-tail elk's hair caddis." He thought for a moment and then said, "But you don't want it to be the first one out. Start with a Royal Coachman, wet or dry, until the hatch gets going, then switch to the elk-hair." Axel smiled at Arlyn's enthusiasm and his intense but disorganized approach. Axel knew that he didn't have any yellow-tail elk's hair caddis flies, but he also knew that Arlyn would want to look through Axel's meager supply of basic flies before offering his own. Axel offered up his single white plastic box of flies to Arlyn and busied himself with adjusting his waders and felt-bottomed boots. Arlyn thoughtfully examined Axel's limited selection and put together a packet of flies from his own supply. On clicking a small, yellow plastic box closed, Arlyn handed it to Axel. Axel put the box away and went back to the cab of the truck and dropped his brown sheriff's jacket on the seat. He grabbed a thin nylon pullover with a hood, as it was lighter and water repellent. He also grabbed a Billings Mustangs baseball hat, his polarized sun glasses and his radio phone. He clicked it on to confirm reception. He placed it in the bib pocket.

Arlyn looked at Axel's pullover and rendered quick judgment, "You're going pretty light for November in the mountains."

Axel shot back, "Want my jacket? Take it. I'm leaving it here."

Arlyn sorted through a pile of sweatshirts, rain jackets and old waders looking for the right piece. Then he picked up Axel's jacket, shirked out of his suspenders and put on Axel's insulated brown coat complete with Rankin County patches and an embroidered name tag. When he got the suspenders back up on his shoulders he looked at Axel, straightened his broad-brimmed felt hat and said, "Let's go, Bro; we're burning daylight."

The men quickly gathered their gear and hiked through the boulder field to reach the lowest of the pools. En route, Arlyn talked about the creek and the spots that he thought would be good today, and how they could work the creek between the pools hard. Axel talked little, with most of his thoughts dealing with the mechanics of moving down the path with his long rod, bulky waders, and boots. Down the path, the men moved slowly with a similar rhythm to their broad shoulders.

They both knew that the highest pool upstream was the deepest and had the biggest fish, but not many of them. Axel knew Arlyn would rather be skunked seeking lunkers than catch ten ten-inchers. Axel's perspective was just the opposite. He was there to catch fish, even if they were fingerlings. They passed through the meadow littered with boulders and turned off the path toward the stream at the lowest pool.

Axel always enjoyed this moment, when Arlyn blocked out the world and entered a virtual trance, concentrating on the upcoming battle with nature. This was a different person from the loquacious drinker, the stumbling drunk, or the hungover, surly electrician. Axel found that with this Arlyn, he himself was more relaxed.

As though driven by a computerized program Arlyn checked the wind, the right shoreline, the water temperature, the left shoreline, the mid-stream flow, and the water clarity. No surface feeding evident. After a silent two-minute assessment, Arlyn flipped his head upstream to the next pool. This one was longer, with darker, green water, signifying deeper runs. Axel knew that Arlyn wanted to fish the pools still further up, so he volunteered to take the two lower ones. He said, "Arlyn, you take the upper two. You go for the big 'uns. I'll take the lower pools. I'll work this one and the first and the stream between 'em."

Arlyn looked up at Axel with a puzzled look, but then quickly agreed as though he feared the offer might be rescinded.

While Axel set up his gear, he could hear Arlyn splashing in the shallow water on his way to the third pool.

Axel smiled at Arlyn's transparency. Especially when fishing, Arlyn was as easy to read as a high school kid.

Axel assembled his rod, strung the line and tied the red-banded Royal Coachman to the leader. He surveyed the small river as it flowed into the pool. He again smiled. Arlyn hadn't coached him like he usually did. Maybe landing the big brown had elevated Axel a step or two in Arlyn's mind. Or maybe Arlyn was focused on the big fish today.

Axel spotted Arlyn upstream dancing over the rocky shoreline en route to the third pool. Axel was pleased that Arlyn was so obviously exactly where he wanted to be and that he, Axel, could be part of it.

After two short false casts, Axel softly laid the Coachman on the water only fifteen feet upstream. He saw the small Rainbow hit it and immediately flip out of the water, as though stung by the unexpected sharpness of the hook. Axel considered trying to pull the small fish straight in rather than playing it on the light tackle with a taut line. In deference to Arlyn and respect to his teachings, Axel worked the small fish as if it were a trophy.

Three fish later, Axel moved to the top of the second pool and caught a glimpse of Arlyn squatting down in the upper pool releasing a fish. He had tucked his rod under his arm and used both hands to hold the fish. Axel couldn't see the fish but considered that it had to be pretty big to take two hands. Axel whistled toward Arlyn who waved back in acknowledgment.

After ten casts at the new spot, which failed to attract any strikes, Axel decided it was time for the elk-hair caddis fly. He pulled in his line, took off his vest and sat down on the rocky shore to change flies.

Axel immediately recognized the loud crack as a shot from a mid-sized rifle, below the high pitch of a .22, but not the boom of a higher-caliber elk rifle. *Off to the right, beyond the path. Not too close, but seemed to be directed this way.* He recognized that the waves of sound were tightly packed without a reflective echo.

Arlyn yelled as he went down in the knee-deep water.

At first Axel didn't connect the shot and Arlyn's yell, as if he'd wrenched his knee while wading. But the yell was enough to get Axel up off the ground and looking toward the upper pool. Axel could only see that Arlyn was in the water and not trying to get up. In a single movement, Axel tossed his rod up on the rock shore along with his vest. Axel wiggled back into the suspenders of his waders and was running full-tilt through the shallow water toward Arlyn. Halfway there, the creek cut deeply into the bank, and Axel was suddenly running in deeper water, lifting his knees up to his waist. He stumbled and fell, and recovered only to stumble again ten feet from Arlyn.

Arlyn was on his side trying to keep his head above the water. Arlyn said nothing and didn't move. Immediately, Axel could see that the upper right arm of the brown jacket had been shredded into a soggy rag, a *red* soggy rag. To Axel it looked like an animal had taken a bite. The wound was a bowl of pulsing blood streaked by white ribbons of connective tissue. *Where had the flesh gone?* "Holy shit," was all Axel could say.

Arlyn groaned. He couldn't hold up his head and he slumped off to the left away from the wounded arm. He opened and closed his eyes as though fighting to stay conscious.

Axel shuffled behind Arlyn and grabbed him around the chest and then dragged him up, out of the rocks into the dry grass. He put his feet higher than his head to get blood going that way. And then he unsnapped Arlyn's bib waders and tore open the sleeve of the brown jacket to get down to the wound. With Arlyn lying face up, Axel straddled him to pull the arm out of the sleeve. His shirt was crimson and sopped with bright red blood. The wound itself was fluid hamburger.

Axel stood up and, as though directing a first aid class, looked up at the sparse trees and said, "Stop the bleeding. Treat for shock." Then he continued, "I need a belt, two belts. Tourniquet this arm now!" He then unbuckled his web belt from his waders and bent over and positioned it just below Arlyn's shoulder and above the wound. He threaded the end through the buckle and then drew it down tight. It slipped on the blood and slid down the upper arm into the wound itself. Axel loosened it and pulled it back up above the gouge and held it in place with both hands while he pulled the belt with his teeth. His hands were covered in Arlyn's hot blood. With this second effort, he made the belt tighter. Arlyn's face contorted in pain and his head flopped back to the left. An image of a severed arm flashed across Axel's mind, but he could already see that the blood flow was slowing. Arlyn wouldn't bleed out on Longbow Creek.

Axel again stood up and looked upstream and down. *No help.* He ran back to the creek, rinsed his hands, unsnapped the pocket in the bib of his waders and retrieved his radio phone. With one punch he was talking to Ange in town. Axel barked, "Ange, sheriff, medical emergency. Arlyn's been shot up on Longbow Creek. Blew off half his arm. Lost a lot of blood. Need a copter here. We're about two miles upstream of the trail head. Federal land. We got to get him out of here fast. You got coordinates there? On the phone? You know where we are?"

"Yes, Boss. Here on the console. Which copter? Forest Service Search & Rescue?"

"No, that would be coming out of the Park. Best we can do is the

MSP helicopter in Billings. Anything else and we could be too late. Got it? See what you can line up. Also, call John Gatlin of the Forest Service. He might have some ideas. Call me in five minutes."

Axel walked back to Arlyn and then ran through the grass up to the trail as though to direct a rescue party. He quickly returned to Arlyn lying on his back with a glassy stare off to the left. Axel placed his hand on Arlyn's chest. The heartbeat was strong.

Axel quickly unbuckled his waders, took off his wind breaker and shirt, and spread them out covering Arlyn's chest. *Shock, gotta treat for shock.* He zipped up the brown sheriff's jacket over them. He stood straight again, hitched up his waders, and craned his neck, looking for help.

CHAPTER 25

(Friday, November 25)

Arlyn lay on his back, eyes closed, nose in the air. His breathing was slow, but deep and steady. Axel noted that his face had more color than ten minutes ago.

"So what the fuck was that?" Arlyn said through his teeth, without moving his lips.

Axel ran over to him and kneeled down. "Somebody shot you. Upper arm. Tore it up pretty bad. You lost a lotta blood. Belted down your arm. I think the bleeding's stopped. Copter coming. We're just gonna stay cool. Half hour we'll be outta here, pronto."

Axel unzipped the brown jacket and slid his hand down under the bulky clothing to Arlyn's heart. The beat was fast, but strong.

Arlyn opened his eyes, moved his head slightly toward Axel, and whispered, "Pronto's cool. I'm here." Then he closed his eyes and rolled his head back. He clenched his jaw with a vague smile and then started humming softly.

Axel had done all he could for Arlyn. The belt was as tight as he could make it. Arlyn was warm, his feet higher than his head. The wound was open but had stopped pulsating with Arlyn's heartbeat. Axel stood up and with his hands on his hips took a new look at the surroundings.

He knew the shooter was long gone, but where had he been? Where'd he shoot from? Axel scanned the creek, the creek bed, and the wispy aspens on the narrow flood plain and the hills beyond. The wind had died and there was no movement in the trees. No sound other than the creek. His mind was moving fast. Was this an accident? A poacher thinking he saw an elk in the creek? Where was the shooter? Had to be upstream on higher ground.

Upstream of the highest pool, Longbow Creek worked its way around a huge granite boulder. Standing next to Arlyn, Axel examined the massive boulder as best he could. It was divided by a vertical crevasse as though a giant had cleaved it with an axe. He nodded his head as he considered how a shooter could get himself to the top, forty feet up. Certainly not up the front wall. Axel moved to his left to trace the top edge of the boulder. On the far right, the big rock tapered off to the point that it went underground. From that point, it would be easy to walk on top of the boulder to the crevasse. He again scanned the possible flight path of a bullet from the top of the crevasse to Arlyn in the creek. Nothing other than a few thin-leaved aspens in the way. He knelt next to Arlyn, tapped him on the shoulder and said, "You OK?"

Arlyn grunted, "Yeah."

"I'm going up the big rock. Back in five minutes." Arlyn grunted a non-verbal reply. Axel high-stepped through the sparse grass and young, thin aspens up to the face of the boulder. He ran along the boulder to the right, to the point where the front wall was only three feet high. He climbed up on the rock and then ran up the slope to where the crevasse opened to a wide crack filled with pine needles, mulch and shallow-rooted, twisted dwarf evergreens. He looked down on the creek and the spot where Arlyn was shot.

Then he scanned the horizon. He saw that behind the rock, away from the creek, was a half-overgrown two-track road, probably from the days of wildcat logging. A fork of the road ran right up to the boulder. Axel saw it as the getaway route.

Before Axel could consider what to do next, Ange called him to report on her efforts and the MSP helicopter's ETA: Eighteen minutes; they just cleared Forest Service Headquarters. Ham's onboard, plus two EMTs and John Gatling of the Forest Service. She asked about Arlyn, and Axel answered that he was conscious and the bleeding had stopped, but he needed a hospital quick. Then she asked him about the shooter—any sign of him, any evidence?

While on the radio with Ange, Axel continued to scan the skyline. *Helicopters? Movements of the trees? Dust from the trail? Nothing.*

"What? No.... I climbed up a big boulder, but ... no sign of a shooter." Axel stopped. Talking to Ange wasn't going to change a thing. Then he started up again as though on automatic pilot. "Had to be a hundred-yard shot. Probably from this huge boulder, forty feet up. Coulda sat here with a tripod, squeezed off one shot, then took off on the backside. Two-track logging road. Haven't seen any evidence of anything yet. Guess there's no chase, but maybe Ham will see something on the way in. First priority is getting Arlyn outta here. Can you get them to call me? I'm going back to the creek. Reception's probably worse down there, but tell 'em to call now. Gotta go."

As he walked back down to Arlyn, he patted the pockets of the fishing vest, hoping to find a cigarette. Axel had quit smoking years ago, but the urge never quite disappeared.

Just as he got back to Arlyn, the radio came to life.

"Cooper here." Axel called into the static.

"Axel, it's Ham. How's Arlyn, over?"

"Right, Arlyn's conscious. Bleeding's stopped, but he's lost a lot of blood." He looked down at his GPS location readout on the phone. "You know where you're going? We're sitting near the creek, a hundred yards from a massive bolder. You'll want to drop on the west side of the creek, near the boulder. Should be easy to spot. I'll meet you there. Hey, look for a possible shooter on the way in. Some two-track roads back here, over."

The radio spit and crackled electronic interference.

"Got it. I got two EMTs, Montana's finest, ready to go to work. We can't be more than a couple miles out. Hang tight, Axe. We'll be looking. We'll get the bastard, over."

"Damn right, we'll get him. Over and out." He stood up, feeling stronger now. With a greater sense of purpose, he started scanning the terrain opposite him. He'd fished Longbow with Arlyn many times, but never looked at it as a crime scene. Everything took on a more sinister appearance. He saw a lot of spots where a shooter could hide. Further to the right, there was a half-mile-wide meadow that was covered in intermittent sagebrush and thigh-high grasses. Behind the boulder and the cliff behind it, the Harlan Range started up in earnest. A snow-covered shelf above the wall was the beginning of the steady march of granite that would eventually lead to Mt. Elliott, towering at close to twelve thousand feet in elevation.

Arlyn held his head straight, had his eyes open and was watching Axel out of the corner of his eyes, but said nothing. Then he turned his head toward Axel and said, "Ain't dead yet, Bro. Guess I'll have to learn to cast left-handed. This bitch is starting to hurt." He closed his eyes and rolled his head back. "Tell the medics I'll be here."

Axel was pleased at Arlyn's humor and brought his focus back to the creek. He wanted to find the spot where the shooter had stood. He could not do any more for Arlyn but find the shooter, and locating the spot was the first objective. On the other bank, about twenty yards downstream, the grasses gave way to a thin stand of young lodgepole pines and a mass of wild rose bushes. Axel figured that if you were looking for cover, the four-inch trunks of those lodgepoles wouldn't offer much, but if one sat low in the thick shrubbery the cover was solid. Axel was scanning the rimrocks of the cliff behind the boulder and the snow field above them when the radio cracked again.

"Cooper, it's Gatlin. Sorry 'bout Arlyn. How's he doing?" He paused and then started up again, "I got the FBI coming as soon as they can get there. They've got another copter and have already left Billings. Could be half an hour."

"John, I read you. Arlyn's going to make it. FBI. I was afraid of that. I've got too much business with them already."

He decided to leave it at that. Gatlin was an old friend and now was not the time to rework Crestfallen. "Axel, give me a break. FBI is the world's best. And straight arrow. It's gotta be federal. You're in the National Forest."

Axel thought of Major Jack Hilton. *Straight arrow? Don't think so.* But he said, "Well, hope we got a local guy. Nobody from Denver. Ya hear me? Is there somebody in Billings you can harness for this, over?"

"I don't know who's coming. There are only 'bout three guys in Billings. Henderson usually gets the Forest Service cases, but it's potluck, whoever's in town today."

"I'll leave that to you. Just whatever happens, don't let this fall to Denver!"

Gatlin continued, "Whoever it is, they're on their way. Hey, weather problems brewing. We got a big nasty Arctic front sliding down from Edmonton, bringing with it lots of wind and snow. Two hours, could be a whiteout. We have to do as much as we can today. We'll be there in four minutes. Over and out."

"Over and out." Axel put the radio back into the bib pocket of his waders. He knew that Gatlin was right. He could feel the weather change. Moving clouds. Temperature dropping. It'd be dark soon, if the snow didn't arrive first. He rubbed his bare arms to generate some warmth.

The light was beginning to dim. Axel again checked with Arlyn, said, "Only a couple of minutes," and then walked out into the creek at about the spot where Arlyn had been. The water swirled around his knees. He wanted to get another sightline to the boulder. He could see the upstream ripple that Arlyn would have told him to fish first. He turned around and faced the boulder and the rimrocks. Axel narrowed the shooter's position to the top of the boulder, within twenty to thirty feet, either direction, of the crevasse. The rimrocks were another hundred yards beyond that. Making double sure he had the right angle, he walked to the shore and gathered a dozen fist-sized river rocks and laid them out in a line on the ground pointing to the shooter's position. Hopefully, there'd be enough light to see the line from above. *It had to be right.*

As he finished, he heard the helicopter. It was landing. Between the gurgle of the river and the swirling wind, he hadn't heard it until now.

The helicopter touched down west of the boulder, the blades whirling to a lazy stop. The pilot kept the engine going at a slow idle.

As Axel went past Arlyn, he quickly touched him on the shoulder. "Medics are here. I can't go with ya. I gotta stay for the FBI. You OK with that?" Arlyn just nodded his head without opening his eyes.

Ham was the first out and ran toward Axel. "Axel! Where is he?" Ham shouted. Over Ham's shoulder Axel could see the EMTs already out of the helicopter and getting their stretcher and materials ready.

Axel pointed back toward Arlyn and yelled so the EMTs could hear over the noise, "Down toward the creek."

As the gear-laden EMTs trotted toward the creek, Ham studied Axel carefully. "Are you OK?"

Axel ignored Ham and yelled at the EMTs, "Arlyn's down here. We've got to get him outta here."

Then Arlyn looked at himself, and indeed he looked unusual in his waders, no shirt, no jacket, and blood on his arms and chest.

"Arlyn's blood. I'm okay," Axel spat out.

Axel turned away from Ham and followed the EMTs to Arlyn. They went right to work and Axel stepped back.

Ham came up to him, put his hand on Axel's shoulder to get his attention and said, "Axe, you go sit in the copter. We've got bottles of water. Get a coat. They'll take care of Arlyn. We can talk in a minute, go sit down."

Axel had never seen Ham so solicitous.

"Ham, we've got to get after this now, if Gatlin's right about the weather coming in. It's now or never." Axel flipped his head to John Gatlin, the last of the helicopter's passengers, who had just looked up at the blackening sky. "I'll get some water in a minute. I guess I need a coat. I think I got a line on the shooter. Top of the boulder, by the crevasse. Either that or a much longer shot from the rimrocks." He pointed up toward the snow-covered rimrocks behind the boulder.

Both Ham and John Gatlin went down to the creek, and Axel went up to the helicopter. He washed off some blood, found an insulated MSP jacket and joined them down at the creek.

"There," Axel pointed to a spot ten feet out into the creek. "Arlyn went down right there, and as near as I could figure, the son-of-a-bitch had to be within twenty to thirty feet of this line." He swung his arm along the line of rocks. "Beyond that, the bigger aspens cut him off on the left and some spruce on the right."

Ham followed Axel's reference line up toward the boulder.

"Either that or somebody lying in the shrubs across the creek, but that strikes me as too close. Easy to be seen."

"Where were you when the shot was fired?" Ham asked.

"Round the corner. Downstream. I don't think you can see it from here. Look where the creek bends back this direction down there. I was about twenty yards beyond that bend, this side of the creek. Shooter never saw me."

"Or … maybe he *only* saw you," Ham said slowly.

"Huh? What are you getting at?" Axel hadn't stopped to consider why a sniper would pick off Arlyn with a single bullet and then disappear. He was interested in Ham's perspective. That Ham thought Axel was the intended target sent a shiver through his back.

Ham started talking out loud. "That looks like a sheriff's jacket Arlyn's wearing. You two are practically the same build, with that bulky jacket on him. From a hundred yards out, nobody'd be able to tell whether a lone fisherman in the creek was five-foot-six or six-six."

"He had a baseball cap on, too," Axel offered, souring at the thought that he was the target. "Couldn't see his face. My face." Suddenly, there were lots of reasons for a sniper, wherever he was.

"Ham, this is not good. I've got too many enemies lately," Axel breathed, barely audible.

"We'll get the bastards, Axe. Whoever they are. Believe me on this one." Ham's voice was edged with earnest intent.

Just then, Gatlin walked up and said, "Wind's picking up. Has got a nasty bite to it, gents. Between the wind, sunset, and the snow, I'd say we've only got an hour." He looked down at his handheld radio. "FBI should be here in five minutes."

Ham filled Gatlin in on Axel's theory about the shooter's position.

"Well, I know this patch. Had a lightning fire out here last year. There is an old Forest Service road that runs between that boulder and the rimrocks. And another one above the rimrocks, just under the snow line," Gatlin said, pointing behind them. "Neither's used much anymore, but it'd be passable with a motorcycle, Jeep, ATV, anything that's got a good four-wheel drive."

"Where do they go? I've never seen either before," Axel asked with a note of surprise. He thought he and Arlyn knew most of the old roads back here.

"Well, these logging roads are like a net. If you know the turns to make, you can get to Route 34 about four miles out of town. But you can get onto the main Forest Service road just one hundred yards the other side of the trail head." He pointed downstream.

Axel's mind was spinning. "Who's gonna know about this road? Know we'd be fishing here?" New questions were flooding his mind.

"Yeah, I don't know who you're thinking of, Axel, but we can't get a copter to chase him. You said the shot was … close to an hour ago?"

"Three fifteen. One hour and seven minutes ago. Depending on how bad the roads are, there's a chance they could still be up here."

"Maybe. Going the other way, up the mountain, there's another way out." Gatlin continued. "We had to use it on a Search and Rescue out here a couple years ago. Goes up to Dead Horse Plateau and down in the Kingdom out east."

"Charlie Ryan's Kingdom," Axel stated flatly, as though it was the last piece of the puzzle.

"Now, don't go jumping to conclusions, Axel," Ham cautioned. "These rough roads crisscross the mountains. Hell, you could probably get to Cody from here without touching a paved road. You start looking for clues that say 'Ryan' to you, and you'll miss whatever's really here." With a long, high-pitched whistle, the helicopter's engine revved up.

Ham turned to Gatlin. "You goin'? The other guys should be here soon."

Gatlin was on his radio phone.

"No, this copter taking Arlyn's going straight to Billings. I'll go back on the next one. Should be here as soon as this one leaves. I just heard that the FBI has assigned Dale Henderson, out of Billings. He's coming in now, but between the nightfall and the snow, he's not expecting too much. He's got a couple guys. Tomorrow we've got some ATVs, a couple of Jeeps and a crew of six guys—CSI, mountaineers, the whole shebang. If the snow doesn't blanket us."

The EMTs had strapped Arlyn to their stretcher, had an IV running to his left arm, and had covered the open wound. Arlyn was alert. Axel grabbed Arlyn's left hand and squeezed it. Then he said, "You take care, Bro."

Axel couldn't take his eyes off Arlyn as they carried him to the copter and loaded him in. Axel bit the inside of his cheek to stop the tears as the helicopter bounced slightly and lifted off into the blustery snow.

Axel nodded as he watched the copter bank and turn toward Billings.

"I can bring out a deputy. Two ATVs. But let's go now, we're burning daylight. And who knows what'll be left here come morning."

As soon as the MSP helicopter was out of sight, the FBI's black helicopter came into view. As it came to rest further downstream, Gatlin left Axel and Ham in order to greet the new arrivals.

Axel and Ham walked up past the boulder to the old road, looking for any kind of clue that someone had been there recently.

Axel climbed up on the boulder again. Away from the edge and out of the wind, pine needles made a soft carpet. He was looking for footprints, and was so absorbed by his study of the ground that he didn't notice Dale Henderson's arrival. The wind was getting stronger. Ham briefed Henderson on what he knew so far.

Then Henderson directed the investigator to scour the area on and around the boulder, centered on the crevasse. "What we're looking for is anything artificial, unnatural. The shooter was likely here for quite a while. He's got to have left some trace. Could've been on horseback. There's probably foot prints, and if we're lucky, even a shell casing. He only took one shot and split. We're not dealing with an amateur." Then Henderson pulled one of the officers aside and told him to go down to where Arlyn had fallen to look for anything that would be useful.

Henderson climbed up the boulder to where Axel was. Axel looked up and nodded when he saw him approaching. They'd met over the years on one case or another. Dale Henderson was certainly better than someone from Colorado. Henderson offered a handshake and a flashlight. In response, Axel said, "Good to have you aboard, Henderson."

Dale Henderson was thirty years old and a thin six-foot-three Montana native who had always treated Axel with respect. He responded, "Sheriff, can't help but wonder if you were the intended target."

"Yep. I'm coming to the same conclusion. The extent of my brother's enemies is limited to saloon owners with unpaid bar tabs and angry husbands. And neither one's gonna go to this much effort. I'd say this well-planned and well-executed shooting makes a whole lot more sense if the target is the notorious Rankin County Sheriff." He paused. Henderson said nothing and Axel started again, "Arlyn and I were fishing. 'Bout a hundred yards apart. He had an old sheriff's department jacket on. While he's a couple inches taller, be hard to tell who's who. Shooter probably didn't even see me."

"I see." Henderson looked down at the creek below them. "'S'that where he fell?"

"Close, I pulled him out of the water. I think this is the line. Better'n nothing, I guess." He swung his arm in front of him, pointed back to the creek and the spot where Arlyn stood.

Henderson only nodded. "It looks like you worked out a pretty clear idea of where our shooter was. One shot. Any chance the bullet still in the body?"

Again, that first moment of finding his brother raced through his mind. "No, I don't think so. Bullet took out half the bicep of his right arm. Never seen a mess like that from a single bullet. Looked more like a shotgun blast."

"Don't worry. We'll find it. We've got some new technology. We'll find the bullet wherever. It's not going anywhere. That current won't pull it down."

Axel said nothing but relaxed a bit as the two men examined the surface of the boulder in silence.

Somewhere behind them, lower on the boulder, a voice shouted, "Hey, I think I've got something!" Henderson trotted down to investigate, leaving Axel alone at the crevasse. He had covered this area before. Rather than searching the ground further, he found himself rechecking the line of flight and trying to imagine the mind of the shooter. He thought about Arlyn and how lucky it was that he was still alive. But the thought that there are people who want him dead wouldn't leave. Axel had suddenly become fully aware of his own mortality. *The MSP helicopter could be taking my body to the morgue. What would happen to all the things I've never sorted out with Arlyn, with Anne. They'd just have to guess as to what I really meant, what my intentions really are.*

Axel walked off the boulder.

Henderson interrupted Axel's ruminations. "Sheriff, we got a fresh scrape on a rock. Deep gouge, fresh, six inches off the ground, and what looks like a cotter pin—three inches long, one leg bent back. Up by the rock. Popped off. Top of the dirt. Fresh. Looks like something hit the rock pretty hard, popped off the pin. We also got what might be

ATV tracks. Big tread. Two lines about four feet apart. You didn't hear an engine, did you?"

"Nothing, other than the shot. Mid-caliber. After Arlyn went down I was splashing through the water. Couldn't hear a thing."

Axel knew his eyes were watery and that his voice was cracking. He kept his focus on the ground in front of him. Henderson turned to go. Only then did Axel say, "Right." He followed Henderson down the slope of the boulder. Axel, the target, the victim's brother, had a flash of self-consciousness and wondered if everyone was watching him. He shook off the thought. Standing up tall to stretch his back, Axel saw a fleck of white under a wild rosebush growing next to the boulder. "Hey, what's this?" he said. He bent over to a half-burned scrap of paper laying in a slight depression out of the wind. He pointed to it, but didn't touch it. Henderson came back and swung his flashlight on it. It was a small band of heavy paper embossed with gold, about the diameter of a finger. The ash of the burned portion was still intact. "A cigar band?" Axel said. Looking closer at the band, he could see in the ash the faint impression of a man's face in profile above a crest of some sort. His heart was racing. He carefully surveyed around under the bush, but found nothing more.

"It looks like it dropped under that bush, Sheriff, out of the wind. Looks charred, like part of it burned. That's gotta be fresh. Fragile. I'll get a technician to photo and bag it." Just then Henderson's radio sounded, and Axel could hear the incoming voice say Hilton's name. Henderson turned his back to Axel, walked further away and turned down the volume on the receiver. Axel was curious, but knew that Henderson would not offer anything about Major Jack Hilton.

Axel stood guard over the band until a federal crime scene technician took photographs, lifted it off the ground with white gloves, and placed it in a tiny, confetti-filled, clear plastic box. Axel moved back up the boulder, off the path. As he was about to turn to go, he saw it. He yelled, "Hey, here's more: a cigar butt. It's still warm. Who smokes cigars these days?" An image of hunched-over Charlie Ryan chewing a cigar popped into his head like some weird cartoon. *Hilton smokes cigars.* Henderson walked up to examine the cigar butt.

"I believe we have a pairing, Sheriff. This is good work."

In spite of himself, Axel was pleased. This contribution was a positive step. "So where is the major these days? Has he got you babysitting me?" he asked. He knew he was not going to get an answer, but *what the hell?*

"No, it was just a routine call. Hilton put in a formal request for a new FBI investigation on the Ryans, and my boss wants to know if I got a problem with a declination. Far as I know, Hilton's back in Denver. There's nothing official out on Crestfallen. I'm not on the case, and won't be if there is one. Got it? I'm here because of this shooting. It's on federal land." Changing his tone he added, "This shooter, if he was right here, he's not as much of a professional as we were thinking. Higher up would be better. Better angle, less interference. Longer shot, but a better picture. A marksman, yes, but sloppy. Hasty. Did he use a brace for the gun? Was he hurrying out of here? Is there any chance he thought you might come after him? How many people knew you guys were going fishing today?" Henderson's rapid-fire questions made Axel think Henderson was trying to distance himself from Hilton and that Hilton was a problem for the FBI. Then Axel had another thought: maybe all this was indeed making him paranoid and he was going to end up trusting no one.

Axel continued to search for evidence of a hasty retreat or a gun-barrel rest or any of the other things Henderson had just spouted off about. Thirty seconds later, though, a huge gust of wind picked up and started dropping big, nasty, wet snow pellets at them.

"Time to get out of this high country, boys!" Ham Frazier's voice boomed from behind them. Axel and Henderson looked at one another for an uncomfortable second, weighing the other's thoughts. "Time to go, Sheriff," Henderson said, "I think we've got all we're going to get."

Axel stood up and raked his hands through his hair. *Time to check in on Arlyn and talk to Anne.* In the increasingly heavy snow shower, he went back to the creek to round up the abandoned fishing gear and get on the helicopter. He wondered if there'd be anything left tomorrow.

There wasn't. The weather system brought in six inches of snow and temperatures in the teens.

CHAPTER 26

(Wednesday, November 30)

Between Axel and Anne, Arlyn had had seventeen visits since the helicopter brought him in. Friday night, Anne wasn't on duty, but by nine o'clock she was back at the hospital to check in on Arlyn and to interpret the medical reports for Axel. Arlyn had lost a lot of muscle and blood. Infection was a real concern, but the bones and ligaments were intact. More than half of his right bicep was missing.

Today, Arlyn was in a positive mood, looking forward to going home tomorrow to see how well he could cast left-handed. He wasn't interested in physical therapy. Axel and Arlyn both knew he would do whatever was needed to keep fishing. Without a word of discussion, the brothers understood that Axel was the shooter's target and he was the reason Arlyn was injured. Axel felt guilty. Arlyn was somehow lighthearted about the fact that he wasn't anyone's intended victim and that he took a bullet meant for his younger brother.

Today, Axel left Arlyn's bedside to go to the Billings Federal Building and sit in on the first FBI evidence meeting since the shooting.

He got to the Federal Building ten minutes before the meeting was set to begin. Henderson had taken the unusual step of inviting him to sit in on the FBI's internal evidence meeting and status call. Axel was reassured by the openness Henderson had displayed.

Axel parked the County's Cherokee in the "Law Enforcement Only" zone of the surface lot and walked into the building, down the ramp to the underground garage, usually reserved for prisoner transport and the occasional federal judge. He tapped his hat to the garage attendant, a uniformed federal employee whom he had never met. The attendant, an older man whose leathery face spoke of years in the Montana sun and wind, nodded his head and said, "Sheriff," by way of greeting. Axel knew that he was on parade and that word that Axel Cooper, the man himself, was coming had obviously been spread through the building. If Axel had any doubts about that, they were resolved ten seconds later when Dale Henderson picked him out of the building's security line for quick VIP treatment.

Henderson was tense. As they stood by the glass wall dividing the screening area from the rest of the building, he swung his eyes right and left, scanning the hall. "Axel, we gotta talk," and seized Axel's elbow and ushered him toward an open staircase. Then he whispered, "Hilton's missing. No one's seen him since last Thursday." He let that sink in and then, as though confirming Axel's thought, said, "Yes, before Arlyn's shooting. We got a nationwide net out. He can't get far."

In order to give himself a moment to think, Axel looked back at the line of people going through the metal detectors. Then he nodded his head and said, "So, what are you telling me here? Is he a suspect?"

Henderson said nothing. Axel suddenly started breathing hard and pushing out the exhaled air through his nose. His face flushed. Then he snapped, "This some kind of goddamn secret? Hell, it sounds pretty incriminating to me." Axel looked up at Henderson for a response, but got none. "I hope to hell he's on your list, or is this some sort of protect-our-own circle jerk. So, where was he seen last? What was he doing?"

Henderson turned away from Axel toward the stairs.

Henderson started talking slowly as he looked away, "Axel, what I'm telling you are rumors. This isn't evidence. You know everybody's a suspect. Today's meeting is about physical evidence, not our suspect list. Hilton's on our list, but you're never going to see it. We've got a fresh, active investigation. We're not to the point of arresting people. There's no smoking gun. What I'm telling you is that one of the suspects is acting strangely. We got two Hilton stories going here. One is that he went elk hunting in the Tetons, northwest Wyoming. Three guys. On ATVs. High altitude. Third morning, Hilton takes the extra gas can and takes off, while the other guys are sleeping. Left 'em twenty miles out in the bush. Left no note. He just split. No one's seen hide nor hair, since. Second story's that he checked himself into a private rehab facility in Seattle, which won't reveal any client names without a subpoena."

"So when do we get some facts?" Axel asked solemnly. He envisioned Jack Hilton lying on the ground, sighting his rifle down on Arlyn from the boulder at Longbow Creek.

"Soon. We've got three guys in Jackson Hole grilling the hunters and an Assistant U.S. Attorney talking to a federal judge in Seattle at eleven today. Rehab could just be a cover story for the elk hunt. Or vice versa. Apparently, he told a couple of his assistants he needed to 'get some perspective' and 'detoxify,' whatever the hell that means."

"So, is that all you've got?" Axel said. "Or do we have something else to talk about? If that's all you got, I'm outta here. My gut tells me I should be down in Jackson Hole checking rentals of trucks big enough to haul his ATV up to Rankin County." Axel could tell that Henderson wasn't saying all he knew about Hilton. The thought passed through his mind that maybe Sven Thordahl was right: we have an unwarranted faith in large federal organizations, including the FBI.

Axel took a step back and glared at Henderson. "Maybe this county sheriff needs to take a more active role in this investigation. This isn't a random, drive-by shooting. I can't say we know who shot Arlyn, but I'll bet that whoever did it is someone we know."

Henderson flipped his head back to cut Axel off.

Kris Bradford, the mysterious Delores, and a second woman were walking down the stairs toward the two men. She held a single three-inch-thick file. Axel recognized her immediately from her squared shoulders, but decided that it was her call as to whether their acquaintance was public. She looked away from Axel and greeted Henderson. Then Henderson formally introduced the two to Axel. His tone said that he wanted the two women to understand who Sheriff Axel Cooper was, and that they should adapt their behavior accordingly.

Axel's uniform included a badge with letters one inch high spelling out his name. He felt that Henderson had gone a bit overboard in his explanation. Henderson had discounted him, as if he'd said, "Beware of what you say. This man is not our friend." The extent and formality of the introduction again confirmed Axel's unique status—a county sheriff cooperating in the investigation into the shooting of his brother on federal land while still considered by many to be the catalyst of the DOJ's worst embarrassment since Ruby Ridge.

As soon as the women were out of earshot, Axel said, "If you'd rather, I can leave now. Maybe the FBI, U.S. Marshal Service and the whole DOJ would just as soon I go away. But the more important story is that somebody shot my brother, thinking they were shooting me. And you know what?" Axel waited for Henderson to look him in the eye. He then said, slowly and emphatically, " I'm going to find that guy, with or without your help, but it would be a lot better if I had it."

Then Henderson responded, "Well, maybe your coming in today wasn't such a good idea. I'm on this case and nobody's got immunity. But you've got to appreciate that any organization's first instinct is to protect itself. The DOJ's not perfect, and we know it, but we're not looking for someone else to air our dirty laundry. If Hilton's the shooter, I'm going to get him."

Henderson turned away to climb the stairs.

Axel reached up and grabbed Henderson's elbow. Henderson turned back so the men faced each other. Then Axel said, "Hey, let's be straight here. I've got nothing, absolutely nothing, against you, the DOJ, the FBI, the U.S. Attorney or even the U.S. Marshal Service. I got put in a bad place by one U.S. Marshal, and ever since then it's been raining crap. It looks like one way or another I've gotten my brother shot. It's hard not to connect the dots. But the last thing I want to hear is that there's some sort of federal effort to protect Jack Hilton or sweep this whole thing under the rug. If protecting the DOJ means protecting Jack Hilton, we've got ourselves a major confrontation."

"Axel, chill. Relax. We *will* find out what Hilton's been up to. We *will* get it right. I told you everything I know. Did you hear that? No, I haven't arrested the guy and I won't until I've got probable cause, just like everybody else. Got it? I thought you'd want to know, professional courtesy bullshit. If you can't handle uncertainty, I'll save myself the effort and tell you as much as I'd tell any other brother of a shooting victim—nada! All right? Are we straight here?"

Axel took a deep breath and held it for a long count. He then exhaled slowly, in an effort to relax. Then he said in a low, soft voice, "Right. Physical evidence. Where are we going?"

Henderson pointed up the stairs, off to the right.

The evidence meeting struck Axel as more of a conclave of forensic scientists than an effort to solve a crime. They spoke in a different tongue. They were totally into the facts without any conjecture. True to Henderson's prediction, they found the bullet in the creek bed. It was of particular interest because of its high lead composition. They were also intrigued by the amount of oxidation. It was an old bullet. The working theory was it was a hand-poured repack more than ten years old. Axel was right, it was a mid-sized caliber usually used for deer hunting.

But the high science had been saved for the cigar band. Someone had assembled a collection of seventy-eight cigar bands and then reduced them to ash without crushing the band. Then they recorded the unique refractive light patterns of each of the bands to compare with the band Axel found under the rosebush.

The senior scientist out of the FBI's science lab in San Francisco had flown in today for the presentation. This was apparently one of the first cases using this new technique. He compared it to matching finger prints. Axel was impressed even before it was revealed that the scientists were 97% sure that the cigar was an El Camino-King Ferdinand, made from tobacco grown in Honduras. A Billings Special Agent had identified the company's North American wholesaler in Tampa and learned from them that the brand was sold through thirty-two retail shops in the five-state Northwest region. None was within a hundred miles of Billings. Henderson closed the meeting with the statement that once the suspect list was developed and pictures available, it would be distributed to all the retail shops. Agents would visit the three closest stores: Bozeman, Jackson and Spokane. The store in Denver would also get an FBI visit.

Axel was pleased to see that there was some progress, and the case was receiving high-level attention. He considered that his displeasure with Henderson had been misplaced. While he could not bring himself to apologize, he was profuse in his statements of appreciation to all the agents. He sensed that Jack Hilton was high on the FBI suspect list, but they weren't ready to disclose that to Axel. On the way out, Axel shook Henderson's hand as they promised to keep in touch as things developed. Axel reflected that he'd probably never see the FBI's suspect list. Driving home, he put together one of his own: Hilton was at the top.

CHAPTER 27

(Thursday, December 1)

Jim Faraday, the Denver FBI agent, called late to the house phone at Arlyn's.

"Axel, gotta talk to you. We've got some new developments. Seems to complicate things. Got a minute?"

"Whatta you got?"

"Looks like Rankin County's a pretty busy place. Crestfallen's just the beginning."

"Well, I'm all ears. What're you talking about? Did you find Hilton?"

"No Hilton news other than we are officially looking for him. He's on the internal apprehend-on-sight list. Don't be talking to the press about that. The real news is *more drugs*. Seems that a pretty new, but heavy, supply line of meth is coming out of south central Montana. Going to Missoula, Spokane, Seattle, and maybe even Anchorage. We caught a runner. Last month, airport security at Sea-Tac got him with a false-bottomed suitcase. Never said these guys were smart."

"So what's the Montana connection?"

"Well, the song he's singing is that he's just a runner for a plant outside Olympia, but there's a new pipeline. Private plane out of rural Montana. Make the stuff and load up the plane for delivery. Airdrops once the money changes hands. Aluminum boxes with little parachutes. Plane loads up an order, takes off, and heads west. Gets GPS coordinates in the air over a satellite phone, drops the box, calls in the time, and flies home."

"That's hard to believe. Where's the plane supposed to be flying from? Couldn't have been Crestfallen."

"That's today's sixty-four-dollar question. All we got is what he's told us. He's local and says he only deals with the Seattle and Olympia guys. Did the Sea-Tac-to-Anchorage run. He's now looking for love from the FBI. His story is that they got two new suppliers. One in Washington east of Olympia and the other in Montana, somewhere between Billings and Sheridan. Both of 'em now operational, flying out meth. Airmail."

"Lotta ground between Billings and Sheridan."

"He's got two more clues. Story goes that the producers just started up a new plant, and that old management, who'd been holding down production, was on the way out. One way or another. The Seattle distributors were looking for a lot more dope outta Montana."

"Old management? Like Charlie Ryan? He was on the way out. Feet first. But Crestfallen wasn't in operation yet. Think they got another site?"

"Well, I'm looking at a lotta pictures of pole barns and gravel straightaways. One of our copters reported a small plane on a takeoff route over Crestfallen. I talked to him. He was taking Hilton to Billings the morning of the raid. He says it came out of nowhere. Nobody's looked into it yet."

"Think Hilton knows anything about this?"

"Who the hell knows what Hilton would be thinking. He *was* on the copter that got buzzed. And he wouldn't know anything about this Washington guy. But it's all over the DOJ internal bulletin board. Since last week. He'd have to be totally out of the loop to miss it. Who knows, maybe he knew something two weeks ago, before they caught this guy. Maybe he uncovered a second site and was bound for glory."

"Let me know when you find Hilton. He needs to do a lot of explaining. Think I'll become a Rankin County airplane spotter."

"I'll let ya know when Hilton shows up, one way or another."

Axel laughed. "So he's made the FBI's 'Wanted: Dead or Alive' list already?"

"Not funny. I'll call you tomorrow."

CHAPTER 28

(Sunday, December 4)

Axel's cell phone buzzed as he walked into the kitchen. It was Fred Rosch, Chief of Police in Grant.

"Axel, heads up! We had a shooting outside the Matterhorn in the parking lot. This morning. The guy's got ID as John T. Hilton, out of Denver. He was hit twice. He's unconscious on life support at Grant Hospital. Too unstable to take him to Billings."

"Holy shit! Hilton! Jack Hilton? You sure it's him?"

"Think so, but I want your opinion. All we got is a Colorado driver's license and a Marine Corps duffel bag, stenciled 'Major Jack Hilton.'"

"Is he going to make it?"

"Shot to the head looked nasty. I haven't heard from the hospital. Second shot to the shoulder. He shot back. A 9 millimeter with two rounds fired was lying on the pavement."

"When did this happen?"

"We got the motel handyman who says he heard four or five shots about 8:35. He was around the corner. He didn't hear anything else. No yells. No doors slamming. No running. Nothing."

"You really think it's Hilton? Folks are looking for him. Last I heard, he was either in Seattle or the Tetons, south of the Park. He coulda been Arlyn's shooter, up on Longbow. Did you get a look at him?"

"Yeah, big guy. Shaved head."

"Sounds like him. No U.S. Marshal ID? Nothing in the room? Been there long?"

"Checked in yesterday morning. Nobody saw him after that. No phone calls through the switchboard. I'm going through his stuff. Called the MSP. They got a lab tech coming down from Billings. Ballard.

Don't know him. Sergeant Warren Ballard. Told me to leave everything in his room where it is."

"You talk to Ham Frazier?"

"Yeah, but he's back in Helena. Wants me to call him when we get a positive ID. See if we can confirm this guy is Jack Hilton. I want you to look at him. Can you come in?"

"Sure, at the hospital? Who's all there now?"

"Nobody's at the hospital. With that head shot, he's not going anywhere soon. Boots Tornquist took the first call from the Matterhorn. I've got him out looking for Hilton's car, if he's got one."

"Well, I'm coming in. I'm out at Arlyn's and I've got to get cleaned up, so it'll be an hour. Meet me at the hospital?"

"Yeah, see you then."

Axel poured a cup of coffee, walked outside and sat on the top step of the porch. He rubbed his unshaven chin. *Hilton shot.* He watched the wind flutter the last few leaves on a nearby aspen. He took a sip of coffee, stood, and headed back into the house.

Inside, he called Dale Henderson's cell phone. The shooting was news to Henderson.

"So why didn't Rosch call us? Christ, he knows who Jack Hilton is. Sure, he's not positive, but I can't imagine that there's many folks shave their head, have a 'John T. Hilton' driver's license, and carry around a Marine Corps duffel bag with his name on it. Give me a break. We got the shooting of a federal officer. Line of duty, we got a federal crime. I sure as hell hope that Rosch isn't looking for his fifteen minutes of fame, 'cause *it's over*. Now, I got calls to make, but no way in hell is this Rosch's case. Hear me? This is Fed. Got it?"

"Dale, loud and louder. If it *is* Jack Hilton."

"Wanna give me odds? From what you told me I'm bringing a whole team down. Sunday morning. They'll love it. Same as Arlyn's. What're you guys *doing* in Rankin County?"

Axel ignored the question.

Henderson started again. "Axel, do a favor for me and Chief Rosch. Call him and tell him to call me. It will avoid the question of why I had to call him and cut the paperwork on my end. You know it shows multi-jurisdictional cooperation, stronger territorial integrity. Bullshit like that."

"Got it. Programs like that got us where we are, *antiseptic interdiction.*"

"Hey, it's my life. Have Rosch call in the next ten minutes and we can forget you and I ever had this conversation."

There were few vehicles on the road as Axel drove toward town. En route he called Ange to let her know he was coming into town earlier than 2:00 PM, as scheduled. He told her that Fred Rosch had called about a shooting at the Matterhorn Inn. He didn't mention that it was most likely Jack Hilton.

As Axel turned off the gravel road onto Route 34, fifteen miles east of town, he looked to his right—the route out to the Kingdom—and wondered what the Kingdom might have had to do with Hilton's shooting. He turned the corner and headed toward town.

The approaching old red pickup looked familiar. The chrome bumper and flat windshield glistened in the morning sun. Axel slowed to take a closer look.

Two guys. The driver in a ball cap, the other in a full-brim hat. Two rifles on the gun rack. As the vehicles passed, Axel turned to see Frank Ryan intent on the road straight ahead of him. Then Axel slowed further and looked for a side road to turn around to follow them.

As he slid through a u-turn, he cautioned himself to be an observer and not to push Frank. No sights, no sounds. He accelerated until he caught sight of the pickup starting to climb the next hill. He slowed, so as to stay a full mile behind, just about the distance between the rolling, twisting hills. He passed Arlyn's access road. The next valley was a deep one down to McNally Creek, sheathed in a stand of cottonwoods.

As Axel dipped into the valley, Frank was on the crest of the next hill. Frank slowed down. Axel slowed further. When he got over the crest, the red pickup was waiting. It was parked on a side road, but facing the highway, ready to turn either direction.

Axel inhaled deeply and regripped the steering wheel.

He passed the truck without turning to look at the occupants; then he focused on his rearview mirror.

Frank stayed put. The next turn and dip of the undulating road took the pickup out of Axel's rearview mirror. He slowed down. His thoughts of what to do next were suddenly interrupted by the expanding image in the mirror of the old red truck coming up fast.

Axel pulled off onto the narrow shoulder.

He didn't stop but kept the Jeep rolling with its outside, right wheels on the grassy slope. He didn't turn to watch as the pickup blew past him.

"Thwack! Thunk!" The noise reverberated in the Jeep. It was like a metal rod smacking the side behind the driver's door. Axel turned to look. The interior back-door liner had a hole in it the size of a lunch plate, exposing its mechanics. He stopped and got out. One shot had hit the left-rear door in front of the rear wheel. The second hit a rear panel just above the wheel: two half-inch holes as round and precise as if they'd been made by a drill-press. Axel shook his head. *Time to move.*

He jumped back into the Jeep, pulled onto the road and called Ange. "Ange, switch on the recorder. You got work to do. I'm at milepost 21 on Route 34, east of town. I've just been shot at by the occupants of an old red pickup. The driver's Frank Ryan. Saw him from six feet. Absolutely positive it was him. Two shots hit the left rear of the Jeep. Probably trying to hit the tire, slow me down. Ryan's heading east on 34. The first turn-off for the Kingdom is at milepost 31. I am in pursuit. I need you to make some calls. Tell 'em all the same thing. I've been shot at and am in pursuit. Who do we have on the road?"

"Our guys?"

"Yes, our guys."

"Well, we got Ollie south on 176 and Carlsen out west, near Greenwall. They're both rolling."

"Great! Send Ollie out here, full speed. Whatever this turns out to be, it could be over before he gets here, but I might need backup. Tell him to watch the curves."

"Got it, Boss."

"Do that now. I'll stay on this line."

He dropped the handheld microphone and gripped the steering wheel with both hands. He could see Frank's pickup. There was no oncoming traffic. He edged toward the center of the narrow road and punched the accelerator.

Ange came back on the line. "He's on his way."

Axel slowed to talk to her. "Good, now call Chief Rosch. He's at the Matterhorn. I don't have his direct number. Call the station, they'll patch you through. Jack Hilton's been shot. The MSP crime lab is en route. They don't need me in town. Tell him I'm not coming in. Then call Ham in Helena. Actually, call him first. See if he can get some help out of Billings. MSP helicopter with rifles and EMTs. Can't see this going down quietly. Tell 'em we're going to the Irish Kingdom, probably the Ryan homestead, south of milepost 31 off of Route 34. Tell Ham to have MSP-Billings call Henderson of the FBI. Maybe they can all come down in an MSP helicopter. We can't go into the ranch without a lot of firepower. Tell Ham to have somebody call me when they're airborne. Got that?"

"You bet, Boss. Be careful."

"You got it. Call you when somethin' happens. Over. Wait, wait. Tell Rosch to call Henderson at the FBI in Billings. Right now. Give him the number. Tell him to call now or the Feds will audit his tax returns forever. Henderson's waiting."

Axel threw the handset into the passenger seat and stomped on the gas pedal, easing the Jeep out to the highway's center line. The county Jeep sped over the winding ribbon of highway. He finally saw the old red pickup.

As the gap narrowed, Axel got a call from Ham.

"Axe, what's going on?"

"Hilton's been shot in town. Frank Ryan passed by me on Route 34 as I was going into town to check him out. Frank's going east, I'm going west. Figure he's a lead suspect in Hilton's shooting. Could be Arlyn's shooter, too. So, I turned around to follow him. He sees me and pulls off, and I pass him. He jumps out behind me, comes by, puts two rifle shots in the Jeep and passes me. I'm still following. Now I'm only a couple of hundred yards behind him. Eastbound on 34."

"What's gonna happen if you catch him? Play it forward. You can't do this alone. Even the Lone Ranger had Tonto."

"Ham, I'm all right. I'll follow them. I don't think they're ready for a standoff on the highway. I've got Ollie coming and, I hope, your copter out of Billings and whatever the FBI brings in. I'm the scout, just following the enemy. Out of range."

"And you stay *out of range*. It'll take an hour before anybody else gets there. Lotta time for things to happen. You talk to Henderson?"

"Early on when all we had was Hilton's shooting. Ange called him with the pursuit. Coordinate with your copter. Hey, we're at milepost 30. Charlie Ryan's place is at 31, but it doesn't look like they're turning. No, they're going by. I'm a good half mile back. They know I'm here. I'll hang back."

"Axe, good. Now cool it. There's nothing to be gained by hot pursuit. Fact they're running means they're not ready to surrender, whatever the crime. Just follow 'em. Keep folks informed. No heroics."

"Right, Commissioner. We just passed milepost 32. Hey, have your copter call. We got a new destination. Wow, they're slowing way down. Turning left, north off 34, just beyond milepost 32. Everything else has been south of 34, back a couple of miles."

"Axe, you've done your job. Now back off! Could be they've shot two people, what's one more? Christ, you might have been their first target. Stay back."

"Roger that. Have the copter call."

Axel called Ange with the new destination.

Axel slowed down and turned off on the side road which snaked its way up a long, high ridge with sharp hairpin turns. Through the road dust he could see the red truck crawling to the top.

Axel stopped as the truck reached the top of the ridge and turned toward him. He watched as Frank Ryan pulled a rifle off the rack and adjusted his window to use as a gun rest. Axel saw the barrel jut out of the window. He loosened his seatbelt and dove to the floor of the Jeep. Frank squeezed off two quick shots into the Jeep's engine. The metal-on-metal collision had a mechanical sound, like shifting gears. The last chug of the dying engine shook the whole Jeep. Axel could hear the antifreeze flowing onto the hard-packed gravel as he counted to 180 before he got up off the floor. Looking over the dashboard he saw that the red truck was gone over the backside of the ridge.

Axel grabbed his scoped rifle from the rack and picked up the transmitter, just as the helicopter called in its ETA of forty minutes. Henderson of the FBI and EMTs were onboard. Axel got out. He slowly scanned the crest of the hill as he moved out from behind the protection of the Jeep. Up the road, he found a game trail that led straight up the hill, while the road went off to the right to a switchback.

He went back to the Jeep and called Ange. "Where's Ollie?"

"Two minutes ago he was eastbound on 34. Milepost 28."

"Tell him to cut the siren and lights. We're further east than Ryan's. Just past milepost 32. Left turn. Northbound. My Jeep's 'bout a mile down that road. Tell him to stop behind the Jeep. I'll meet him there."

Axel went back to the trail. He carried the rifle with one hand as he crouched over, carefully moving up the narrow, steep, rocky path. As he approached the crest, he lowered himself to the ground.

The scene below was a long, flat valley parallel to the ridge. The ridge was topped by a rugged line of limestone outcroppings, palisades. The road was way off to the right, and there he could see the lingering dust clouds from the pickup. A hundred yards down the back slope was a cyclone fence, topped with barbed wire. Off to the right, there was a green gate and inside that a round-roofed metal building. No sign of the truck or the men.

Axel turned to look back to his Jeep to see if Ollie had arrived. Not yet. He scooted back down from the ridgeline and walked off to his left to get another angle on the compound.

He kept a watchful eye on the access road, both off 34 and at the crest of the ridge.

He scrambled up to the crest to check out the new angle. The view was now a full panorama of a small airport. A small single-engine plane was parked in front of the round building. The pickup truck was parked behind it. There was a single narrow runway, opposite the round building, running the length of the valley floor. It cut through several cross-ridges, making it look like a small-scale expressway through the mountains. On the left side of the runway was an open-walled equipment shed. It held two small tractors and two tanker trailers—trailers much like the anhydrous ammonia trailer at Crestfallen.

Axel lay down, pulled his rifle up to his shoulder and, through the scope, sighted in the building. Two men came out. The man in the wide hat was waving his arms. Max McCreary. Frank Ryan ran across the runway to the equipment shed as Max went to the airplane.

Axel looked behind him to the access road. No Ollie.

Frank started up one of the tractors, hitched a trailer to it and then hitched up the second trailer. He slowly drove the rig across the runway into the round building as Max loaded a large aluminum box onto the plane and climbed into the pilot's seat.

Axel stood. *They would get away.* Behind him, he heard the gravel crunch of Ollie's squad car stopping behind the Jeep. Axel snatched up his rifle and ran down the steep slope toward the Jeep.

Ollie was out of the patrol car. From thirty yards away Axel yelled, "Oll, this is an airport. Maybe a meth plant. Grab a rifle and chain cutters. Hilton's shooters. They're looking to fly away."

The two men ran up the hill and stood on top of the ridge. No reason to hide.

The airplane's engine was running, but slowly. The plane wasn't moving.

Axel and Ollie went down to the fence and Ollie cut a three-foot vertical slice into the steel mesh. He pulled the flap back and Axel squeezed through. Then Axel pulled the flap from inside the compound as Ollie slid the rifles through, then himself.

Frank ran out of the hangar and looked up at the lawmen at the fence. He ran up to Max's window, waving his arms as though to push the airplane away from the hangar. He ran back into the hangar as Max revved up the engine and the plane slowly rolled forward, toward the runway.

Axel pointed to the equipment shed on the left side of the runway. "Ollie, run down to the shed. If the plane starts to take off, shoot out the front wheel. You can get within thirty yards. Stay behind the old tractor. Got it? The front wheel." He handed Ollie the rifle.

Ollie looked up at Axel with a furrowed brow.

"Do it!" Axel commanded.

Ollie went down the steep grade in a half run, half controlled fall. He angled for the back of the shed. He worked his way behind the shed and then up the far side to the front corner. He waved back to Axel, and then he crouched behind the parked tractor.

The plane rolled out onto the runway and turned away from Axel.

Axel waited. Ollie waited. The airplane sent out a high-pitched, steady drone, but didn't move.

Axel scanned the sky. No clouds, no wind, no helicopters. He gripped his rifle in one hand and the long-handled wire cutters in the other and set off on a slow, cross-hill course to the hangar and Frank Ryan.

Frank burst through the side door at a full run. He wasn't running toward the plane. He was running away from the hangar.

The fireball blew out the side door and lifted the roof, while propelling the wide overhead front door out past the pickup onto the runway in front of the plane.

Frank turned and ran toward the plane. He slipped and nose-dived on the hard-packed gravel apron. His pistol clattered across the runway.

The second explosion lifted the back edge of the roof and folded it back against the front half, which stayed in place. A blue fireball rose above the roof, followed by leaping flames.

Axel focused on Frank and ran up to him with his rifle forward.

"Stay right there! Put your arms straight out!" Axel picked up Frank's pistol and tucked it in his belt.

Behind him the pitch of the engine increased to a screech, and Axel could hear the wheels rolling over the tarmac. He didn't look back, but stepped closer to Frank.

The plane increased its speed down the runway. Axel wanted to turn and watch, but he had Frank to manage. *Come on, Ollie!*

Fifty yards down the runway, Ollie lay in the shadow of the old tractor. He squeezed off two successive shots. Two hits. But the plane continued to pick up speed, and then suddenly it slumped forward onto the damaged tire. The plane slowed down, but the engine speed surged. The plane rocked back, nose pointing upward. The rear wheels stayed on the ground as the front wheel lifted off the pavement. The plane moved forward, picking up speed, and aimed toward the open skies.

Two hundred yards down the runway, the plane suddenly flopped onto the front wheel. The flat tire shredded and smoked as the plane careened to the right off the runway. The wheel's single supporting shaft collapsed and the plane nosed into the ground and spun round, angled back toward the shed. The blades of the single propeller shattered on the ground. Ollie charged the disabled aircraft.

Axel stayed ten feet back from Frank. "That Max?" he asked.

"Max," Frank said into the ground.

"Looks like quite an operation. You're good at blowing up stuff. You do my house?" Axel asked.

"Yeah, Halloween surprise."

"Crestfallen would be small potatoes compared to this. Airmail delivery!! Hilton know about this?"

"Hilton's an independent operator. He was looking to be a hero. Aging Boy Scout. He figured it out. Is he dead yet?" Frank asked.

"Not yet, but he's got a good start."

Axel heard the welcome sound of an approaching helicopter. Out of the corner of his eye he saw Max crossing the runway, hands up to his shoulders. Max was followed by Ollie. Ollie's rifle was pointed at Max's back.

"The Feds will take you, but tell me now—you guys shoot Arlyn?"

Lying on the ground, Frank turned his head up toward Axel. "Just how dumb do ya think I am, Sheriff?"

"You don't want my answer. Did Hilton do it?"

"Sheriff, I don't know who the fuck shot your brother. All I know is you shot mine."

CHAPTER 29

(Tuesday, December 6)

Sven was up before dawn and ate his oatmeal in solitude while looking out at the dark, empty barnyard. He watched as the wind swirled the dust in the yard.

Lately, Sven was up early every day and out on the ranch with his ATV before Randy and the crew had a chance to ask him what his plans were. He also liked having the ATV out of the barn, especially now that the county sheriff had an interest.

Walking out the door, Sven was hit by a blast of cold air. The recent cold snap added a bite to the wind. He turned his face and kept walking. Since his speech, he felt cut off from his family, Randy, the hired help, townsfolk, and the other old ranchers. The Internet was even less satisfying. Everything there was in the extreme, of the moment, and full of self-righteous outrage.

"The Sven Speech," as Hank Anderson at the *Courier* called it, was described as a call to recognize and appreciate the differences between Montanans and the rest of the world, the rest of the country, and maybe each other. Sven was surprised by Anderson's positive review, especially considering Anderson came from Ohio, a flatlander who spent his energy putting words on paper. No mention of vigilantes or the removal of federal authorities. He liked the modest amount of attention and was pleased that he had said what he had, but he didn't feel that he'd made an impact. He thought that everybody had already made up their minds on the issues or, for one reason or another, really didn't care. He told Megan that she'd done a great job, but he might as well have been talking to the wall. Chester had given him a smiling nod and a wink, about all Sven could expect. *Finally, I've done something that my too-smart-for-his-own-good son doesn't totally disapprove of.* He had reread Hank Anderson's review and smiled. *But, no more speeches. No more bombings. No more shootings. No more vigilantes.*

For today's morning exploration, Sven had decided to cruise the upper range, back against the county forest preserve into a few canyons—make sure all the loose cattle had been rounded up, check on the wolf carcass, and maybe take a drive up to the mine—up the front side, the day hiker's trail—just like your average Joe. See if they'd started again. Since the explosion, he had been fighting the magnetic attraction of the mine—the criminal pulled back to the scene of his crime.

In spite of the cold, the ATV started up right away and Sven was eager to get the noisy machine away from the ranch houses. The wires were clean. No tampering. He raced off in the cold wind toward the lower pasture, down the main road. The ATV kicked up a cloud of dust behind him. With the calves sold off, the remainder of the herd would be in the lower pasture. And, as he expected, they were collected by the creek, near the highway, as though they enjoyed watching the traffic. Just before he got to the main road, he slowed down and turned west to go cross country. He made it across the field on the hard, dry ground and forded Bridal Veil Creek. Then he cut up and over a series of ever-steeper foothills, gaining altitude. The ATV slowed under the strain but was able to handle the sharp rise. Three miles out, he turned back to see if he was being followed and to get a view of the ranch from the mountainside. The town was already bathed in the sun's horizontal beams, but Mt. Elliott still cast its shadow over the ranch. Sven decided to double back to the wolf's box canyon from the high side—a longer trip than the streambed approach, but perhaps a chance to meet the rising sun earlier at the higher altitude, then down into the canyon, through the creek, then over to Bridal Veil, and then back up the county trail to the mine and the falls.

He met the sunshine after a steep climb across a rocky slope. He pulled the brim of his hat down to cut the glare. Then moving slowly across the slope, he hit a patch of the loose shale and he slid off a bit sideways, a controlled slide. He leaned into the hill, just like he'd do with a horse, and was tempted to put his uphill foot on the ground for added stability.

Slow and easy, he made it across the shale stretch and stopped thirty feet from the edge of the cliff overlooking the deep shaded canyon and the tomb of the wolf. He pulled on the ATV's emergency brake and swung his weak right leg over the vehicle. In spite of living a lifetime on the ranch, he had never viewed it from this spot. He considered what the wolf's route across this ridge might have been. That warm October day seemed like ages ago, before the ride to Bozeman, before the mine explosion, before his speech. And long before he started chasing Sheriff Cooper.

Sven shook his head and turned back to the ATV. He swung his leg over, eased off the emergency brake, and shifted to low gear. The machine rolled slowly forward on the loose rock. Sven turned left, downhill, away from the cliff. The transmission gave a solid, low-pitched thunk as the gear engaged. Just then Sven heard a new noise; a single metallic crack like a crowbar hitting a rock. He figured it was just a rock, popped up by a tire, hitting the undercarriage.

Unknown to Sven, the steering control arm had sprung free from the front right wheel and slapped against the rocky ground. The cotter pin to hold it in place wasn't there to do its job. The handlebars were turned away from the canyon, but the right wheel didn't respond. The ATV slowly drifted to the left, but not enough. Sven squeezed the hand brake and jerked the handlebars to the left. The left front wheel responded while the right wheel was still aimed at the edge of the cliff. The machine's weight was on the right wheel. The right wheel rolled forward, down the ever-steeper incline. The left front wheel skidded sideways on the rocky ground.

Sven let go of the handbrake in order to regain traction, but the machine continued to the right. When the right front wheel reached the sharp edge of the cliff, Sven grabbed the emergency brake lever and pulled it up toward him. The rear wheels locked, but the ATV slid forward. Sven let go of the handlebars altogether and leaned hard to the left. As he pushed with his good left leg to jump off, the front left tire and the right rear lost purchase on the crumbling edge of the sheer canyon wall.

Sven extended his left leg, raising him in place, but the right leg—the wounded, slow-responding, right leg—stayed with the machine as it cascaded over the edge in a shower of loose gravel. The man and machine were united in a twenty foot freefall, but after a twirling bounce off a granite outcropping, Sven was alone for the last forty feet of a rolling tumble.

He beat the ATV to the valley floor only to have it land on top of him. His head was under the left wheel, as though the vehicle was trying to squeeze out any remaining life in him. The echo of the crash reverberated in the box canyon and then, as the rising sun just caught the edge of the sheer wall, there was the rustling of a trickle of dislodged rocks cascading to the canyon floor, retracing Sven's fall.

They found him just before nightfall. There was no question that he was dead.

CHAPTER 30

(Friday, December 9)

The first real snow of the year fell overnight. It had been predicted and the Rankin County plows and sand trucks were out before dawn. It was cold. This snow would stay a while. As Axel swept the six inches of powder off the pickup, he wondered just how much had fallen in town and if Anne would have any trouble driving down from Billings in the afternoon.

Route 34 east of Grant had just been plowed when Axel started his drive in from Arlyn's.

Slowly climbing the last hill before the bridge, he called the office. "Ange, so how bad is the snow? Anything serious?"

"Well, in town we got 'bout a foot. Three wrecks reported. Nothing serious. Nobody hurt. Busy morning. Henderson's looking for you already. He talked to Ollie, but he wants you to call him. He's at the FBI-Billings office already. He said to call either before nine or late afternoon."

"Got it. I'll call now. Any problems with any of our units?"

"No, not really. We got the wrecks covered. Snow hasn't messed things up too much. Ollie's already gone over to the garage to turn that smashed-up ATV over to the Feds. Then Hank Anderson popped in just before you called. He said he'll catch you later this morning. He's wrapping up the week's edition and says he wants a couple of juicy quotes. The FBI in Denver put out a press release late yesterday. He left us a copy. He wants your reaction to it. Other than that, not too much going on. I guess the ski mountain got over two feet and they're going to open the upper lifts. Should be good for the weekend."

"Henderson have an update on Hilton?"

"Maybe for you, but not for me. Seemed to me he was more interested in how much snow we got than anything else."

"Did he say anything about Thordahl?"

"Not a word."

"What else is going on in town?"

"Well, they closed school over in Greenwall. The furnace went out last night. Topper said that their step-down transformer blew out near the wind farm west of town. But power should be back up by noon. The boys are scheduled for a ball game tonight over there. Might play it here or reschedule."

Axel crossed the Vermillion River Bridge.

"Well, I'm almost there. See you in a while. Think I'll swing by Hank's first. I need some good press."

Standing at the front counter of *The Rankin County Courier's* office on Broadway, Axel quickly read the FBI press release. It struck him as an attempt to fit Hilton's actions into a comprehensive federal crackdown on meth production. It stated that Hilton had suffered "extensive, life-threatening injuries." But he was already out of the Denver hospital and at a rehab facility. The release gave him credit for the initial discovery of the Irish Kingdom's Palisades operation. Axel and Ollie were noted, as they had been in Monday's release, for their initiative in pursuing and apprehending Frank Ryan and Max McCreary.

As Axel looked up from the page, Hank Anderson asked, "So, Sheriff, what else needs to be said? Come on back; I'll buy you a cup of coffee."

The men went back to the drab, windowless employee lunchroom and Hank poured them cups of coffee. They huddled around the single, small table.

Axel sipped the hot coffee and said, "Well, what they forget to say in all the releases is that Hilton is the most complex and manipulative federal employee since J. Edgar Hoover himself. I think he knew about the Palisades operation weeks ago and was trying to strong-arm Charlie Ryan into closing it down. He was trying to get it closed down *before* anybody else in the federal government even knew it existed."

Hank shook his head in disbelief and said, "Why would he do that?"

"Be a hero. Go out strong. Round up all the bad guys all by himself. His only job was to apprehend Bob Johnson, the Minnesota fugitive. Charlie Ryan offered up Johnson a week before the raid. But that didn't fit Hilton's vision. He was out for a big score, especially after he figured out there might be a second plant. He wanted to report that he'd closed down one operating meth plant and stopped another from starting. Hooray for Jack Hilton!"

"How could he ever imagine that he could do that by himself? There had to be ten guys in the Kingdom in on the Palisades deal. They weren't going to give up without a fight."

"Well, the only angle that makes sense to me is that Hilton went to Charlie after the Crestfallen raid, but before the Colorado National Guard invasion, and tried to make a deal. Maybe a free pass if he co-operated. In order for any deal like that to work, Hilton had to keep the FBI in the dark. If *anybody* else knew about the Palisades, the deal's off and Hilton's on the carpet for not reporting the Palisades operation when he first knew of it. He's dead meat."

"A deal?"

"Two strange guys, neither of whom can control anybody else, tried to negotiate a comprehensive deal. First, Charlie's got the upper hand. He knows he's dying and he's trying to clean up and clear out of the drug business in one fell swoop. Maybe he thought he could close down the Palisades without anybody ever knowing it ever was there. But after the plane takes off, Hilton has a stronger hand and he pushes Ryan to close down the Palisades operation immediately. But Ryan pushed back. So Hilton brings in the Colorado National Guard to tear down Crestfallen. Almost out of spite."

"What was that about?"

"I think that Hilton was under a lot of pressure and tried everything he could think of to get Ryan to close down the Palisades. Lots of self-imposed pressure. Certainly, the shootings at Crestfallen raise its profile. The delivery plane takes off and almost hits Hilton's helicopter. Hilton sees it and the wheels start turning. Maybe the FBI copter pilot reports it and somebody at the FBI starts asking where the plane came from. More folks get interested in Rankin County. The real kicker, though, was a report out of Seattle last week that somebody is *already* running drugs out of south-central Montana and using a small airplane to do it. That report was on the internal Department of Justice billboard last week. Wonder if our copter pilot saw it."

"Whoa, but you don't know if anybody at the FBI was up to speed?"

"Don't think they were there yet, or they would have done something. Hilton was the only one that put it all together. And he was in a hurry to wrap it up before anybody started asking questions. Hilton had to know that Charlie was losing control over the whole operation. His health was getting worse. Charlie talked to Frank and Max about Hilton's offer. Frank and Max weren't ready to close down their Palisades operation, regardless of what Hilton knew about it. And when Charlie died, Frank and Max figured that any deal Charlie made was off and went after Hilton. Hilton tried to muscle them into submission and they pushed back."

Hank nodded his head and said, "So Hilton's a man with a big secret."

Axel continued, "Frank and Max quickly figured out that Hilton knew too much *and* wasn't sharing it. So getting rid of Hilton eliminates their problem. At least for now."

He flipped the press release onto the table. "This makes it seem like the discovery was the logical result of the Fed's everyday business."

Hank slowly nodded his head. Then he said, "Wow, that's pretty wild. So you think Hilton was out to negotiate a private deal with Charlie Ryan—but they couldn't keep it a secret."

Axel smiled. "I've got three other alternatives but what I gave you is my best shot. The FBI might get some stories out of Frank and Max, basically what Charlie told them, but unless Hilton recovers and talks, it's anybody's guess as to what really happened. See what you can get on the Seattle dope-runner they caught last week. I'd rather not be your source for that or any guess about a deal between Hilton and Charlie. Call Henderson at the FBI in Billings. He's in the office 'til nine. Called me already today."

Hank said, "I'll do that. Hey Axe, I got another angle on this. Do you think Hilton was somehow *in* on the meth operation? Crestfallen being a red herring, almost a cover-up?"

Axel shook his head. "That's alternative number three, but I don't think so. I think he did what he did to promote himself. I don't think he was running dope or blackmailing Charlie. He was in for his glory. I have to give him some credit for that. He was out to close 'em down."

Hank said, "I guess, but is any of this ever going to get resolved? How's Hilton doing?"

"This press release is the latest I've heard. Seems he's still got most of his marbles and is improving day to day. Brain injury can be anything," Axel said.

Hank wrote a quick note on a small pad. Then he said, "I just can't believe Frank and Max—thinking that they could blow away Hilton and their troubles would be over. They were dumber than Willy running out of the ranch house."

Axel took a sip of his coffee and said, "You can say that again."

Axel pushed back his chair and stood up. Then as Hank stood up, Hank said, "But you gotta believe they almost got away with it. They toss Willy, the start-up boy, to Hilton to make him go away but *keep* the air-drop operation. You think Willy'd keep quiet? I have to think he knew about the Palisades operation."

Standing by the table, Axel replied, "Sure he'd take one for the family, 'specially if grandpa got him a light sentence. But here's one for you. Do you think he knew we were coming that night to Crestfallen? I figure Charlie knew, or at least that a raid was imminent. And he'd tell Willy."

Hank took a sip of coffee and rubbed his hands together. He said, "Charlie had a real heart of stone. He lived with a lot of pain and expected everyone else to have a painful existence. The kid was a pawn."

"Well, we'll never know what went on between the two of them. Can't imagine Frank or Max saying much on that," Axel said.

Hank stroked his chin. He looked straight at Axel and said, "But even if Crestfallen went as planned, Hilton couldn't let the Palisades keep operating."

"Well, that's the second layer. Once Hilton saw that plane it's a whole new ballgame. Christ, he could've reported it immediately and been the team player. But he saw it as an opportunity to make up some ground he'd just lost with Crestfallen. He could give it a pass and save it for another day. Get Charlie to phase it out. Or, one day he wakes up and claims he found some new evidence and reports it to the FBI. After Ryan died, he had to figure that Frank and Max would be after him."

As Axel turned to leave the room, Hank shot him a laser-beam stare. "Whatta you have on Sven Thordahl?"

"I got nothing that you don't already have. Today I'm sure your paper will report him to have been an outstanding citizen. Took a header on his ATV." Axel abruptly walked to the door. Without looking back he said, "Thanks for the coffee. Gotta go."

Back in the truck, Axel called Henderson.

Henderson started right in, "Hey Axe, we got a confirmation of Thordahl buying cigars over in Bozeman. Specialty tobacco shop. Old Cuban guy says Sven'd come in once every six weeks or so. Bring in his granddaughter sometimes. Only bought King Ferdinand cheroots. Says he only had two or three customers for them. Expensive. I talked to Ollie and sent some guys down to take possession of the ATV wreck. We're going to have some mechanics look at our cotter pin. I expect we'll find that it came from Sven's ATV. We haven't done anything new on ballistics, but Sven's son says he used to load his own shells, ten years ago or so."

"So you're pretty firm that Sven shot Arlyn?"

"Well I'm pretty sure, but we can't indict a dead man. I've gone to a grand jury with less evidence and won convictions from juries."

"So what's public?"

"Public? Dude, nothing's public. I'm doing local law enforcement liaison work here. You won't see anything in *The Billings Gazette*. This has got to stay under your hat. If Arlyn wants to talk, I can come down and lay out what we've got. But as far as the public's concerned, Sven Thordahl died a Montana legend."

"So, are you done with Arlyn's shooting?"

"Well, we'll work over the boys from the Kingdom once more, just to make sure that they're not involved, but I'm convinced Thordahl did it. All I got left is the ATV and whatever we can get off his computer.

So, today I've got the cigar and weak ballistics. But that's enough for me."

"So, how many guys you got from the Kingdom?"

"We've got ten arrests. Seven guys, three women. Question is, who do we indict for attempted murder? So far we've got just Max and Frank for that, but that list could grow. We'll get some more good stuff from the folks we arrested. Not everybody in the Kingdom was keen on the meth business."

As he was about to hang up Axel asked, "Anything new on Hilton?"

"Yeah! Just got a call from Denver. The man never ceases to amaze me. Day before yesterday, he couldn't move his left side. Today he's back almost to normal. Some guys in Denver went to see him at the rehab place. He's up, out of bed. Walking with a walker. Still sloppy on the left side, but he can get around. Still can't talk, but he can communicate."

"That's good news. One way or another, he broke this whole thing open."

"Damned right. And I'm sure he won't let us forget it. Hey Axe, I gotta go. Need to be in Columbus in an hour. I'll be back at you if there's any news from the Kingdom gang."

"You coming down soon? Maybe you, Arlyn, and me can share a private cup of coffee."

"You got it. I'll let you know."

Henderson signed off.

Axel drove to his office wondering what Arlyn would think about the news. He just might let it rest.

Axel parked the pickup in the side lot and walked into the Rankin County Building through the front door. He nodded to or talked briefly with several people as he went down the main hall. He felt like he was gliding.

He opened the inner door to the sheriff's office to find Ange and Ollie at her desk, reviewing the new FBI press release.

On seeing Axel, Ange jumped up from her chair. "Hey boss, *you* are the man of the hour," she exclaimed.

"So how's that?" Axel replied, as he swung his head from Ange to Ollie and back again.

"Well you've had four more calls already. A real 'hit parade': the governor's office, Ham called twice, and Anne called to ask if you're available for an early lunch. And remember Henderson."

"Lunch? What's she doing driving down so early?"

"Well, she told me she wants to be here early so she can squeeze in a snowboard lesson before the lifts close."

"Are you serious? I don't think she's snowboarded in her life. Man, this snow makes people crazy. Lunch? Guess so. She calling back later?"

"Yeah. She said she'd call at nine thirty or when she gets to Everhart. Whichever comes first."

"I already called Henderson, but what's with the governor? Since the last time I talked to him, there's been a whole lot of shooting goin' on."

After a long moment, he said, "What's he want? He didn't call himself, did he?"

"No, he's got a young guy who called to set it up. They want to know if you can call back right at ten o'clock."

"Well, I guess I can do that," Axel said. "So, Ollie, why are you back so soon? Thought you were out delivering Thordahl's ATV."

"Well, I was, but the Feds got here early. Signed over the wreck and that was it. Road's clear up north. Snow peters out 'bout halfway to Billings."

"Well good. Looks like we got enough action here for a good day's work." Axel looked out the window at the snow on Broadway and then turned back to Ange. "Ange, what's Ham up to? Sounds like he's messing with the governor again. Any hints?"

"Well you know Ham. He can be pretty emphatic, like the world's coming to an end. He did say you should call him *before* you talk to the governor."

"Figures. You can bet that he's up to something." Axel looked down at the press release on the counter. "Here's some real news. Henderson says that today Hilton's up out of bed and walking again. With a walker. Still a little floppy, he said. Not talking yet. You can't keep a good man down." Axel smiled.

Ange and Ollie looked at each other in silence, both knowing that Hilton was not among Axel's favorite people. Axel walked across the room toward the door to the hall, then he turned back to Ollie and Ange and said, "Let's see what Ham's got to say."

Axel got a cup of coffee, settled in behind his desk, and called Ham in Helena.

Ham opened with, "Axel, promise me you'll approach this with an open mind."

"This? What are you talking about?"

"Well Axe, I think it's fair to say you attracted a lot of attention this fall. Positive attention. And the governor's noticed and wants you to consider a step up."

"Ham, it's me, Axel. Tell me what you're talking about. And I'm not looking to step anywhere. Believe it or not, there's a lot going on in Rankin County. Criminy, I don't even have a place to live, other than Arlyn's. I got a lot of work to do this winter."

"Axel, well I may have overplayed my hand, but I recommended you to the State Police Board. You remember. It's oversees the MSP. It's not a big deal. Quarterly meetings in Helena. Maybe ten or fifteen hours a month total. Go over the budget, review changes in procedures, ratify opinions of the Disciplinary Board, oversight. You'd be my boss. No public hearings. You can get a good peek at state government. Get to know some important people. Lots of visibility. And you actually get paid. Well, next year you get paid."

"Ham, come on. Why'd you do this? Man, you've *got* to have better candidates."

"You're a great candidate. A Montana hero. Rankin County's too small to keep you."

"So how many candidates you got?"

"Axe, you're it. One for one. Governor might have somebody, but he asked me for advice and I'm recommending you. Now he wants to talk to you. You at least have to call him and go to Helena. After that, if you still don't want to do it, fine. But you gotta talk to him. OK?"

Axel was silent.

"Axe, you still there?" Ham asked.

"Yeah, I'm here. What have you got me into?"

"Well look at it this way: this is just another event in your life. You did this, you did that. You became who you are, and because of that stuff happens. Some not so good and some really good. This is a good thing."

Axel did not respond.

Ham continued, "Axel, this could be important and fun. Talk to the governor."

"Yes Commissioner. I'll talk to the governor."

"Thanks. You won't regret it. Hey, I hear Hilton's on the mend."

"Yeah, good news. Henderson told me an hour ago. Hilton'll be back at us in no time."

"Well he can stay in Colorado, as far as I'm concerned. I wish him the best, but…"

"You and me both."

"Axe, now you behave yourself with the governor."

"Ham, I'll do what I can. Talk to you later."

Axel hung up the phone, looked at his watch, and smiled.

END